Jump Into…

DEATH WEARS
RED ROSES

Ivy C. Leigh

JumpRope Chronicles

JERSEY PINES INK

Cover art— Dar Albert, Wicked Smart Designs

Interior design—River Cove Production

The publisher is not responsible for websites or their content that are not owned by the publisher

For information, address the publisher at: JerseyPpinesInk.com

ISBN: 978-1-948899-21-5

Dedication

To my creative friends who inspire me

Quotations

Truth is so obscure in these times, and falsehood so
established, that, unless we love the truth,
we cannot know it.
—Pascal

"All is a riddle, and the key to a riddle..
.is another riddle."
—Emerson

DEATH WEARS
RED ROSES

JERSEY PINES INK

Before —

MAR-SEE-AH SPEAKS

Mar-see-ah, who possesses the gift to see things that are hidden from others, once again seeks to divine the life and loves of that dear little central New Jersey township with the puzzling name of JumpRope.

Her hands shift the smooth river stones, instruments of divination, the choice of each stone guided by the spirit of the Native American wise man, one of the original proud peoples of the land.

Mar-see-ah pauses as a vision forms of a dark-haired woman.

Who is this? Mar-see-ah wonders.

Like you, says Little Bird, the daughter of the wise man. *Danger to see, yet not understand.*

Mar-see-ah tenses. If this woman is gifted as she, yet unaware of her power, she might say something she'd unconsciously seen in another person's mind. If she unknowingly revealed something hidden, it could end in disaster.

Unable to see more, Mar-see-ah wills the darkness away and opens her mind to what is clean and bright. She smiles as she sees a long-held desire reaching fruition. And there . . . stories revealed, stories told, love offered and accepted. Love and secrets.

Secrets bring danger, says Little Bird.

Danger to the woman who could be like me? asks Mar-see-ah.

The answer was silence.

March comes in like a lion and goes out like a lamb
Old Proverb
Or sometimes, March comes
in like a lamb and roars out like a lion

Chapter 1

The month of March came lambing its gentle way through JumpRope Township, New Jersey, softly breathing over streets and sidewalks, hills and dales, meadows and fields, moving on to the long lane that led to the ranch house belonging to Pilar Fanshawe.

The house was built in the 1960s with cream-colored clapboard and a red brick chimney. It was one-story, but it looked like two because of the high peak over the combined living-room-dining room that had a sky-high ceiling. A lower peak above the front entrance had a fanciful Juliet balcony with a windowed door that went nowhere. On one side and toward the rear of the property, an azalea garden bloomed pink and white where there had once been a swimming pool designed to resemble a woodland pond.

It was Thursday. Pilar Fanshawe, who had been widowed for twenty years, was dressing to attend her first dinner with the Voodoo Club, a group of six women who sparked their evening by meeting with a professional psychic who worked at the restaurant.

"The ladies are no longer looking at me as someone to shun," Pilar said to Max Osterhagen. Max had not moved in, but he stayed at Pilar's often enough so that people who were interested in that sort of thing mistakenly believed he was in residence.

"And why would they shun you?" he asked from his place on an upholstered bedroom chair. He enjoyed watching Pilar dress. He found her to be an exceptionally lovely woman. In her early forties to his late forties, she was a never-ending delight. After being a widower for six years, Max was once again ready for marriage and he wanted it with Pilar. But there was something she had not shared with him, something that was holding her back, so he was moving cautiously.

"You know the big reason why they shunned me," she said.

Max smiled. "Yes. You told me about it as if it were a confession."

She turned to study him. "You didn't seem to see it that way."

"I didn't. You shouldn't judge yourself by what people say or might say. You acted as you did for a good reason. And it's in the past." He settled more comfortably in his chair. "What is the second reason the ladies might shun you?"

"My association with Jessi Spellman. It was a flaw of mine to find her amusing. I wouldn't have been amused had I known better. I directed her to a service whose propaganda piece helped her snatch your seat on Town Committee."

Max, trim and compact, his brown hair and neat mustache beginning to glint with strands of silver, answered with his usual good humor. "In retail, the customer is always right; in politics, the voter is always right."

"You know you were the better choice," Pilar said.

"As a resident, I still have a hand in," he said.

By profession, Max was a long-distance truck driver, which suited his ability to be comfortable in his own company for long hours and allowed him to enjoy the changing scenery and to meet new people. Also, his late wife's banking family had been politically involved. Knowledge from that plus his travels gave him a broad perspective.

Watching the way Pilar held her hair, he said, "Yes, pin it up."

He liked seeing the tender nape of her graceful neck.

Her hair upswept, Pilar applied a vivid lipstick. She often went overboard with cosmetics, but the dramatic color went well with her current vintage costume, a broad-shouldered black suit.

"I know what prompted the club's invitation," she said. "That old photo you had of State Senator Fergusson cuddling with his underage stepdaughter. You said I could do whatever I wanted to do with it. I gave it to Francine Smithers. She and her club members are still holding a grudge against the senator because of the way he snubbed them. They apparently found the photo fuel for their vendetta, if that's the right word."

Max nodded. Years back, when on vacation with his late wife, Lois, she recognized Fergusson on the beach with a young redhead. From their behavior, it was obvious that she was his girlfriend. Lois knew the man because he was an agent in the insurance company that served her family's bank. The fact that his amorous activities appeared in the background of one of their vacation photos had merely amused them. They hadn't known then that the redhead was the man's fifteen-year-old stepdaughter. Max hadn't recalled that particular photo until the JumpRope ladies became enraged at Fergusson, who had gone into politics and was now the state senator for Melton County, where the town of JumpRope was located.

He saw Pilar off with a kiss and then stood looking after her little yellow Mazda as she headed to the meeting. He wondered if the women would try to tangle her in what she'd called their *vendetta*.

No matter, he thought with a smile. Pilar would make up her mind and do what she thought best to do.

Chapter 2

$\mathcal{P}$ilar drove to the town's Main Street which led to the Teddy Bear Tavern and Grill, where the monthly Voodoo Club dinner meetings were held. She knew the club's name came when a gentleman friend of a member joked that the psychic portions of the meetings were nothing but "voodoo." The group picked up on it because the idea made them smile.

The club probably treated this psychic business like a parlor game, sitting around the table holding hands while someone pretended to read the future. Did they realize she had no interest in the supernatural? As an interior decorator, she enjoyed decorating herself in costume-like fashions, her distinctive style impressing clients. Her oft-times exotic choices, with old-fashioned ropes of beads and gypsy-like blouses and full skirts, might have led the club members to believe she favored tarot cards and crystal balls.

Her smile faded as she considered her conversation with Max. She believed him when he said the actions that had harmed her in the eyes of many didn't matter to him. Max, honest and straightforward, was a man who meant what he said. It was so good that she had met him when she was finally able to take part in a true relationship. Even so, it was hard not to remember her past.

Back then, widowed a year and still mourning, she was food

shopping while her son, Alexander, was in his kindergarten class. When she came from the market with her full grocery cart, she saw Bryce McCarty on a bench under the store's portico. His son had also been in kindergarten and she knew him because of carpooling. A dreadful accident had recently destroyed Bryce's life. He'd been notified at work that his wife and son had died when a drunk driver struck her car. The only survivor had been their infant daughter.

Glad that he still had his daughter, she'd reflected that if she hadn't had young Alexander to raise after her husband died, she might have been tempted to end her life.

Bryce was looking at the contents of his shopping bag and mumbling to himself.

Curious, she moved her cart near him. He looked up. "Why did I buy this?" He said it as if she might have the answer.

"What did you buy?" She sat on the bench beside him.

He pulled out a box of cereal made of flakes and bright-colored marshmallow shapes. "It's my son's favorite."

"You were thinking of him when you bought it," she said.

"Yes, only—" His voice broke and he fell silent.

After a pause, she said, "Tell me about him."

"He's so bright, so very bright." Bryce related examples of things the boy said, and things they had done together. He spoke in the present tense as if the boy still lived.

Abruptly, he shook himself. "They tell me what to do, what not to do, especially not to do this. Thinking of him, talking of him. They say I must move past it, but—"

Pilar spoke from her own experience. "They think it's helpful to tell you that, but it's not."

Nodding, he stood. Clutching his shopping bag as if it were precious, he turned abruptly and made for the parking lot.

Several nights later, he rang her doorbell.

"I don't know why I'm here," he said when she answered. "I'm sorry. I'll leave."

He looked and sounded desolate. Pilar felt he was close to the end of his rope. "Come inside," she said and stepped back so he could enter.

Once inside, he broke down, sobbing as he spoke of his wife and his son. His daughter, he said, was with his sister in her home.

"I don't know my baby daughter, not like I knew my son. She's getting care and love from my sister, who has two small children. Staying with her, she'll have a brother and sister. They say I should live for my surviving child, but she won't remember me. What I do now will make no difference to her."

Hearing his words as an indication that he might end his life, Pilar took him into her arms. If she questioned her behavior, she need only think back to when she and Vincent were first married. His brother, the only other living member of his family, had died of a sudden illness. Pilar had held Vincent in her arms and given him the comfort he needed. In their bed, he had said in a grief-stricken voice, "I don't know what I would do if I didn't have you." She had touched his beloved face and remembered thinking that if he hadn't had her; she prayed he would have had somebody else.

With Bryce, she thought, she had temporarily become that somebody else. Another human being to listen and comfort, to hold him as he wept without shame, and to answer the need that proved life still had meaning.

Whatever their time together might be called, it hadn't lasted long and had served its purpose.

Several months later they met by chance.

He told her his mother was staying with him to care for his daughter while he worked. "I'm getting to know my little girl," he said. The photo he pulled from his wallet showed a happy infant, old enough now to sit up as she gleefully waved a toy.

"A sweetheart," Pilar said.

"That she is," Bryce answered with pride.

Months later, she saw him again and was pleased to see none of the shadows that had weighed on him so heavily when he'd first come to her door.

"I've met someone," he said.

"That's good," Pilar said. They smiled at one another, with no need for further words.

Her thoughts of the past and later associations were distracted as she entered a section that gave her a distant view of the multi-gabled brick mansion of Menno DeGroot, the site of the first recorded JumpRope murder in the 1800s.

Menno claimed he'd come home from an evening at the Spyglass Tavern to find his wife dead in their bedroom. An astute constable found that Menno was the one who had done the deed. He took his own life by poison before he could stand trial.

A crime solved too quickly to need the kind of clairvoyant assistance the members of the Voodoo Club possibly believed in, Pilar thought as she arrived at the restaurant.

She saw Francine Smithers in the parking lot, frowning in the darkening March evening. She wore a smart-looking coat. Francine was brand-name-proud. Pilar figured that during the evening, the woman would find a way to call attention to the designer.

"I was afraid you might not come," Francine said as Pilar stepped from her car. "The club members would have been disappointed."

Pilar smiled. "Did my invitation have anything to do with that photograph I gave you?"

Francine, who disliked being anticipated, said briskly, "Come along and find out." A short woman with square shoulders topping a squat body, Francine motored ahead, opening the door and leading the way.

The Tudor-style tavern had two huge banquet rooms in addition to a bar and several smaller dining areas, all with beamed ceilings, stone fireplaces, and walls with entertaining murals of quaint villages populated with cuddly teddy bears. The tavern, owned by Chef Theodore "Teddy" Baird, a chunky, round-faced man, had not only given his nickname to the establishment but by making his business logo a teddy bear jumping rope, he had tied it in with the name of the town.

Still trailing Francine as they approached the club's small dining room, the word *gables* intruded into Pilar's mind. It was like a voice speaking to her. The word repeated: *gables*. Pilar broke step long enough to cause Francine to impatiently glance over her shoulder. The phantom voice ceased.

Pilar caught up to Francine, still wondering about her weird experience. The only connection she could think of was just having glimpsed DeGroot's many gabled mansion.

In the club room, she was greeted by four of the club members. Toria Dahlgaard, in her early thirties, was engaged to the mayor. Nancy Lou Withers, and Amy Newton in their twenties, were the two youngest members. Nancy Lou was a pediatric nurse at the Melton County Hospital, and Amy could be hired when Nancy Lou knew of a new mother who needed extra help at home. Iris Roundtree, the Town Hall floating secretary, was in her sixties, the same age as Francine.

Darlene Gage was the last to arrive. Without preliminary, she said, "Do you know that two Peach Acres houses have collapsing foundations?" Fiftyish, blonde and resolutely trim, Darlene was in charge of the JumpRope property maintenance, construction, and zoning department. She ruled with an iron hand with no time for velvet gloves. She took an empty chair, grumbling the word, "Developers!"

Commiserate murmurs all around and hidden glances. Long-divorced Darlene despised developers, yet the latest one to come into town, suave bachelor, businessman-engineer, Acer Wolfgang, was patiently and persistently pursuing her. People were laying bets. The smart money was on Acer, a man as charming as he was wealthy.

The waiter took drink requests as the ladies chatted.

Pilar heard Amy and Nancy Lou discuss, with cheerful enthusiasm, the celebrity news on the Internet. They seemed fascinated by an award-winning singer's highly publicized affairs.

Smiling to herself, Pilar thought that the singer probably had more relationships in a few years than she'd had in twenty. Not that the town folk would believe it. Far more interesting to speculate about a scandalous widow who had entertained men.

What they didn't understand was how alone her husband's death had left her. She and Vincent had enjoyed entertaining but no matter how fond they were of their friends, when it was just the two of them together, they were complete. As for her life after he was gone, their brilliant son, Alexander, who had earned his doctorate in English literature at age twenty-four, saw her as an embarrassment. He once said she swooped in on the broken-hearted men like a warrior-healer in a drama from ancient Greece. What he hadn't understood was that in caring for others, she had found healing for herself that now allowed her to develop a relationship with Max.

Francine, a retired high school math teacher, who was in charge of the meeting, rapped on the table, then turned to Pilar, "Our group was delighted with the old photo of State Senator Fergusson and his stepdaughter, Leslie, but we haven't decided the best way to use it. As you probably know, three of our club members belong to the Ladies Civic Group and three belong to the Joint Emergency Squad and Fire Department Auxiliary. Both groups devote many volunteer hours to worthwhile projects and customarily invite dignitaries outside the community to town events. Fergusson never accepted *our* invitations, yet he appeared at a committeeman's funeral, and he appeared at the January township reorganization meeting to swear in Jessi Spellman to a seat on Town Committee, so—"

Interrupting, Amy jumped up, her cheeks pink with emotion. "Tell it like it was, Francine. It was about winning elections and gathering campaign funds. He needs financial backers for his long-range plans: to win a seat in Congress, and then run for president. We have nobody in town to throw money at him so why was he here making a big deal over Jessi Spellman? I'll tell you why. Darlene discovered Jessi lied and told him that Acer Wolfgang had financially backed her for her committee run. He came to play up to Jessi with the idea that she would assure him Acer's support."

Darlene spoke up. "Acer has no use for Jessi and her schemes. She and her husband, Arnie, are creating a restaurant on property that adjoins the old Mather farm where Acer is constructing houses. His water feature and landscaping will separate his property from hers.”

Nancy Lou, her copper-brown complexion set off by face-framing natural curls, said, “Nobody who’s dealt with Jessi thinks much of her—except her husband, Arnie. He worships her.”

Francine, miffed by Amy’s interruption, grabbed the reins again. “Our concerns have become more serious. Fergusson believes a married candidate has a better chance of being elected. Leslie is now of age, and her mother has been dead for years, but voters wouldn’t like a candidate marrying his stepdaughter. We’ve learned that Fergusson plans a marriage of convenience that will allow him and Leslie to continue their games with no one the wiser. If voters knew the hanky-panky started when Leslie was fifteen, they’d rightfully see it as child abuse. Pilar’s dated photo of Fergusson snuggling with his underage stepchild is proof of his behavior, and now, Pilar, we need your help.”

Pilar frowned. “Isn’t the photo enough?”

A flush rising along her throat because it embarrassed her to say negative things, Toria said, “Having the photo isn’t enough. We would need to let people see it, like putting it on the Internet. That’s something like Jessi Spellman might do. We don’t want to create a scandal, but if Fergusson is a bad person, we want to find out.”

Pilar said, “Why not give the photo to the reporter, Joyce Jane Gilbert? You should have invited her to your meeting tonight, not me. Reporters have the job of finding out things and putting them in print.”

“We did think about giving it to JJ,” Francine said, using Joyce Jane’s nickname, “but the mischief with his stepdaughter is probably only one part of his tawdry life. We want more information. Your son, Alexander, is dating a girl whose grandfather is among Fergusson’s New York supporters. Alexander does writing on the Internet and knows how to research gossip. It’s called bogging.”

“Blogging,” corrected Darlene.

“Blogging,” Francine echoed emphatically as if she’d said it right in the first place. “We invited you here because we want you to ask Alexander to check out Fergusson.”

Pilar sputtered a laugh. “You want him to be a spy?”

She was tickled by the notion of Alexander as an undercover agent. Five-foot-eleven and burly, he'd once been so shy around women that he'd made up a girlfriend to save face, but things had changed. His girlfriend now was the heiress, Solstice Windsor. Pilar recalled times when he'd been told that instead of writing plays that he couldn't get produced, he had the voice of an actor. Maybe a character's role as a secret agent wasn't so farfetched after all.

Chapter 3

With the business about State Senator Fergusson settled, meals were served. Appreciating the company more than she had expected, Pilar looked forward to dessert. Teddy's had the most delectable chocolate cake. She was savoring it in her imagination when plump and cheerful Iris, who sat next to her, began explaining how the individual sessions with the psychic, Mar-see-ah, would proceed.

Pilar drew back. "Individual? I expected her to join us at the table."

"Oh, no, that would be like a séance," Iris said, the expression on her round face earnest. "These are personal readings."

Pilar felt increasingly uneasy as Iris explained. "We go one by one to see Mar-see-ah in another room, and when everyone is done, we each report and try to make sense out of what she said, which can be mysterious. But it's so much fun!" In her innocent enthusiasm, Iris didn't notice Pilar's lack of it. "The odd thing is, you'll think what Mar-see-ah's said doesn't mean anything, but later, something will happen and you realize she was on target."

Pilar was glad of the distraction when the waiter appeared with a large tray of desserts and selections were made

The sessions with the psychic began. Nancy Lou was the first to go.

Talk around the table turned to the May dedication of the new war memorials, but Pilar, paying scant attention, realized how uncomfortable she was with the idea of a private session with a psychic. She didn't accept supernatural abilities, but she did believe in intuitively reading people. How many interior decorating jobs had she won because she'd sensed what clients really wanted despite what they'd said? A person billing herself as a "psychic" must have developed these skills to a high degree. Pilar had no intention of allowing anyone to scratch around the edges of pain and guilt she'd kept hidden for twenty years.

Several members had gone out and returned, and then it was Pilar's turn. A placid expression concealing her turbulent emotions, she left the room and headed in the direction where she had been told the readings were held. Her path led to a dimly lit alcove.

Her eyes adjusting, she saw an ordinary-looking middle-aged woman with graying hair seated at a small table. An empty chair angled out invitingly on the opposite side. This was Mar-see-ah? Well, what had she expected? An exotic face and a jeweled turban? She considered the woman's name. Pilar bet people used to call her "Marsha," but "Mar-see-ah" was more dramatic.

The psychic blinked as if the sight of Pilar had caught her by surprise, then she smiled and invited Pilar to take a seat. "You're a guest with the club tonight?"

"Yes, but I'm not interested in a reading. I only came out because I didn't want to be rude to the members."

Mar-see-ah nodded and said gently, "It isn't necessary to have a reading. Go to the bar for something to drink. When you come back, I'll tell you some innocent thing to say to the others. You won't have to worry about being rude."

Her mood lifting, Pilar proceeded to the bar and ordered a brandy. At ease, she idly looked at the mural on a far wall. It showed a storybook town with a teddy bear reading a newspaper while jumping a rope turned by two other bears. She smiled, knowing the bar was a hangout for reporters of the daily county paper, the *Melton Monitor*. Their patronage had earned the bar the nickname, "News Room, Booze Room."

When deciding it was time to return to Mar-see-ah, Pilar stood and abruptly heard the words *gables* and *peaks*. She knew the words came from inside her head but as before they seemed as clear as spoken speech.

Stunned, she sank to her seat again. Aware of the murmur of conversation from those clustered around tables and soft music from speakers behind the bar, she wondered what could have inspired the phantom voice? Her gaze returned to the mural. The painted town showed buildings with peaked roofs and gables. Okay, but why would what she saw come to her in unearthly words?

After an uneasy moment, she wondered how long people stayed with the psychic. She hoped no one would come looking for her. On her feet once again, she retraced her steps back to Mar-see-ah. The woman stepped to meet her. "I should explain the procedure before you return to the others so you know what would normally happen. You would sit opposite me and I would hold your hands." She reached and gently touched Pilar's hands.

Pilar felt an unexpected warmth. Startled, she looked up.

Still touching Pilar's hands, the psychic said, "You have —"

Pilar tensed, uncertain of what she would hear next.

"—a great deal of intuition," the woman finished.

Relaxing, Pilar smiled. "Yes, it's a help in my decorating business, sensing what people want. My son says I can see into his head, but that's simply because I'm his mother."

Mar-see-nodded. "Of course. When you return to the others, tell them the words that came to me when we met were, *Look for the light.*" Her hand fell away from Pilar's, and then she said, "I suspect you might not believe this, but random thoughts, images, and even sounds, can carry serious meaning."

Pilar stared. This sounded too close to hearing the words *gables* and *peaks* as if spoken to her.

Mar-see-ah smiled. "You also might be interested to know that when I was young, my name was Marcia, pronounced Marsha, with two syllables." In a more serious tone, she added, "Take care from this day on. If anything worries you, you can always get in touch with me here."

Pilar thanked her and left, feeling dazed. Mar-see-ah's explanation about her name had to be a coincidence. The woman *couldn't* have known about her earlier thoughts.

When with the others again, no one seemed to think she had been away too long. At ease, she found her chocolate cake as enjoyable as she had first anticipated. After everyone had finished their psychic session, it was time to report what Mar-see-ah had said.

Iris was told something that the group members finally decided was like saying, "Little pitchers have big ears." Everyone knew Iris's job with the township put her in a position to hear just about everything that was going on.

When it was her turn, Pilar, with a shrug, reported, "I was told, 'Look for the light.'"

The group seriously pondered over what Pilar knew was a random phrase. Toria finally said, "I suppose it could mean you will come to an understanding about something."

Iris leaned forward, eagerly. "I know! It has something to do with your decorator business! The right shade of paint, dark or light, or maybe the right ceiling fixture for a room you're fixing for somebody."

"That could apply," Pilar said. Iris's cheerful naiveté settled the matter. Mar-see-ah was all savvy show business. How foolish to have felt anxious. As for the phantom words, she had imagined them. Having been uneasy about meeting a professed psychic, she had worked herself into a nervous state.

The Voodoo Club evening concluded and the women prepared to leave. Francine took her coat from the rack, saying, "You can't go wrong with a Calvin Klein fashion," a comment received by the others with knowing smiles.

As Pilar headed home, she thought about Alexander and the notion of him doing an investigation. She would invite him and Solstice, to dinner and discuss the idea of them investigating Senator Fergusson. Whatever they decided, they would have a pleasant evening, thanks to the club. She should send them a thank you card.

Approaching the center of town, she saw Sable's card shop still lit although neighboring shops were closed. Thinking of the moment she'd had with Mar-see-ah, she smiled, remembering she was supposed to look for the light. In any case, the shop was an opportunity to purchase the card she'd been thinking about. Sable, a talented artist who worked with greeting card companies as well as selling cards, often kept her shop open late. She was a procrastinator and was always catching up on things she'd ignored as time slid by.

Pilar parked at the curb and entered the shop. She called Sable's name. There was no answer. She felt a flash of alarm, then figured Sable must be in her workroom in the back. Heading there, she moved around a display case and gasped when she saw Sable and a fallen stepladder on the floor.

A heavy-set woman, Sable had apparently been on the stepladder when it fell, taking her with it. She'd landed hard, striking her head. Bleeding from the head wound, she lay sprawled under greeting cards she must have pulled from an upper shelf. Her eyes in death were open in a wide, unseeing stare. Around her body lay a garden of cards that pictured red roses now blooming in spilled blood.

Chapter 4

Jessi Spellman was furious with State Senator Earl Fergusson.

How dare he treat her like a stranger? Hadn't he come to JumpRope to swear her in when she was elected? She was not only a Township Committeeperson, she was a woman the senator had wined and dined at his estate. What had happened to their beautiful relationship? She was also buddies with his wealthy New York State pals who wanted to bankroll Fergusson's political future. He needed his friends, so why was he blowing her off?

When she had last called his office, the fourth time in two days, his secretary once again told her he was "busy." No reason, like being on the senate floor (an expression she'd recently learned) or in an important meeting, but just, *busy.*

Jessi fumed. Too busy to speak with *her*?

It was early on Friday morning and Jessi was driving through the bright sunshine to the JumpRope business district and Sable's card shop. Now that the weather was good, progress was being made on the crappy old buildings that would become a five-star restaurant for her husband, Arnie. Good-hearted Sable had created an advertising flyer for free.

Jessi was still insulted that her plan to flip the property to Acer Wolfgang had failed because Arnie had been determined to quit his title search business and be a chef in his own restaurant. Normally mild-mannered, and not much to look at, when Arnie put his foot down, he could be ferocious. Jessi thrilled as she thought what a man he could be. She had finally gotten interested in the idea of a restaurant—or at least interested in the theme she'd come up with.

She was naming it "Carousel." In the course of a title search, Arnie learned that in the 1800s JumpRope had been home to the McKinnon Amusement Park and Circus. The park had a Ferris wheel, a carousel, and an amusement arcade.

When finished, the restaurant would offer three dining spaces: a Fifties-style luncheonette in what had been an old garage, a Twenties-style cocktail lounge in the new section between the garage and an old barn, and inside the barn, a Gay Nineties banquet hall, with more dining on a roped and tasseled balcony that overlooked the tables on the main floor. A lighted, revolving carousel would sit atop the restaurant roof. There would be three ponies with riders dressed to represent each of the period styles of the three restaurants.

Was that not the product of a mastermind?

She stopped at a light and glanced up to the rearview mirror to admire her reflection, kiss-kissing at the sight of her pretty little face: her skin so white, her hair so black, her eyes a flashing green. The light changed to a matching green. *Green*, the color of money, her favorite color. Jessi approached the card shop and slowed her vehicle. There was yellow tape across the sidewalk and police cars in the street. What was going on and where was Sable? Jessi had made arrangements to arrive early because Sable promised to be there. She should be outside chasing the cops away. Had she pulled one of her forgetting tricks?

Jessi had taken a color copy of the Sable's flyer home to show Arnie and he'd loved it. She took a photo of it for social media, but she also wanted flyers to post around town and to mail. Why pay for the copies if Sable let her do it for free? She'd run them off on the shop's color copier and have hundreds ready to announce the opening date of the Carousel Restaurant and all its marvelous features.

She'd been counting on Senator Fergusson chipping in for the envelopes and postage. He'd talked about using the restaurant as the county base for his district political endeavors. Only now, he wouldn't even come to the phone.

Furious with the senator all over again, Jessi parked, grabbed her ad copy, flung her small, curvy body from her car and crossed the street to Sable's shop. She hadn't gotten up early for nothing. No way would she tolerate a delay.

"Excuse me, Committeewoman Spellman." One of the cops had stepped forward to block her way. "I'm sorry, but if the card shop is your destination, it's closed."

The cop was big and dark-skinned. Alfonso somebody or somebody Alfonso, first or last name, who cared? He at least knew who *she* was.

She looked up into the officer's face and flashed her cutest smile. "I know it's before hours, but I have business here. It's not closed to me."

"I'm afraid it is. There's been an incident."

"What are you talking about?"

"An accident," he clarified. "Miss Kilgallen didn't survive."

Jessi gasped. "You mean she's dead?"

"Yes, Ma'am."

"Is her body still in there?"

"No, Ma'am."

"Okay. I didn't want to see her, anyway. All I want to do is use her copying machine."

"I'm sorry. The shop is closed until the investigation is completed."

"What investigation? Was there a break-in?"

"I don't have additional information, Committeewoman Spellman. The owner is dead and the shop is closed. I regret any inconvenience."

"Oh, sure, you regret. Is Chief Parkerson in today?" He'd better be, she thought. That's why she paid taxes.

Alfonso nodded. "Yes, Ma'am, the Chief's on the job."

"Then call him on that shoulder mic and tell him I need to get inside this shop immediately."

Alfonso took a breath and then did as she requested.

Jessi, tapping her size four shoe, heard crackly gobbledygook and assumed her directions were getting answers. Finally, she heard a voice that could only belong to the police chief, Allen "Slim" Parkerson."

"Yes, Sir," Alfonso said into the mic. He tapped something to silence the device and looked down at Jessi. "The Chief said you can meet him at Town Hall later this morning if you have questions."

Jessi stared in disbelief. "You mean I can't go inside the shop?" The next words tripped off her tongue so effortlessly that she amazed herself. "I have work to do for Sable that I promised to finish for her this morning. It was horribly important to her. If she's dead, it's even more crucial. You have no idea the trouble you'll be in for holding this up."

"The Chief said—"

"Yeah, yeah." Fuming, Jessi turned her back on him and returned to her car.

Her tires screeched as she roared off. At first, she had no destination in mind. And then she had a thought.

The chief said he would see her in Town Hall later that morning, so maybe he wasn't there right now. If he wasn't, she could tell the person on duty at the window whatever she wanted.

She smiled triumphantly at her quick thinking. The police department had a color copier. If the cops were keeping her from Sable's machine, it was only fair that she used theirs. If they didn't like it, they had nobody to blame but themselves.

Chapter 5

That same Friday morning, Colonel McDuff, U.S. Army, Retired, headed to his favorite spot along the Hitchmile Stream to spend a few hours fishing and to escape from thoughts of poor Sable Kilgallen. From all accounts, she had died the evening before in a fall from a stepladder in her shop. Although Sable was a fairly young woman, she had not been built for standing on ladders. The Colonel ruefully glanced down over his grey mustache at his portly figure and decided the same could be said of him.

Iris had telephoned him the previous evening to give him the news. Pilar Fanshawe had stopped at the card shop on the way home from one of their hocus-pocus dinners. The emergency people had been called and the news had gotten around quickly, as bad news always does.

Over the years Sable had done some very nice artwork for the JumpRope Historical Society, of which the Colonel was the proud curator. He thought of her dioramas that illustrated the British attempts to burn down the historic Spyglass Tavern and the Presbyterian Church, their efforts routed by the militia. These occurrences were as fondly regarded by the Colonel, a Revolutionary War re-enactor as if he had been part of the long-ago action himself. Of course, Sable didn't have the dioramas ready in time for the event for which they had been promised. Volunteers had to complete the painting. However, none of them could have created the dioramas. That was where Sable had excelled, and this was no time to be critical. He hoped there would be a decent community turnout because he didn't think Sable had any relatives. A lonely funeral was a sorrowful thing.

After parking his car on the road's wide shoulder, he carried his gear along a trail to his favorite fishing spot. Although this section of the Hitchmile Stream was only seven feet wide, the force of the water around a curve had scoured a hollow where fish enjoyed the cool depth. There might be walleyes there but the Colonel didn't expect to catch any. All he wanted was to sit on his favorite boulder and smell the water, hear the birds and watch the antics of frogs and turtles. After a peaceful morning, he would feel ready to go on to the museum and open it up for a busy day of sorting through donated old photos and documents from a house that had been emptied.

He reached the grassy area bordering the stream. It was currently dry, but the Hitchmile was famous for flooding after every hard rain. The Colonel was disappointed to see plastic and paper trash strewn along the stream's skimpy shore. Some careless person had enjoyed a picnic then dumped their leavings instead of disposing of them properly.

Grumbling, he bent to pick up a discarded bag and used it as a receptacle for the trash. He was even more disappointed to find a tin can with drying worms stuck inside. That had been bait, which meant the litterbug had been a fisherman who should have known better.

He carried the bag to what he fancied as his boulder even though he knew he was probably only one of many who had adopted the same outcropping. He dropped the waste bag where he wouldn't forget it and sat, a contented man able to look back on a reasonably long and happy life. Good early years, a successful military career starting in Korea in 1950, and a warm marriage. The Colonel hadn't enjoyed being alone after the death of his wife, but his friendship with Iris Roundtree was a renewing miracle. He smiled, thinking of Iris's cheerful smile and the tender moments they shared. His contentment would reach perfection if only Iris would agree to be his bride.

Thinking of that happy possibility, he affixed his bait to the hook, stood, and stepped to the edge of the water where he cast his line as far out as possible. He was about to step backward to resume his seating place when a flickering downstream caught his eye. A dragonfly. Caught by the insect's shimmer, the Colonel squinted and followed its flight until it landed on a floating object and then was lost in the sunlit glitter where the water swirled around the object.

The Colonel moved closer and decided he was seeing the toe end of a rubber boot floating in the stream. Probably worn by a fisherman, more ambitious than he, who had waded out in the water. He conjectured that the wearer had stepped into a hole deep enough to fill his boots. He'd slipped free of the footwear to avoid being pulled down. The misstep had probably dunked the owner and earned him a snootful of water. By the time the poor fellow stopped coughing, his boots had drifted and were lost until one snagged on something.

Where the mate was, the Colonel didn't know, but he could at least pull this one to shore. Otherwise, it was just one more piece of junk that didn't belong. Reeling in his line, the Colonel cast it toward the boot. After several attempts, he managed to hook it somewhere under the water, but he couldn't pull it loose.

The Colonel decided the boot was snagged on a submerged log that had floated down stream after the last storm and gotten stuck. To get enough oomph into his pull, he needed to be out further, but he didn't want to get his feet wet. To dislodge the boot without stepping further, he needed something sturdier than his pole. Laying it on the ground with the hook still caught, he rummaged in the nearby brush until he found a sturdy broken-off branch. Returning with the branch to the stream's edge, he began in earnest to dislodge the boot so he could reel it in.

Poking into the water under the boot, he gave a hard shove and something budged. A log, just as he had thought. He jabbed again. There was something about the second shove that was different than he'd expected. There was motion just under the surface. The object he'd made contact with seemed less solid than a log. He gave another shove.

The water swirled and this time the thing that had been just under the surface broke through and into view. A much larger, bulky object, floating, turned gently with the current. With a gasp, the Colonel stepped back, the branch falling from his suddenly nerveless fingers.

The boot was not lost.

It was still being worn by its owner.

Chapter 6

The JumpRope Township's mayor, Holland (Holly) Kingston Jr., was in his Town Hall office early on Friday even though it wasn't one of his regular days. His phone was ringing non-stop with people wanting information about the death of Sable Kilgallen.

Whenever anything bad happened in the close-knit community, residents needed a combination of information and reassurance. The mayor was the person they called.

The town was too small for Holly to be there full-time. His regular job was being the Supervisor of Melton County Engineering and Public Works. Small-boned and five-foot-seven with his shoes on, he was stronger than he looked. He had started with the county road crew when he was twenty-one and worked his way up to management. Except for occasions when he was on the road with a crew, his professional dress for both jobs was business attire, sparked off with one of his colorful art-themed neckties.

Later that morning, just as the calls about Sable quieted, he received a call from Pilar wanting to know if it was true that Rufus Neilson had drowned. Holly had just received word himself, and now, starting with Pilar, he knew the calls would start all over again this time about Rufus.

"It's true, Pilar, I'm sorry to say. It was a terrible accident."

"Thank you," she said and hung up.

Holly had heard the tremor in her voice and remembered that

Pilar's husband had drowned years before. Now this, happening after she'd found Sable's body must be putting her in a terrible spin.

Sable had been known because of her card shop, but Rufus was a lifetime resident with a family that went back for generations. All who had eaten at Krupple's Diner were acquainted with Rufus and his pals, the Old Geezers, a self-named group of WWII veterans who parked themselves on a long bench near the diner entrance. They wore matching black wool *Geezer* jackets regardless of the weather and entertained themselves with private jokes and comments about the people passing by.

Eating a vending machine lunch, Holly continued to take calls from residents as well as the media. Weary, he was looking forward to an evening with his fiancée, Toria. She would be waiting for him to pick her up at closing time at the county records building where she worked. He was thinking of which restaurant they would choose for dinner when Slim Parkerson, the town police chief, stopped in.

"Hey, bud," Slim said. "Busy day, huh?" Dressed in a short-sleeved blue uniform, Slim leaned his tall, rangy form against the door jam. His dark blond hair was rumpled from going at it with large, long-fingered hands that had once mastered a basketball and now mastered bullies, drunks and lawbreakers who disturbed the peace of his town. Slim's eyes were a light blue-grey but shadowed as they were by brows and lashes, their color was often a mystery.

"On my way to see Rufus's son, George," Slim said. "If you can spare a half-hour, want to ride shotgun?"

"Glad to," Holly said. He'd been wondering when would be a good time to call on the bereaved man.

George had been alone after his wife's death until he sold his house and moved in with his father, a widower in failing health. George had to have known Rufus's days were numbered, but the old man's drowning must have come as a cruel surprise.

Holly and Slim had been best friends since elementary school. Slim, now six-foot-four, had always been tall. Holly had always been pocket-sized, but their friendship had endured. Nobody enjoys visiting the bereaved, but Holly knew Slim had already spoken with George earlier in the day.

When they stepped outside, Slim headed to his Dodge Challenger instead of the chief's car. "So this visit is personal, right?" Holly said when they were on the road.

"Maybe," Slim said. "You've been on the phone hearing what everybody thinks happened to Rufus. What's the word?"

"Nothing you haven't heard, I guess." Holly smoothed his necktie, a Van Gogh field with a blustery sky to suit the windy days of March weather and the present turmoil. He wondered what Slim meant by *maybe*, but he figured he'd soon find out. "I heard the same thing from a number of callers. Rufus woke up wanting to go fishing. He had coffee with his medicine at home and then George drove him to Krupple's for a wrapped breakfast sandwich and orange juice."

"Did he have it poured in one of the cups from his collection?"

"Yes, according to habit, Rufus brought one of his sports memorabilia cups for the juice. George drove to the Hitchmile Stream, watched his father go down the path leading to the water, and then continued on to an appointment. This was around eight-thirty this morning. George was supposed to pick his father up at lunchtime only by then, it was too late."

"And the speculations?" Slim said.

"People heard that the pills Rufus took made him light-headed. Maybe he was in the stream and 'got overtook' as one person put it. If he went down, his boots would have started to fill. If he wore his Geezer jacket, it would have sucked up water and weighed him down."

"He was wearing the jacket," Slim said.

Holly winced. "Those wool jackets had felt letters and numerals like the guys wore in their high school heydays. Sad to think the jacket that meant good memories had contributed to Rufus' death."

Slim made the turn leading to George's street. "Anything more?"

"Nothing that you haven't already heard. Rufus supposedly was becoming increasingly confused. He'd started wandering outside at night, trying to find people and places that no longer exist. George had installed a door alarm." Holly turned to look at Slim. "Any particular reason you want to know what I know?"

"I figured you hear impartial stories about what he did this morning, and you did. I found the kind of cup Rufus had in his collection broken and tossed in the bushes."

"Whoa! That's mean. Rufus prized his cup collection."

"Yeah. He'd stop people in front of the diner, hold up a cup with the name covered, and challenge them to identify the player who was pictured."

"I played along, even when I knew," Holly said. "Harmless. But maybe it got under some kid's skin. The Geezers were always laughing and saying how the young generation didn't know what real music and real heroes were." Holly frowned. "You're thinking some kid went wandering this morning, maybe cutting school, found the cup, and thought it would be a joke to smash it?"

"Don't know for sure, but since it's the only cup found on the site, I figure it belonged to Rufus. I want to ask George to be sure."

George Neilson, a retired auto salesman, was seated on the front porch of his father's 1910 yellow, four-square house on a street of similarly styled vintage homes. He was of average height with close-cut, sandy-colored hair and a pale narrow face. Holly, whose hobby was painting, always thought that George's coloring came from a narrow wedge of the color wheel.

"Kitchen filled with women in it, stocking me up on food," George said with a weary sigh. "Good to see some fellers for a change."

Holly and Slim both nodded. The passing of a JumpRope resident caused the members of the Joint Fire and Emergency Auxiliary and the Ladies Civil Group to vie in bringing the tastiest casseroles and desserts to bereaved families.

After shaking hands and expressing sympathies, Slim and Holly took seats on old metal-backed porch chairs. George spoke as if he still couldn't believe what had happened.

"He was as right as rain early today," he said with a faraway stare. "He wanted to fish and I said fine. It was a break from him hanging all day in front of Krupple's."

"What number was he?" Holly asked, keeping the topic on Rufus, but from a happier time. He knew that each Geezer jacket sported a different number. Some observers claimed it referred to the wearer's best year, and more than one theory offered inventively smutty details.

"Number 23."

"Know what the number meant?"

"Secret sealed tighter than Fort Knox," George said with a smile as weary and drab as his coloring.

Iris Roundtree stepped from inside, greeted Holly and Slim, and asked if anyone wanted refreshments. Getting no takers, she said to George, "Can you tell me when the funeral will be?"

"Dad always said he wanted to be cremated. I liked the idea of him buried next to Mom at Sycamore Shade, but I guess ashes can be buried the same. With his history of heart trouble, his doctor said there would be no need for an autopsy. I should never have left him by the water. Should have stayed."

"You had no way of knowing what would happen," Holly said.

"But he drowned!" George said, suddenly showing emotion. "If he felt woozy and just slept away on the beach, all peaceful like, that's one thing. But he was in the water, probably in a panic, crying for help that never came. His doctor said the shock of immersion probably knocked him out. An autopsy wouldn't prove if he knew or not." George shook his head. "That's when I decided to go along with the doctor's advice. Going along with cremation, too."

"Following a loved one's wishes always brings comfort," Iris said, clasping her plump hands in a prayerful gesture.

She looked ready to say more and Holly braced for her to come up with problems caused by dead people whose last wishes weren't followed, but all she said was, "Rufus's death has been so upsetting."

Holly figured this comment was partly on behalf of her friend, the Colonel, who was probably still shaken from finding the body.

Iris returned to the house and Slim opened a parcel he had brought from the car. It revealed a tall plastic cup that had been broken, one side still attached to the bottom, the other side a separate piece. It was the type of cup sold with drinks at fast-food restaurants, only this one was from the 1970s. It bore a picture of Leroy Keyes, who had been a Philadelphia Eagles running back and safety.

"That's Dad's cup! Who smashed it?" George stared fiercely at Slim. "One of your officers stomping around?"

"No, my officers don't go stomping around a scene. The cup was in the bushes off the trail."

"That makes no sense." George's face twisted. "Dad was a fan of the Philadelphia Phillies and the Eagles. He treated those cups like gold, but he didn't let them sit on the shelf. He got a kick out of using them. This morning, he had his juice in that one. It should have been with his other fishing things, not broken and tossed in the bushes."

George let more emotion show about the damaged cup than he had about the death of his father. Holly had seen this before, the bereaved fastening on some small thing because the enormity of the loss was too big to handle. He knew Slim had seen this a hundred times more than he had.

"Some rotten kid must have done it," George said, his hands clenched. He glared at Slim. "I want to know who. You send that cup to have any prints identified. I saw it in Dad's hands this morning. I want to know who smashed it."

"I'll send it to the lab," Slim said. "They'll do their best,"

"Got dinner plans?" Slim asked Holly when they were back on the road.

"Yes. Toria and I are heading out of town to somewhere where nobody ever heard of Sable or Rufus. Want to come along?"

Slim, who had no one steady since his fiancée, Lana, had broken off their engagement the previous year, shook his head. "It's Friday night.

Couples all over the place wherever you go. Thanks but no thanks to tagging along with you and your Victorian lady."

Holly didn't argue. Once Slim made up his mind it was stuck in concrete. But the comment about Toria annoyed him. Good-natured verbal shots had been part of his and Slim's relationship since they were kids, but ever since Slim had accidentally discovered that Holly and Toria had separate rooms on an Atlantic City weekend, he'd jab him about it now and then. Okay, so Toria was an old-fashioned wait-for-marriage girl. So what? Holly considered her worth the wait. And if Slim was so smart, how come he was now alone? Not that Holly would say that—it would cut too deep. So, he said, "George sure got emotional over that cup. Will you send it to the lab? Even if there are prints, you can't print all the kids in the school for purposes of comparison."

Slim showed a faint smile. "Yeah, that would have the parents after me with torches and pitchforks. I'll send the cup. Probably get nothing from it, but I said I would." His smile faded. "George's temper about the cup surprised me, too. I guess feeling angry about the cup is better than crying over serious things he can't change."

Solstice had her own painful past that she preferred to keep secret but she had finally told him. She'd been the daughter of a young couple who had fled their homes, disowned their parents, and lived like vagabonds. After Solstice's mother died, her father disappeared after leaving her with people who turned out to be sex and slave traffickers. When Solstice escaped from her last place of bondage, she'd found her way to Brooklyn, New York. She and Alexander met. With his help, she'd been reunited with her only living relative, her wealthy grandfather. She still suffered problems because of her difficult past, and despite her vastly improved circumstances, she'd kept her position with a city trade publication.

When Alexander had emailed her at work to see if she'd go with him to his mother's house, she'd shot back, "count me in, skippy."

Alexander smiled at her lowercase habit. She was a proofreader who received satisfaction from ignoring rules she had to follow at work. As for calling him "Skippy," when they first met he had told her not to call him "Alex" because he didn't approve of nicknames. Laughing at his stuffiness, she never called him *Alexander*. Instead, she'd dreamed up names for him from A-Z.

He felt good about her. She was a strange and difficult girl, but she was *his* strange and difficult girl.

They arrived at his mother's ranch-style house in time to see the fiery globe of the March sun sinking into trees bordering nearby farmland. It made the scene worthy of an elaborate stage set.

As he and Solstice climbed off his red Honda and stowed their helmets, Pilar opened the front door and called a greeting. They crossed the porch under a roof façade with a balcony and a windowed door that was just for show. Alexander always thought the house matched his interest in the theater: illusions, charms, and hidden truths.

Pilar gave him a hug and a kiss on the side of his bearded face and then turned to Solstice, tousled from their motorcycle ride, a fragile gamine with the sweet combination of huge brown eyes, the dark brown of maple syrup, and short-cropped hair, the pale brown of maple sugar. His Maple Girl.

Pilar gave Solstice a warm welcome but made no attempt to embrace her. Solstice shied from being touched and Alexander knew that his mother somehow sensed it. She'd once asked him about it. He'd lied and said it was because of her scoliosis, that spinal twist that elevated one of Solstice's shoulders higher than the other.

"Really?" His mother had said in that tone that told Alexander she didn't think that was the real reason. His mother always seemed to know stuff. It was annoying.

Now she asked, "Have you two had dinner?"

At least she didn't know *that,* Alexander said to himself.

Pilar smiled as if she'd read his thoughts "I have dinner almost all ready. You must feel grubby from that motorcycle ride. I should have my head examined for giving you that machine. And you started driving it when it was still winter!" She shook her head, her crystal earrings catching the light. "But why am I prattling? You two put your things away and take a few minutes to wash off turnpike dust."

"Good idea," Alexander said, thinking his mother never prattled and it showed how shaky she was. He had planned to treat her to dinner but belatedly realized that any nearby restaurant would have people asking her about finding Sable, or worse, talking about Rufus.

He led Solstice, carrying her backpack, down the long hall to the guest room, where she'd slept before.

During dinner, he spoke about a theater workshop he'd joined. Determined to become a playwright, he'd decided to learn more about winning over an audience. Surprisingly, he'd ended up filling in for the director for an amateur performance.

Alexander noticed his mother aimlessly fiddling with two of the ceramic tiles from a set of vintage coasters she had on the table, angling them together to form a triangle, running a finger along the peak, seemingly unaware she was doing it. What was going on? Her head had been slightly tilted, almost as if she listened to words only she could hear.

He asked her if she had any new decorating commissions. She did, and as she spoke of work, she eased back and ceased playing with the coasters and seemed more relaxed.

Pilar listened as Alexander talked but she was also thinking about him and Solstice. Earlier, she had watched them go down the hallway to their separate rooms. Did they visit each other in the night? Not her business, but they hardly seemed the typical couple. She'd seen Solstice resting her head against Alexander's broad chest when they watched TV or a movie. Sometimes she'd twine her fingers in his dark brown beard, but she'd never seen Alexander with both arms around her. It appeared that while Solstice could touch him, he couldn't touch her, at least not without her permission.

Sighing, she decided to simply be glad they had come. Max must have arranged it because she knew Alexander originally had other weekend plans. She was upset over the deaths, especially the drowning, but Max didn't know why it hit her so hard. She prayed he never would.

During dessert, Pilar asked Solstice when she'd last seen her grandfather, who had a three-bedroom home on Central Park West.

"We'll be seeing him soon. He told us that when the cherry trees bloom it's like seeing a fairyland from his window. He'll call when the time is best to see them." Her face flushed with pleasure as she spoke about the elderly man.

"That sounds lovely," Pilar said. Then, in a deliberate off-hand way, she said, "Oh, I have a question about the fundraiser your grandfather attended last year for New Jersey's State Senator Earl Fergusson. You've probably heard that he intends to eventually run for Congress?"

Solstice nodded. "I know what you're talking about, but my grandfather simply went along with his crowd."

"Oh," Pilar said, disappointed. "I was hoping to hear he'd been a Fergusson flag-waver because some women of the town are seeking information about him. Let me tell you more." Laying the background, Pilar explained why the ladies were annoyed with Fergusson. "It was petty business at the start, they were just in a snit, but then they gained a piece of information that made their questions more serious."

She leaned forward as she spoke. "Fergusson's second wife was a widow with a daughter. She and Fergusson separated but didn't divorce. She took the daughter, Leslie, with her, but after her death, Fergusson took the youngster into his home. She's grown now, but she still lives with Fergusson and serves as his hostess when he entertains. But here's the thing . . ." Pilar paused for effect. "The club women have a photograph that hints at a physical relationship with Leslie when she was only fifteen."

Solstice jerked as if she'd been touched with a live wire. "How old was she when he first took her to live with him?"

Seeing the girl's distress, Pilar said calmly, "I read that she was seven when the mother and Fergusson separated. She had to be a young teen when she returned to live with him."

Solstice's brown eyes had widened and her little face had gone so pale that her freckles stood out like cinnamon sprinkles.

She burst out with, "Leslie was abused!"

The thought exploded in Pilar's mind: *and you were, too.*

She froze for an instant. Was this thought any different from the eerie *gables, peaks* nonsense that kept intruding? For a moment, she wasn't sure, but then she quickly scratched out the idea. This insight was logical. It came from simply adding up facts, such as Solstice not wanting to be touched and her current vehement reaction.

The young woman's next words confirmed Pilar's intuition.

"Tell me what you want me to do." Solstice's eyes glittered fiercely and her hands were clenched. "If Fergusson abused his stepdaughter, I'll do anything to help nail him to the wall."

Chapter 8

$\mathcal{R}$ufus's far-flung family finally gathered for his funeral. The arrangements for Sable, whose passing had come first, weren't yet settled. She had no family and if she had a will it hadn't been found. The ladies of the JumpRope Women's Civic Group and Ladies Fire and Emergency Auxiliary (Sable had belonged to both organizations) offered to pay the funeral expenses with the expectation of eventually being reimbursed by the estate, but things were moving slowly— which some privately noted was a fitting tribute to Sable's practice of procrastination.

In the meantime, the attention was on Rufus.

His send-off began with a time to express sympathy to the family before the service at the First Presbyterian Church. A shorter service would be at Sycamore Shade Cemetery when his ashes would be interred followed by a luncheon at Rufus's home. The little money he had left would be divided among George's four siblings. George's share was the house where he had lived with Rufus. The oldest, George had been the only one willing to take on the responsibility of their increasingly frail and confused father.

At the church, George, red-eyed, handkerchief in hand, was garbed in a tan suit that blended so well with his coloring that only his white shirt collar and cuffs showed where his complexion ended and the suit

began. He was comforted by the companionship of his friend, Eunice
"Neece" Van Doran, a quiet JumpRope widow, who wore old-fashioned
dresses and had her graying hair permed in tight curls. She and George
were seen at Krupple's Diner after church every Sunday for chicken
dinner and every Wednesday for the London broil special. What this
staid-appearing pair did with the rest of their time together nobody
knew and nobody cared.

The historic church had two side aisles and a center aisle. The
family members were positioned across the front, facing the assembly,
and divided into two groups to make space between them for the cloth-
shrouded table holding Rufus's Number 23 Geezer jacket, a photo of
Rufus in his younger days and the urn containing his ashes.

To control the traffic, visitors were guided to the open door leading
to the right aisle to walk up and offer condolences to the Neilson family
members and to respectfully pause at the urn. The music was staid
organ hymns being played just loud enough to keep the whispered
platitudes from being clearly understood, which hardly mattered
because platitudes were platitudes. Once visitors had completed their
duty they either took seats to wait for the funeral service or made their
escape.

Slim Parkerson had paid his respects to the family and then went
down the center aisle and took a seat near the rear. It was a Saturday
and the funeral gave him quiet time to lounge back and view the people
of his town in this formal setting.

In the front yard of the church the Geezers "still on top," as one of
them put it, were gathered under the branches of an oak that wouldn't
give shade until later in the season. They looked forward to the
memorial luncheon and agreed with the family's plan to donate Rufus's
jacket to the Historical Society, but they didn't like it that the church
music was gloomy instead of being the lively hymns that Rufus would
have appreciated. Their discussion of suitable tunes disintegrated into

Chapter 7

That evening, Alexander Fanshawe was in his Manhattan apartment packing a duffle bag. He'd finished his latest assignment, applying old film quotations to a bunch of Internet animal photos; a chimp touching another chimp's face, captioned, "Here's looking at you, kid," and a fiercely combatant looking squirrel standing with paws clenched like fists, captioned, "Go ahead, make my day."

One assignment he didn't like was dreaming up snarky wisecracks for pregnant celebrities who'd been telephotographed wearing bikinis. Always feeling too big and awkward but brighter than the other kids, Alexander never felt he fit in. He had grown up being the butt of too many jokes to enjoy playing Fashion Police.

Having shoved his original plans off the stage, he was heading for JumpRope out of concern for his mother. Max Osterhagen had called, saying he had to leave on a truck run and he didn't want Pilar to be alone. She'd found the dead body of the card shop lady and then learned that Rufus Neilson had drowned in the Hitchmile on Friday morning.

Alexander had recoiled from the news. His mother, usually unflappable, had been the one to find his father's drowned body twenty years before. Around the anniversary of his death, she still went into seclusion. Alexander, who had been little at the time, had no recall of his father's death. All he knew was its terrible effect on his mother. He wasn't sure how this visit would go. He'd asked his girlfriend, Solstice, to come along.

recalling comical lyrics from various drinking songs and other musical examples of low humor.

The conversation broke off when Number 33 elbowed his nearest companion and directed attention to the lime green pick-up truck with a Maryland license plate that had bounced to a stop before the church.

The driver's door flung open and a sturdy woman with gray hair spiraling from her head like unfettered bedsprings emerged. She wore a red printed blouse over a hefty bosom, snug white jeans on over-generous hips, and yellow tennis shoes with no socks. A cigarette was held between the gnarled fingers of one hand.

"Who's that?" asked Number 41.

"Nobody local," said Number 15, wagging his balding head.

"That's a whole lot of woman," Number 33 noted appreciatively.

"Rufus was holding out on us," cackled Number 19, who then started coughing uncontrollably. Number 41 pounded Number 19 on the back as they all watched the impressive female figure barrel toward the church, mount the steps and disappear through the open door.

The woman was brought to a screeching halt inside the vestibule by big-framed, bewhiskered Chuck Newton, Assistant Funeral Director who was serving as an usher.

"Sorry, Ma'am," Chuck said, indicating a sand-filled bucket located a step outside the door. "You'll have to dispose of that cigarette."

Her response was to lick the thumb of her free hand, sizzle the cigarette's glow then toss the snuffed butt into the sand bucket and swipe her thumb on the thigh of white jeans, leaving a dark smudge.

"Okay now, Sonny?" Her tone was belligerent, her voice rough from decades of smoking.

"Good with me, Ma'am," Chuck said. "Please follow the directions of that usher to your right." He motioned toward a black-suited man guiding visitors to the right-hand aisle.

Ignoring the directions, the woman resumed her head of steam, plowed into the sanctuary and up the center aisle, shouldering past those on their way out. At the front, she came to Neece Van Doran where she halted and said, "What the hell kind of sister are you? Why didn't you let me know Sable Kilgallen bit the dust?"

She didn't speak loudly, but the organist, sensing a stir in the crowd, had craned his neck and saw an unkempt-looking stranger on the verge of attacking Neece, who was a parishioner and generous giver to the church, which meant she helped pay his salary. Stunned, he forgot to keep playing.

Everyone who had been speaking in the approved hushed tones fell silent, straining forward to see and hear what was going on. Recovering, the organist launched into another hymn, playing louder than before. Now, only those nearest to Neece heard her response.

"Claudine, I'm sorry, I never thought to say anything. How did you find out?"

"You want the whole story?" Claudine challenged.

Francine Smithers, whose sharp ears heard the conversation, moved from her pew and firmly grasped Claudine's arm.

"I can assist you," Francine said. "Come with me."

From his seat, Slim Parkerson had watched the stranger, a tough-looking older female with wild hair and a red blouse that glared like a stop-light, bulldoze her way up the center aisle. Someone from George's past? He then saw the woman ignore George and confront Neece.

The organ music stopped. Even in the hush, Slim was too distant to hear the conversation between Neece and the stranger. The music resumed. Francine spoke to the woman and then led her down the center aisle, passing Slim on their way out of the church.

He shook his head. Who in fresh hell was that woman? And what had Francine said to her? He caught motion off to his left as Officer Donny DeGarmo slipped into the seat behind him.

"Sir?" Donny said.

"Yeah?" Slim said over his shoulder.

"I saw that female's car when she stopped," Donny said in a low voice. "It didn't seem right, the way she acted. I got her plate number."

"Good thinking," Slim said.

As people filed from the church to attend Rufus's interment, their minds were on the woman who'd burst in. Of all the nerve, interrupting a funeral. And poor Neece! She'd looked ready to have a heart attack. Had they heard right? That blowsy creature was Neece's sister? And how had Francine Smithers gotten the interloper to leave?

The women from the Auxiliary and the Woman's Civic Group, except for Darlene, who had an appointment, and Francine, who was still in the churchyard with the stranger, high-tailed it to George's house to have the funeral food ready when the mourners returned from the cemetery.

When Francine arrived, the group peppered her with questions about the rude creature she'd confronted.

"Her name is Claudine Hackamore," Francine said. "She told me she was driving from Maryland to take a neighbor to a doctor in New York City. At a New Jersey rest stop, Claudine saw a newspaper headline with the name of the town where her sister lived." Francine wrinkled her nose. "It said, Flippin' and Dippin'—two deaths in JumpRope, NJ."

"What?" cried Iris.

"Yes," said Francine. "The newspaper told about the flip, a woman's fatal fall from a ladder, and the dip, a man drowning. When Claudine saw that the dead woman was Sable, she was so shocked she almost needed the bathroom again." Francine sniffed, and then added, "She used a crude word for going to the bathroom."

"Awful," said Iris. "A newspaper turning death into a joke."

Francine nodded. "Claudine asked her companion to look up JumpRope obituaries on her cell. There was nothing for Sable, but there was one about Rufus with Neece's name listed as a family friend. Claudine left her companion at the rest stop and found the church. She came in to ask why Neece hadn't told her about Sable's death. She also told me that Sable had promised to send her a check only it never arrived."

"Something Sable probably put off," Nancy Lou said.

"Francine, how did you get the woman to leave?" someone asked.

"I told her I knew things about Sable's affairs and could help."

"She believed you?"

"Enough so she gave me her name, address, and phone number."

Amy said, "Do you believe Sable sent her a check?"

"She must have had a reason to burst into the funeral and practically attack Neece, so I suppose it's true," Francine said.

After murmurs about Claudine's terrible behavior and praise for Francine's actions, the topic switched to Pilar Fanshawe.

"Poor Alexander had to come all the way from Manhattan," one of the women said. "Pilar should have stayed home. Her husband drowned and she never recovered. She should have known the funeral of a drowning victim wasn't good for her."

"Alexander's odd but he's good to his mother," another woman said absently. She was giving one of the salads a critical look. It contained chopped tomatoes with pieces of their cores carelessly left in.

"Did you see how Pilar acted outside the church?" said another. "She stopped and held up both hands with her fingertips together. I thought she was praying, but she started talking about the shape of the roof."

"The church has an A-line roof," Nancy Lou said.

"That's what she was talking about," the woman said. "The shape. Tents, peaks, gables, and so on. Nonsense. Alexander finally got her to move on, but he must have been embarrassed."

"That's not the worst of her embarrassing behavior," said a redhead, busy with the casserole dishes keeping hot in the oven. "Max Osterhagen seems so nice. Does he know about the men Pilar has had in her bed?"

"You don't know for sure they were in her bed," Iris said.

"Oh, please!" The redhead rolled her eyes.

"Those men Pilar made friends with had all suffered tragedies," Toria said. "There was a man from here whose wife and son died in a car crash, and one from Melton, who lost his family in a terrible fire."

"Pilar suffered the loss of her husband and had to raise her son alone," Iris said. "She was trying to help others who were hurting."

"Mattress medicine," quipped Amy. "I once asked Vivian Mather, before she married Nero Gibeau, what she thought about Pilar's former relationship with him. Nero was young enough to be Pilar's son!"

"Only you would have the nerve to ask," Nancy Lou said, her brown eyes wide. "What did Vivian say?"

"She said she loved Pilar because she'd saved Nero's life."

"Saved it twice," Toria said.

Annoyed, Francine spoke. "I never saw anything so brazen as Pilar standing up and facing a crowd at a Town Committee meeting and announcing that Nero Gibeau had spent the night in her bed."

"Remember the circumstances," Amy said. "The beaten dead body of a newcomer was found in the woods. Nero's behavior was sometimes odd because of what he'd suffered in the service. That made some people think he was the killer, plus, he wouldn't tell the police where he'd been on the night of the murder. He was too much of a gentleman to involve Pilar. People in the crowd at Town Hall shouted that they wanted him arrested. That's when Pilar stood and told them he had been with her that night. And you, Francine, calling Pilar brazen is a rotten thing to say. She was brave. In my book, she's a hero."

Stung by Amy's remark, Francine stayed silent, but her eyes blazed.

"If only Pilar would lay off the vintage clothing," the redhead said. "Most of the time, she looks like she's in costume."

"Speaking of costumes," said Nancy Lou, "That Claudine person looked like a bag lady. Neece's dresses are old-fashioned and so is her tight perm, but she always looks nice."

"Claudine's after that check," Francine said importantly, getting the attention back on her, where it belonged. "I know her type. She'll be hanging around until Sable's affairs are settled and she gets her money."

Chapter 9

With the funeral luncheon over, Darlene drove to her appointment with Acer Wolfgang. He'd invited her to see the progress of his upscale development on the former Mather farm, now called Mather's Woods.

She felt a bit guilty. Although she had hotly criticized developers, she had privately decided Acer was not what she'd first assumed.

They had met at a JumpRope event more than a year ago. He was a cosmopolitan Manhattan multi-billionaire. When he wasn't being entertained at some society event, he was traveling by private jet or holding corporate sessions aboard a luxury liner on the way to some European conference. She'd learned that much from the Internet, but nothing about his early life. When he continued to seek her out, she decided he wanted a friend in her position so she would excuse his development's shoddy workmanship. The cold shoulder she'd given him fell far below freezing.

Over time, she came to see he was too proud to take shortcuts in time and materials. When he did something, he made it his best. Earlier that year he had asked her to save him a seat at a wedding. It occurred to her that as she distrusted him because of his position in the world, perhaps others sought him out for the same reason—not in friendship, but for whatever advancement could be gained. It might mean that Acer could be as lonely as she.

Still, she had a bone to pick with him. Today would be the day.

She arrived at the former Mather House where he'd said to meet. On the first floor was his office and the development's showroom, where he'd created a parking area for prospective homeowners to see a scale model of the layout and meet him in his office.

Acer stood beside a silver-toned Bentley Flying Spur. She pulled in beside him. As she stepped from her second-hand Toyota, he came forward, smiling in welcome. Tall and handsome, his dark hair was attractively feathered with gray at the temples. Instead of what she thought of as one of his power suits, he wore a light jacket over a tan open-collar shirt and darker tan chinos. Casual, yes, but a movement of his arm revealed one of his unbelievably expensive watches.

She was soon riding beside him in his luxurious vehicle on the way to his development site. They spoke of various JumpRope matters and then moved to the two unfortunate deaths.

"You knew them personally?" Acer asked gently.

"I knew Rufus, but not well. I do know the town's going to miss seeing him among his Geezer friends gathered on the bench in front of Krupple's Diner. I knew Sable better. A talented woman, skilled in art. Another sad loss for the town."

He turned the car smoothly into what had once been Mather farmland which had grown into a forest over time. Unlike the typical developer, Acer hadn't razed the land. A large number of mature trees were left standing, enhancing the sites.

He came to a stop at a clear body of water constructed for drainage. A wooden dock was presently bordered by fencing and keep-off signs but she could visualize it transformed into an attractive pond. The distant background showed thick plantings of evergreens, a buffer between his property and Jessi's. She saw a section with houses under construction. One had a porch with tall columns.

Here was her moment. She drew a breath. "That looks like a southern mansion. Pilar told me you weren't building tract housing with models for buyers to choose from. You're selling lots for custom-built homes, with you, the builder." She narrowed her eyes. 'When we met, I thought you were a run-of-the-mill developer. You later knew the trouble I had with houses in the town's previous two tract developments. Why didn't you tell me you lwere doing something different?"

He smiled. "When I realized the conclusion you'd jumped to, I decided to wait until I could show you."

"I wouldn't have believed you." He had a way of turning things around, didn't he, not sure whether to be annoyed or not. Yet she had to admit she could be negative, and yes, judgmental. Life had given her enough lemons so she no longer tried to make lemonade.

"True, you wouldn't have believed me, but now you have proof. The owner of the home you noticed has purchased double lots for gardens landscaped in a southern style to match the house."

"You're original plans hinted at nothing like that," Unconsciously, she'd used her brisk code-enforcer tone.

He chuckled. "The plan showed the layout, the streets, the lots, and the water retention basin. I couldn't show how it would look when finished because it's a work in progress."

When they returned to the Mather House, he showed her drawings and photos of the various architectural styles that buyers wanted.

"What this?" she said about one of the photos. "It's like a wealthy man's hunting lodge on a lake. Why would they want it built on land that's in a small town, rather than in some woodland?"

"The buyers, an older couple, want the advantages of living in a modern environment, yet when at home, they'll enjoy the serene atmosphere of a mountain retreat, plus a water feature in front to more closely represent the feeling in that photo."

She frowned. "You can build this so it looks as if it belongs here?"

Pretending to be insulted, he said in a lofty tone, "They wouldn't have purchased three lots if they hadn't known my reputation."

Recognizing that he was teasing, she said with mock humility, "I'm so sorry, please forgive me. I forgot to whom I was speaking."

"Don't ever forget it again," he said, and then, as they stood looking at one another, they burst into laughter.

* * *

Darlene returned home, thinking over the time she'd spent with Acer until he'd received a call that had taken him back to Manhattan. Remembering his teasing, which had always annoyed her, she realized it hadn't bothered her at all that day. She felt that they had turned some sort of corner, but didn't know where it might lead.

Before she could think about it further, Francine called.

"The lawyer who wrote Sable's will had been found," Francine announced without preliminary. "He's in Melton. We need to see him now. I'll pick you up and explain on the way."

In her car, Francine said, "The lawyer, Earnest Cobb, wanted to speak with representatives from both the JumpRope Woman's Civic Group and the Ladies' Fire and Emergency Auxiliary. I'm the Auxiliary President and you're the Civic Group's treasurer and once wanted to be a lawyer. You're the best one to go with me. We have to see him today or wait two weeks for his return from a vacation."

At Cobb's address, a home office, the mailbox was shaped like an open-mouthed shark. His welcome mat read: "I'd Rather Be Fishing."

Earnest Cobb answered the doorbell giving them a wide smile. He wore a T-shirt that stated, "A Reel Expert Can Catch Anything."

Ushered in, they all took seats, and then he said, "Not that any death is a good thing, but the timing for this was perfect. I was just back from a trip when I learned of Sable's passing and I'm shortly off on another trip."

"Now, about Sable's will." He lifted papers from a desk. "Sable's father and I were friends from way back. I knew her as a child. Her family was all gone when she moved to your town. She consulted me when she started her greeting cards business and I'm the executor of her will. I'll do my part with legal filings but I'm soon out to sea after a prize marlin in Los Cabos, Mexico, so . . ." He showed a childish grin as he flourished papers. "Sit tight and don't let the boat rock. You ladies are going to get the biggest catch of your lives.

"* * *

"I still can't believe it," Francine said to Darlene on the way home. "Sable's entire estate, including the shop building and her home, both paid in full, are to be divided equally between the Fire and Emergency Auxiliary and the Civic Group. Cobb was right about us sitting down. If we'd been standing, we'd have keeled over."

"What floored me," Darlene said, "was how casual Cobb was about his role as executor. He should be involved, every step of the way. Instead, he's putting it all in our hands, but still looking out for himself. He's passing the job of executor over to the beneficiaries without formally resigning, so he still makes his commission."

"At least he'd prepared the required legal papers for us to sign. He said his assistant would file them immediately."

"It's amazing what Sable has done for our two organizations," Darlene said. "We both agreed to pay funeral expenses, but too much had been up in the air to make plans. Now that we're in charge, we can follow through on funeral arrangements. And we should let Claudine Hackamore know."

Francine scowled. "I'll call her when we decide on the date."

Later, after a date was decided, Francine called Claudine, who said she couldn't attend because her truck had broken down and wouldn't be fixed in time. She then started rambling about her need for money.

Francine told her she was sorry about the truck and gave a quick goodbye, not wanting to hear Claudine start complaining about the check that had never reached her.

Chapter 10

$\mathcal{P}$ilar arrived at Sable's funeral at the Smith and Snow Funeral Parlor. She'd been mortified over her behavior at Rufus's funeral. Thank goodness Alexander kept her from making an even bigger fool of herself. Now, with her usually calm manner, she signed the guest book, spoke to the ladies of the women's groups, who served as greeters since Sable had no family, and then moved to the open casket.

Sable rested on blush-pink satin, her blonde hair gleaming and her pale blue chiffon shroud flattering her coloring. Pilar agreed with the ladies that Sable would have been pleased, considering the circumstances. The service featured lovely music, and comments from the mayor, and other attendees. They then reassembled at the Sycamore Shade Cemetery for the final ceremony, where the Business Association had prepared a large wreath for Sable's final resting place.

Mingling with other mourners, she heard about Sable's generosity with the two women's groups. Responding appropriately, she hoped she was redeeming herself compared with her confused rambling at the funeral of Rufus. A luncheon at Teddy's was to follow the burial ceremony, but Pilar went home. She feared that murals at Teddy's showing peaked-roofed houses might set her off again. She didn't understand the phantom-like words that kept coming to her, but she wasn't taking chances.

Chapter 11

That evening, Holly drove to Toria's, intending to take her out for dinner because she was flying out the next morning to see her mother in Texas. The woman had wanted to be involved in Toria's wedding, yet she'd canceled two previous visits, so they had never made plans. Holly didn't know what was going on and Toria didn't want to discuss it. Resigned, he figured she'd tell him when she was ready.

When she welcomed him inside, he discovered she'd ordered Chinese food. That went well with his plans because there was something else he wanted them to do that evening. Take-out or not, she made it a special meal, using her best tablecloth and the English Rose pattern china that Holly had given her that past Christmas.

He still found it hard to believe that when he'd first met her, a tall, shy girl with brown-green eyes and fly-away brown hair, he'd thought her plain—except for the blushing. Back then, she would color up over nothing. He then discovered that what brought the brightest flush to her cheeks was being close to him. They'd gotten to know each other and now, he and Toria were a couple. It was going to be even better when her engagement ring was joined by a wedding ring.

During the meal, they discussed their respective days. After Sable funeral, Holly returned to his office. Toria, Nancy Lou and Amy went to Jolly's Yesterday's Treasures.

"Amy was hunting for old-fashioned phones for a play Chuck's little theater is going to do. She found two pink princess phones. Perfect for a play set in the 1960s. Oh course, Jolly gave her a hard time about the price."

Holly laughed. "Keeping up his reputation as the town's miserly grump. I bet Amy had something to say to him about that. When we're together with Amy and Chuck, we have a great time, but she never hesitates to speak her mind."

"She sure did that with Jolly. He ended up giving her the price she wanted and then, with no haggling, she bought a tube of Tinker Toys for a child in the family she's currently helping out."

"Guess both Jolly and Amy ended up satisfied?"

"Yes, but someone who isn't satisfied, is Francine. This is about money that Claudine said Sable owed her. Francine wants to learn if Sable just put it off or wrote the check and forgot to mail it. Your dad, Sable's accountant, said it wasn't listed in anything he's seen, He figures the details of her financial information are in her card shop office. Francine got the key from the lawyer. I promised to go look."

Holly was puzzled. "If Francine figures there's information in the shop, why isn't she rushing to find it and show how valuable she is?"

"Because the information might be on Sable's computer. Francine uses a cell phone for calls and texting, but when she wants to do something with a computer she comes to the library when I'm volunteering. She pretends she could do it herself but I'm faster. She doesn't like admitting she doesn't know how to do everything."

Holly grinned. "Typical Francine."

"I told her I would look for it when I return from Texas."

After cleaning up together after the meal, he said, "I'd like to go to Sable's shop for a painting I bought months ago. She was framing it."

"Something she painted?"

His eye twinkled. "Yes, your Valentine's Day gift."

"You gave me flowers and candy. They were perfect."

"Thanks, but you were supposed to get this too. Sable promised to have it ready on time but you know her procrastination. Maybe it's ready and she never got around to telling me. We should go now to look and you can keep your promise to Francine. Her key wouldn't get us in. The insurance company agent changed the locks on after Sable's death. The shop is filled with insured merchandise. There may be other shop keys floating around. He didn't want to take any chances."

"If Francine's key doesn't work, how do we get in?"

Holly lifted his phone. "The agent is expecting my call. He lives in JumpRope. He'll meet us there."

On the drive to the shop," Toria asked, "What's the painting about?"

"You'll have to wait and see,"

She pretended to pout. "OK, be mean. I'll change the subject. Did Slim learn anything about fingerprints on Rufus' cup, or how it had gotten smashed and thrown away? Talk about being mean!"

"Nothing yet about the cup, but there's trouble in George's family. When Rufus started failing, his family wanted him in a nursing home. Rufus refused. When George sold his own house and moved in with his father, he solved the problem. His grateful siblings agreed George could have the house when their father died. Now, they're thinking George is getting more than his share. One sibling said that George got money from the sale of his own house, so why should he now have their father's? They want to sell the house and divide the proceeds among the siblings, of which there are four, not including George, who has been living rent-free with all his food and expenses paid by their father's pension."

Toria frowned. "None of them wanted the responsibility of their father except George. Their plan leaves him with no place to live."

"They said he could use his own money to fix that."

Toria sighed. "Families! Glad Sable didn't leave a mess like that."

The agent met them and they were soon inside the shop.

"I'll leave you two here," he said to Holly. "No sense me hanging around. If I can't trust the town mayor, who can I trust? I'm heading to the diner for an after dinner dessert. Call me when you're ready to leave."

After he left, Toria smiled at Holly and said, "Well, Mr. Mayor, I notice he didn't trust you with the key," Her smile faded as she looked around at the racks of commercial greeting cards and a gift area holding stuffed toys, ornaments, and decorative calendars, plus a display of Sable's original greeting cards. With sadness, she thought of Sable no longer able to enjoy creating and using her artistic gift.

Hey!" Holly said, putting his arms around her. Are you thinking this is spooky because somebody died here?" "Not really." She rested her cheek against his shoulder.

She was five-nine and he was about two inches shorter. The height difference used to bother her, believing it meant she'd have had no chance with him. She not only liked his brown-haired, blue-eyed good looks, she admired his handling of people in public meetings and how skillfully he got things done. He was amazing. But she'd been too shy to even talk with him and probably never would have if he hadn't come to the county records room where she worked and needed help researching a property.

She'd soon discovered their height difference made no difference to him, and after they'd been dating awhile, she'd gotten the nerve to show up wearing high heels—red ones. He'd said he loved how she'd looked. That's when she knew she wanted to belong to him forever. Unconsciously, she ran her thumb over the diamond in her engagement ring. And that would happen. She just had to get a few things straightened out first.

Holly smoothed her hair so the fine strands weren't tickling his face. "If you're not scared, hon, what the trouble?"

"It just feels like we shouldn't be here."

He chuckled. "An anti-trespassing gene? If Darlene finds out, she'll want to clone it and inject it into the entire population. But aren't you curious about the painting?"

"Yes, and also finding Sable's records for Francine, but—" Feeling better, she smiled. "My painting comes first."

Holly grinned. "That's my girl." Moving aside a curtain that divided the shop from an area of long tables and art supplies: oils, watercolors, acrylics, chalks, colored pencils and inks. "Here's where she created her original work."

His voice took on a reverent tone as he led Toria into the space. He was known for his colorful art theme neckties and he was serious about art. "Sable invited me to make space for myself here if I wanted, but my apartment attic hideaway is more my speed."

Toria spotted a rough sketch of a flyer Sable had made for Jessi's restaurant. "Oh, look," she said. "Jessi's calling it Carousel."

With a wry laugh, Holly explained how Jessi took a flyer into the police department office and used up all the colored toner in the printer to make herself advertising copies without paying for them. She claimed she'd only done a few, but Officer Farley said she was there for a good hour. He knew she was on committee so he figured it was okay."

A wall rack with frames stacked sideways caught his eye. He moved to look at the items and said, "Whoa! Here it is. My name on it and a receipt. Sable framed it but never told me." Turning to Toria, he said, "Happy belated Valentine's Day." He flipped the frame around so she could see the painting and then handed it to her. It was a soft, almost magical, blur of colors with a dark blue silhouette showing a couple embracing in a mystic scene.

Toria's eyes widened. "Oh, it's so beautiful."

"It's one of her Aurora Borealis series,"

Toria touched the surface. "The paint is thick and there's fabric."

"Right. She laid acrylic paint on heavily with a knife and worked in ribbons to enhance the 3-D effect. Look at these." He showed Toria colored photos of Sable's aurora borealis work with silhouetted figures in the foreground. "She was making a name for herself in Ocean City, Maryland, where she went each year."

"These are adorable," Toria said. "Silhouettes of children with balloons for a kid's birthday, and, oh, look, a bride and groom—"

Holly saw her staring at a wedding scene. He took a breath, then asked, "When you see your mother, you're going to settle the details about our wedding, right?"

They planned a June wedding. They had their marriage license, good for six months, at the urging of Holly's father, the previous mayor. The older man had horror stories of couples who'd forgotten about the document's three-day waiting period until it was too late. Holly and Toria had the license and the dates reserved for the church and the reception at Teddy's, but nothing else, including the reception menu.

Her face constricted. "I think my mother has health problems."

He moved close. "Is this what you didn't want to talk about?"

"Yes. She says she wants to help with the wedding plans, yet there's all this stalling." She spoke in a low voice. "Illness is the only reason I can think of to explain her behavior. I'll know after this visit." She shook off her gloomy mood. "I have my Valentine's gift and now we should be looking for Sable's financial records. Where's her computer? I hope she didn't use a password."

"I think her office is in the back room, but I've never been there." He opened the door as he spoke and found the wall switch. He and Toria entered and gasped. It was as if they had entered a world of clutter, with cabinet doors papered with sticky notes.

"Oh, my," Toria said sorrowfully. "Probably notes of things she didn't want to forget, only they didn't help."

Holly saw a counter with an empty surface next to a printer/fax machine. He called it to Toria's attention.

She said, "That's a place for computer. Did the police take it?"

"No idea. Maybe it's out for repairs. Let's not touch anything and leave. Slim's off on a long weekend to his sister's place in upper New York State, but I'll call his cell after I get home." Holly didn't want to upset Toria, but he was thinking that despite the new lock, a thief might have gotten in.

At home, Holly called Slim and explained why he and Toria were in the shop, and added his concerns about the absent computer. "Did your men remove it?"

"No reason for it. Out for repairs makes the most sense. Hate to think anything else" There was a silence while he thought and then he said, "I'll have my men make sure there's no sign of a break-in although that's not likely. And to stay on the safe side, tell Toria to say nothing except to say the locks were changed and she couldn't get in." Then Slim said, "And by the way, is she ready for her visit to Texas?"

"I'm taking her to the airport tomorrow, but I don't know how it's going to work out."

"What's that mean?"

Holly told him about Toria's concerns for her mother.

"I've been wondering," Slim said. "Being your best man, it seems things are moving slow. Back when Lana and I were still getting hitched, she had her gown, the date fixed with the church, the catering arranged, plus down payments made on everything including music, flowers, and a limousine, all done way ahead of time."

Holly sighed. "Toria's parents have been divorced for years. I've not met either one. Her mother remarried, but not her father. Toria doesn't seem interested in seeing him and won't say why. He doesn't live far away, only in Delaware."

"Sounds like trouble going way back. Have a clue as to why they broke up?"

Holly shook his head. "No. My father knew them back when Toria was young. He said they seemed a perfect family. When she started high school she stayed with her aunt here in town because her father had a new job in Delaware and her mother had gone for a visit in Texas. Neither ever returned. Word eventually got around about their divorce. Toria's parents took turns having her live with them until she was in college. By the time she graduated, her aunt had died and Toria inherited her house and that's where she's lived since then."

"Find out what went wrong between her and her parents,"

"Good advice," Holly said.

Slim chuckled. "That's my job, protect and serve."

Chapter 12

$\mathcal{F}$riday morning, the Ladies Civic Group met in their usual location, the first-floor trustees' room of the Sycamore Shade Cemetery caretaker's house. The new caretaker lived on the second floor, formerly the apartment for Chuck and Amy Newton. Now that Chuck was an Assistant Funeral Director with Smith and Snow Funeral Parlor, they'd moved to a larger place, better for them and their growing son.

The meeting was originally scheduled to plan the Memorial Day parade, including a discussion of new veteran monuments to be placed in the park adjoining the historical museum. To that end, wives, widows and mothers of veterans were invited. And now, because of Sable's bequest, members of the Joint Fire and Emergency Squad Auxiliary were also in attendance. The two organizations needed to discuss the sale of Sable's house and its contents.

Francine was feeling anxious and angry with herself. When Claudine complained about a missing check Sable was supposed to send her, why hadn't she asked how big the check was? It made her feel stupid and she hated that. She remembered how good it felt when she'd been praised for smoothly guiding Claudine away from Rufus's funeral. Francine knew people counted on her for information and knew she always did the right thing. She had a reputation to uphold. If that check was for a huge amount, it would eat into Sable's bequest for the two women's groups. People would say, "Guess Francine doesn't know as much as we thought she did."

Holly's father, Sable's accountant, couldn't find a record of the check, and when Toria had gone to look at Sable's shop records, she said the police were keeping the shop closed. Under the circumstances, Francine decided the best thing was to say nothing that would remind anyone about it, but she was still angry with herself.

Why hadn't she asked Neece, who might have known something about it? Too late now. Had Neece had stopped driving? She had come to the meeting with Lillian Brent and Lillian's sister, Esther. She knew Lillian and Esther lost a brother in Korea and Neece's husband died in Vietnam. Neece was sixty-two but looked older. She'd taken early retirement as a high-school secretary and quit her volunteer job as the treasurer of the Baptist Church when both had upgraded their computers. She'd said she was too old to learn anything new.

Cindy Hoyt, the Civic Group's president, called the meeting to order and said, "You are probably all aware of the bequest Sable's made to our two women's organizations. Our groups organize and work at special community events, such as the recognition of Memorial Day."

As planned, Cindy then said, "Now, Francine Smithers, of the Fire and Emergency Auxiliary will say a few words."

Hiding her inner concern, Francine stood, thanked Cindy, and said, "Sable's bequest is of immediate importance. If we have the house cleared out and sold before we have to pay additional taxes, it will benefit both our organizations and the town in general."

"That makes sense," said eighty-year-old Lillian, nodding her head of wildly colored red hair. "And I'm glad there's going to be monuments for the men who served in the more recent wars."

"And I'm glad the Mather family can pay for them," said Lillian's sister, Esther, whose hair was its natural downy white. Always sour about newcomers, she added, "That Vivian Mather Gibeau came here and now wants her father's name added to the Vietnam memorial because he was a Mather even though he didn't live here. And she also wants a new marker for the war her husband served in."

Ignoring Esther, Daisy, who ran the bakery, asked, "Where's Olivia Bunker? Her daughter was in the Gulf War."

"She's not home yet from Maine," Caroline Kroll said.

Francine raised her voice to get the meeting back on track. "We should put the sale of Sable's house in the hands of a realtor. The furnishings and other items can be disposed of in a big yard sale."

After discussion, it was decided to have the sale on the third weekend of April, starting on Friday evening and all day Saturday.

With the date settled, someone said, "Since Pilar seems to have quit doing the JumpRope Jive, a crying shame, we should see if she can advertise the sale, and it can be put it on the town activities page and social media."

Francine volunteered to ask Pilar to create and publicize the event.

With that settled, there was a lull, in which Cindy asked Neece, how George was managing the conflict about his father's house.

Looking as if she'd been roused from a nap, Neece blinked, the sausage curls in her tightly permed gray hair bobbling like miniature action figures.

"He's doing all right," she said in a vague tone. "He's the oldest, you know. He takes their fussing in stride."

Another veteran's widow asked Francine, "You've been talking about Sable's bequest. What are the details?"

Francine stood again. "We will have the income from the house sale and its contents, the numbers to be determined. As for the rest of her holdings, such as what's in her shop, and the income from her commercial card sales and paintings, there's a lot of paperwork to go through."

"Right, paperwork," Amy said, looking at Francine, who still stood at the lectern. "At the funeral lunch for Rufus, you told us that Claudine said Sable owed her money. How much was she talking about? We should know the amount."

Francine gripped the edge of the lectern, for once not knowing what to say.

"That Claudine!" Neece interrupted in a loud voice, suddenly looking wide awake. With a gesture that made the printed pattern across her ample bosom wave, she said, "She's been nothing but a trial to our entire family. She ran off with some biker when she was fifteen and disappeared for years. Then she showed up, looking a mess and talking like she'd grown up in some mountain place where people had no education. She was soon off again with somebody else. When our parents died nobody knew where she was. By the time my husband and I moved here, I figured she was gone for good." She sighed heavily. "Then Sable brought up her name. Seems they met when Sable was in Maryland with her painting. Don't know why the two of them hit it off. Can't understand it. Claudine's my younger sister but when she does show up, she acts like she's the oldest, in charge of me. I don't want her here hounding people. For all I know, she made up the whole thing about the money. It would be just like her. Fortunately, she didn't want much so I settled it with her. She's back in Maryland and we won't hear from her again."

Francine inwardly sighed in relief. She doubted that dowdy Neece had extra funds, so the amount of money could have been much. She'd been worried for nothing. Still, Neece deserved credit for her actions.

Importantly, Francine said, "Our thanks to you, Neece, for taking care of the matter. It was a splendid gesture."

"Yo!" called Amy. "Let's hear it for Neece!" She started to clap and everyone joined in.

As Francine left the meeting, she admitted it had worked out very well. They were done with Claudine and now she'd call Pilar.

When Pilar heard what was needed, just the date, the time and the location, she quickly agreed. "I'll spark it up with clip art and bright colors and put it on sites for local readers. I'll put it on social media and also print out flyers and distribute them."

Pleased, Francine headed home. Everything was fine although the cheer had been for Neece and not her. And, in the future, she would watch out for Amy Newton's big mouth.

Chapter 13

$\mathcal{P}$ilar felt content as she designed the flyer for the sale of the contents of Sable's house. Contentment was good, she thought, but it wasn't the same as happiness. She remembered once being truly happy, a young woman's joy. A time when the door of death seemed so far along the twisting corridor of life it was hard to believe it waited at all. Then that trapdoor of ice opened beneath the feet of her young husband, drowning him and nearly drowning her sanity as well.

She'd managed to get a grip on herself. No mother can care for a child and stay in seclusion at the same time. What did Alexander remember? Very little, she hoped. Perhaps this year she'd have the strength to forgo that barren week when she allowed herself to remember everything she wanted to forget.

Her thoughts moved to Max, who was away on a truck run. Had he come along sooner, she would have rejected him. He was too sound in mind and body, too resilient despite his pain over losing his wife. He wouldn't have needed her. Yet by the time he'd appeared, it was like the sun coming out after prolonged darkness. Instead of continuing to hide from light and warmth, she had been able to receive it. But a shadow from her past still lingered. Max wanted more from her than she could give. Her long-hidden guilt and shame remained too powerful for her to fully open her arms.

The phone rang. It was Max. After a warm greeting, he asked, "How do you feel about roses in your yard?"

"That would be wonderful! I started a walkway I wanted to line with roses but I didn't get far last year. The place where I want to put them has clay soil. It's hard to dig and must be enriched. Why do you ask?"

"I'm at a flower market that's selling out. How about I get a dozen bushes, mixed colors? We'll see about that soil when I come home."

They talked a bit longer. After they hung up, Pilar thought about his words "come home." He had the house in town that he and his wife bought years before, but now, "home" to him meant her ranch house,

On the road with the new plants, Max thought about Pilar. Someday they would live in the house she didn't want to leave. He understood clinging to treasured memories. It was where she and her late husband had lived and where they had brought home their newborn son. Max had his memories of his late wife, but he had handled them differently.

He and Lois had married in their twenties, living in the city where she worked for her family's bank. He had his truck driving career which was made more profitable thanks to his associate's degree in business. They expected children but were in no rush. They'd wait until their early thirties. Lois planned that when their children arrived, she would stay home with them in a place away from the city's hustle and bustle, yet not too far from its advantages.

They had searched for a property in a well-run town with nice homes, good schools, enough local business to supply day-to-day needs, and outlying areas of trees and meadows for a true country atmosphere.

They found what they wanted in the town with the amusing name of JumpRope and purchased a house. It would be an investment, rented until their children arrived and they would settle there.

When their thirties arrived, Lois couldn't become pregnant. Busy with her career, it didn't bother her overmuch. Max wanted to know if there was anything wrong with either of them, but doctors found no reason for Lois's failure to conceive. She didn't wish to adopt and Max agreed for her sake. Time went by. They enjoyed being together and their affections never wavered. They were content until an undetected aneurysm stole Lois's life.

Shattered, Max sold their city house where the good memories wounded him. He moved to the JumpRope house that was fortunately between tenants. He couldn't stay lost in sorrow. His trucking business forced him to get out, see new scenes and meet new people. Slowly, he began to take an interest in the town. He became involved and even served a brief stint as a committeeman.

He'd first noticed Pilar when he was six years a widower. Attracted by her graceful beauty and intrigued by her costume-like clothing, he arranged to meet her. Gradually, they became friends and then a couple in all the ways that means. He was certain they loved one another. Beyond that, he would wait and see.

Pilar was delighted with Max's rose bushes. She stood nearby as he made the ground ready along the path she'd designed. He easily lifted shovel load after shovel load of heavy earth to the canvas he'd spread the ground and mixed in soil enrichment to cradle the plants when they were set in place.

Appreciating his strength, she admired his handsome face with its neat mustache. Recalling a Spanish proverb: *Kissing a man without a mustache is like eating an egg without salt,* she smiled, thinking how she enjoyed his kisses.

When the first bush was in place, well-watered and heeled in, she exclaimed, "It looks even better than I expected."

He leaned on the shovel. "Ready for eleven more?"

"As long as you keep working I'll keep thanking you."

He grinned. "Later, maybe you can show me. I've heard that actions can speak louder than words."

"We shall see about that," she teased, her eyes bright.

Max laughed and went to the house to bring out cool drinks.

Alone, Pilar admired again the first addition to her new garden walkway. She noticed an instruction tag had come loose and now lay on the ground under a few fallen petals.

As she leaned to pick up the tag, she suddenly had a vivid memory of finding Sable's body and seeing drops of her blood spattered on flowered greeting cards. Stunned, she watched the rose petals on the printed card in her garden transform into drops of blood and the printed tag became blank.

The vision, or whatever it had been, winked away. Rubbing her eyes in confusion, Pilar could only think that in her shock of seeing Sable's body, she had missed something important. Her subconscious was bringing it to her attention. Her muscles tensed as she came to a fearful conclusion: Sable's death had not been an accident and the blankness of the tag sent a message that her killer was someone unsuspected.

Appalled by her run-away thoughts, she struggled to rein them in. If she didn't, what might happen next? A branch on the ground might transform a fishing pole, and she'd take it as a sign that Rufus's death while fishing had been another crime?

Nonsense, she scolded and realized her problem. In the restaurant, Mar-see-ah had implied that she, Pilar, could see things hidden from others. Ridiculous! What she'd just experienced was nothing but a trick of an over-active imagination.

There had been two deaths, yes, but they had been dreadful accidents, not murders.

Chapter 14

Slim scowled as he strode around Sable's card shop. Home from his visit with his parents over the weekend, he was following up on Holly's phone call. His men had found no signs of a break-in but in the back room office, there was a blank space next to the printer where a computer should be.

A call to the insurance agent told him there was no computer in the back when he'd done his inventory. The agent recalled it had been an old, bulky thing. In his opinion, if Sable had wanted an office computer, she would have recycled the old one and looked for something new.

That made sense to Slim, especially when he saw at the shiny cash register/computer at the counter in the front of the shop. But where was her missing cell phone, which he'd previously determined wasn't in her home?

In the office again, he studied the sticky paper notes decorating every available surface and a jumble of magazines devoted to art. A disorganized mess. The phone could be hiding anywhere. On that thought, he opened the drawer under the printer. To his surprise it was empty. Puzzled, he opened other drawers. Empty. The same for the drawers in the filing cabinet.

Had Sable, admired for talented artwork and criticized for procrastination, decided to turn over a new leaf—get rid of the clutter in her back room office and make it as neat as the sales section? If so, she hadn't lived to finish the job. Logical, perhaps but it didn't feel right to Slim. He turned his attention to searching for the phone. Not finding it, he turned to a stack of mail Sable hadn't gotten around to opening. In it, he found an overdue bill from her phone service provider.

After returning to his office he called the company and learned that wherever the phone was, it was turned off. A requested copy of her incoming and outgoing calls showed nothing suspicious. But there sure was something suspicious about her missing files. If Sable had decided to get organized, she would have pulled out papers to sort, gotten distracted, and pushed them into a corner to deal with another day. Regardless of how long it took, there would have been records to keep. So where were they? Could someone have snuck in the back room while she was busy with customers, cleaned everything out and moved it out the back door with no one the wiser? She might not have even realized the papers were gone. Only why would anyone want them? It made no sense.

He'd previously worked on a crime where a magazine writer's records were taken. It had been for a reason that no one expected and was a surprise when it was eventually figured out. Maybe a solution to this would appear, but he couldn't think what it could be. Besides, there was something hc had to now for Caroline Kroll.

The previous week, she'd been concerned about her neighbor, Olivia Bunker, who hadn't come home from visiting in Maine and hadn't responded to phone calls. After she and Slim had talked she decided that Olivia, who had an independent streak a mile wide, was still away and simply ignoring her phone.

Now her concern was her missing cat, Shadow, and she needed his help. He figured the animal was simply off on a springtime prowl— Mrs. Kroll probably thought that too, but she was lonely and it gave her an excuse to call him.

In his vehicle, he figured that by the time he arrived, Shadow would have shown up. She'd apologize for calling for nothing and invite him to come in for a little visit over coffee,

Kroll's home was on a narrow rural lane. There were only two houses in that section, Mrs. Kroll's and Mrs. Bunker's, both surrounded by woodland. Lots of interesting places for a cat.

When he pulled into the driveway Mrs. Kroll stood outside with the gray cat in her arms, a sight that confirmed his earlier opinion.

The woman was tiny with bluish-tinted white hair. Although the spring weather was pleasant, she wore a too-big, heavy jacket. He figured it had belonged to her late husband.

"Well," Slim said with a grin as he stepped from his vehicle. "I see you found Shadow. Or did he show up on his own?"

She looked ashamed. "I couldn't find Shadow this morning so I thought he might be in Olivia's garage. He's gotten in there before. I took the keys that Olivia left with me and opened the garage door. Shadow was there." She paused, then added in a shocked tone, "And so was Olivia's car!"

"She's home then?"

"You don't understand. I pretended Shadow was still missing after I found him. I didn't let you know because I was afraid you wouldn't come if I was fussing about Olivia again."

"Mrs. Kroll, I would have come." The answer seemed simple to him. "Mrs. Bunker probably arrived home late last night and is still asleep."

"Sleeping past nine in the morning? Olivia? Never! Now I'm thinking the car could have been there for days. Olivia could have come back while I was away on a visit. If she'd been home, why haven't I seen her?"

She looked fearfully toward the Bunker house. "I'm afraid something terrible has happened."

Slim frowned, thinking this wasn't turning out how he'd expected. "Did you knock on her door and try her phone?"

"Yes, but she didn't answer either one. I have her keys, but I was afraid to go inside. That's why I really called you." Setting the cat on the ground, she reached into the jacket pocket, pulled out a ring of keys, and thrust them at Slim.

"You have to look!" Her face puckered with emotion. "She could have fallen, like Sable Kilgallen." Tears started rolling down her cheeks.

"She would have laid there helpless, praying I'd come over, only I never did." She broke down in sobs.

"Ah, jeez." Slim stepped forward and put an arm around her. She sagged toward him and he thought she was going to slip right down to the ground, so he used his other arm, too. She was so hunched and little that her head only came up to the bottom of his chest.

Voice muffled against his shirt, she sobbed out her worst fear. "She could be in there dead."

"No, no," he soothed, but now, he was a bit worried too.

The woman straightened and stepped back. "Just go look. I'll sit on my porch. Maybe I'm being foolish, imagining the worst."

"Okay," Slim said. "You sit and I'll see what's what."

Standing at Olivia's front door, he rang the bell, hearing it chime inside. He waited. No response. He knocked and waited. No response. He found the correct key in the ring, heard the click of the lock, and gave the door a push. Because you don't just invade someone's house without warning, he sang out a hello, called Mrs. Bunker's name, and identified himself as he stuck his head in.

He stepped back as the smell rolled out.

He shot a glance toward Mrs. Kroll, hoping she hadn't noticed his recoil. "Going in," he said, calmly, turning so she wouldn't see when he sipped on gloves from his pocket and clasped a hand over his nose. He didn't have a lot of experience with this sort of thing as a small-town cop, but he'd had enough; besides, any country boy knows the reek of something dead.

A few minutes later, he was calling all the right people for backup.

Olivia Bunker, wearing what had once been a nice slacks and sweater set, lay stretched out on the top cover of her fully made bed. It didn't take a lot of cop savvy to know she had been home and dead for a lot longer than just a few hours.

Chapter 15

The next evening, Holly was at Newark airport when Toria's plane landed. He stood waiting when she emerged from the walkway, an overnight bag in one hand. They each rushed forward, the bag dropping as they clasped one another. She felt so darned good in his arms, he thought, and smelled good, too.

wedding business

She always smelled good, but this was a new scent. He sniffed. "I guess you're now my Texas wildflower."

She smiled. "I'm still your New Jersey wildflower, but what you smell is something new from Texas."

"Whatever, I like it." He picked up her bag, wanting to ask about her mother's health and what had been accomplished with the wedding plans, but she hadn't come from her flight bubbling over with good things to say and she looked tired, both worrying signs.

After they collected her big bag, they left the parking garage in Holly's blue Ford crew cab truck and headed toward the highway.

"Has anything interesting happened while I've been away?"

"Not interesting, but sad," he said. "Slim found Olivia Bunker dead in her house. Briefly, he told her about the circumstances, not mentioning Slim's unanswered questions about Sable's missing files and phone.

Toria tried to lighten the conversation by telling Holly about her flight home. She'd been on the window seat of a three-seat row, and the woman in the middle started asking the man on the aisle for crossword puzzle answers.

"He gave her a couple of correct ones but then gave her words that wouldn't fit or were just plain wrong. I think he didn't want to be stuck entertaining her all through the trip."

"I bet you knew the right words."

"Mostly, I did. She turned to me and I tried to help. When the puzzle was finally done, she took a nap."

"Bet you were glad."

"Well, I wanted a nap myself, so then I could take one."

He smiled. That's my girl, he thought, always willing to help somebody. Despite his smile, he was tense. He wanted to know about her mother's health, but he didn't want to ask questions until she'd had a chance to relax and had some food in her stomach.

He called ahead to a restaurant he knew, requesting a table where they would have privacy. After arriving, they were led to banquette seating in a corner. The table had a white cloth, the lights were soft and there was soothing music.

"This is really nice," Toria said after they'd ordered beverages. She'd asked for hot tea. "I don't feel like having a big meal. Maybe a bowl of soup and crackers."

An invalid's meal, Holly thought. He was hungry but still didn't feel like eating. Crazy. But if he was going to be any good to her, he couldn't be dragging around like a famished squirrel. He ordered ale and grilled rib-eye steak with mushrooms, plus an appetizer of seared scallops with sauce to be served with the meal. He knew Toria liked them. Maybe she'd perk up and start nibbling.

As the waiter left, Holly was wondering what to say when Toria dove into a subject that she had never discussed before—her parents."

"My mother and father are obsessively private people," she said. "I felt I should respect that, but it was unfair to you. I was mistaken about my mother having an illness." Toria's weariness seemed replaced by brittle energy. Her hands were clasped tightly, the knuckles white. "My mother was keeping a different secret. Remember I told you that she'd remarried? I barely knew my stepfather, Dave, but he seemed to make my mother happy." When Holly nodded, she came out with her bombshell, "Dave died of a heart attack this past January."

Stunned, Holly blurted, "And your mother never said anything? Why keep it a secret? You talk on the phone with her every week."

Toria's expression revealed conflicting emotions. "I should be mad at her, but it's so pitiful I can only feel sorry. If you want to be mad at her, be my guest."

"Why should I be mad?" Holly started wishing he'd ordered something stronger than ale.

"Because that's why she's been stalling about the wedding plans. When we decided on a June wedding, she wanted to be in on everything. Back then, she agreed that my father would walk me up the aisle, but after Dave died, she realized she would have to be alone when she faced my father at the wedding. That's when she started stalling."

They stopped talking as their beverages arrived. When the waiter left, Holly asked, "Why wouldn't your mother want to face him?" This, he thought, was a conversation they should have had a long time ago.

"There's nothing wrong with him, not really. Or my mother, either. The problem was me." Toria looked away, as if ashamed. Her voice dropped so low he could barely hear her. "If they hadn't had me, they would probably still be married."

Holly blinked. He'd heard that children of divorced parents sometimes took the blame on themselves, but this was ridiculous. Toria was an intelligent, mature woman. Surely she realized her childhood impressions were false. Then he remembered how she was when they'd first met, dressing in drab greys and browns, skirts and tops too big and too long. Only gradually had she started dressing to show herself off to the best advantage. Was it really so hard to believe that negative feelings caused by parents could linger into adulthood?

He tried to think of what was the best thing to say, when she blurted, "I hate my wedding dress!"

Not waiting for his response, which was a good thing because he didn't have one, she rushed on. "I let my mother persuade me to choose a dress I didn't want." She blinked back tears. "My mother liked it because she thought it was a style my father wouldn't find fault with, but it's all wrong for me. Horrible! The last thing I did before I got on the plane at the Dallas airport was to call the shop and cancel the dress. I told the bridal consultant the wedding was off!"

Toria's last sentence hit Holly like a blow to the stomach. *The wedding was off?* He felt his blood pressure fade and himself fading right along with it, then he heard what she was saying next.

"I had to tell the poor woman something!" Now she was blushing with the embarrassment of telling a lie. "When my mother picked out that dress, the consultant said it was one of her favorites. I couldn't insult her and let her know I didn't like it."

Holly found his voice. "Of course, you couldn't." He spoke with remarkable calm, considering he was thinking that Toria had no idea of the power she had over him, how she could tilt his world with a few unintended words.

"And now," she continued, "I have to start wedding dress shopping all over again." She reached out a hand to clasp his. "You've been so wonderful and patient with all the delays. All I've done is wreck everything. I need a dress, but at this point, I'm too burned out to even think of what I want."

If the waiter hadn't arrived with their food at that moment Toria would have probably burst into tears. It gave Holly some time to think. By the time the waiter had left, his wits were working. Taking a notebook and pen from his breast pocket, he slid around the seat of the banquette until he was by Toria's side.

"This has been your problem," he said to her, satisfied with how her tearful expression had changed to puzzlement. Dramatically he poised his pen over a blank page where he quickly sketched the shape of a female mannequin.

"Now—what was wrong with the dress your mother wanted?"

"What?"

"Just tell me. Describe it. What was wrong with it?"

Toria started to laugh. "It was puffy, with huge fat sleeves."

"Like this?" He sketched huge, ballooning sleeves.

"Yes. And a wide skirt made of ruffles." She watched him draw. "No, no," she said. "Make them worse. Carnival in Rio ruffles."

He scrawled a few more exaggerated lines and said, "And now for the hat and veil." He lifted his attention from the pad to look at her. "And when we're done with the dumbest dress, you'll figure out the smartest dress and know that's what you want."

Continuing with the carnival theme, he drew a big round hat and sketched outlandish flying veils. All of a sudden he realized Toria wasn't looking at the drawing anymore, she was looking at him.

He looked up and into her eyes.

"I love you, Holly Kingston," she said. She was laughing, but there was a catch in her voice. "The heck with the smartest dress. What I've already got is the smartest guy in the world."

She threw herself into his arms, and if her elbow tipped her water glass into her bowl of soup, neither one of them noticed nor cared.

Chapter 16

Slim lifted the next morning's *Melton Monitor*. The front-page headline jumped out:

THINGS HAPPEN IN THREES

JJ Gilbert's article reported the latest JumpRope death, that of Olivia Bunker: "Two tragic accidents and an apparent, equally tragic, suicide."

"Thanks a lot," Slim said to JJ several hours later when she sashayed into his office to see if there were any updates. "Making us sound like Death Town, USA."

"Town of Drug Errors," JJ said, tossing her head, making her ponytail swing over one shoulder. "Two deaths from prescription drugs. Mrs. Bunker had an empty sleeping pill bottle next to her bed and Rufus had a history of getting his heart medicine snarled up."

Slim just looked at her. He wasn't going to argue and he wasn't giving information. He'd wait until he had a toxicology report on Mrs. Bunker.

"And that still doesn't answer who might have been hanging around the Hitchmile on Rufus's last morning," JJ said. "I was there when you found the cup. Ever get a report on it?"

"No," he said, shoving his chair backward on its casters so he had more room to slump back and thrust out his legs. "And you better not stir up more rumors in print."

"I'd just be reporting facts," she said. "I could have put a lot more in about Mrs. Bunker. The more people thought about it, the more they could see that she had been planning on dying for some time."

"I heard. Getting rid of possessions she'd saved for years."

"Right. She was a major contributor of household items to the Civic Group's yard sale last year. Then there was her frog collection! Nobody understood at the time, but I suppose it makes sense, now," she said, remembering.

Before Olivia had left for Maine the previous fall, she'd gone on a house-cleaning binge. People were shocked to hear she'd dumped her treasured collection of frog ornaments in the trash. Why not donate them? She had no trouble explaining. "I got tired of dusting. Collecting frogs was fun, but the joy of a collection is finding matching items. Donating them all together would defeat the purpose for anyone else." That was Olivia, JJ thought. Doing things her way to the very end.

Slim was thinking they would probably discover there was a health problem she'd kept a secret. Aloud, he said, "Mrs. Bunker's only relative, her daughter, Harriet, up in Portland, Maine, doesn't know about her mother's death. The Portland police looked for the daughter after I called with the news. According to neighbors, Harriet and her husband are on a camping trip. For now, she's unreachable."

"Sounds like she's as independent as her mother. Now, I've got another question, but on the same subject. I saw some of the scenes from when Sable's body was found. Saw the flowery greeting cards around under her head. Roses in blood."

Slim sat up straight. "How'd you see evidence photos?"

JJ folded her arms and looked smug. "Reporters can't reveal sources. I also saw withered red roses in a vase in Olivia Bunker's bedroom right next to that fateful bottle of pills."

"Yeah." He didn't know why, but while waiting for the medical examiner to officially proclaim her death, he'd wandered outside and found a red rose bush alive with spring blossoms, which somehow made the tragic scene inside even sadder. Another thing he'd taken into account was that Olivia wasn't dressed for bed. An accidental overdose seemed more likely to happen at night—wake up groggy and take another dose, which would be too much. But suicide? Knowing people would eventually find her, she would probably want to be fully dressed.

To JJ, he said, "You wormed your way into seeing evidence photos. You sure get around don't you?"

"Doing my job," she agreed sweetly. "And now I ask, were there any signs of roses, like a few red petals, where Rufus was found?"

"Jeez, JJ, give it a break. What are you after? A headline about some imaginary killer leaving red roses as a signature?"

She shrugged. "If the vase fits. And you didn't answer my question."

With patience he didn't usually have, he said, "No, there were no roses, not a petal of any color where Rufus was found."

As he spoke, he saw that as usual, JJ's attire was casual, a lightweight jacket over a *Melton Monitor* T-shirt, her long legs encased in skinny jeans. The same tomboy as always. He remembered her trailing after him and her brothers, making a nuisance of herself when he was at their house. Deciding to switch away from the deaths—instead of tossing her out of his office, that is—he said, "Your cabin ever dry out?"

"Finally." She adjusted easily to the switched topic. "Would be great if Darlene's smart guy ever gets around to engineering a solution to the flooding. If that happens, I can put my front porch back on."

"Darlene's guy? Wolfgang?"

"Who else? He's been after her since they first met."

"What's the attraction? Darlene's got a harder line on rules and regulations than most cops."

"If she was a male cop, you'd applaud her grit and determination."

"That, plus her lack of humor and touchiness. No thanks." Slim couldn't argue with how Darlene did her job, but he'd never warmed to her, which was apparently the way she liked it, not only with him but with everybody. He returned to what JJ had said earlier, and asked, "You really plan on rebuilding your porch?"

"Sure. And you know how pretty that location is when it's not half underwater." She looked pensive. "I sit on my porch with a cup of coffee and enjoy looking at the Hitchmile Stream. My own little wonderland." She shook herself and stood. "But I'm making no improvements until the flooding is conquered. I can't afford to do it twice." At the door, she turned back and added, "If I ever get it done, I'll throw a party. If you feed me hot news, I'll put you on the guest list."

"Holding my breath." He grinned, baiting her, waiting for her to grin back at him. There was something about that little gap between her two front teeth that he liked even though she could be a royal pain.

There. There it was, *that smile*, and then she was out the door.

The following Monday, Harriet Bunker Johnson returned home from her camping trip to learn about her mother's death. Harriet immediately traveled to JumpRope. Accompanied by her balding husband, they'd made funeral arrangements at Snow's and now they were in Darlene's office. The supposed reason was that Harriet planned to sell her mother's house and wanted Darlene to inform her of township requirements for making the sale. It soon became obvious that Harriet's true mission was to make it clear her mother had not committed suicide.

"Mother did *not* take deliberately take too many pills." Harriet spoke firmly, her oval face, surrounded by a crop of curly brown hair, was flushed with emotion. She held a sheet of folded newspaper in one hand and made chopping motions with it as she spoke as if striking down rumors.

"I read the article in the *Monitor* and heard the talk around town. Mother was cleaning out the house because she planned to move to Portland, near me. Before she left for home, she was extremely excited about the move. She was *not* planning to kill herself. She was only in her sixties and in tip-top shape. She joked that she might even get married again."

Harriet's eyes filled with tears and her silent husband pulled her close for a moment before she straightened. "I don't know when Mother started taking sleeping pills. It was an over-the-counter medicine. The excitement of moving must have kept her awake at night."

Darlene was thinking that if Harriet didn't know about her mother needing sleeping medicine, she didn't know the woman's mental state as well as she claimed.

Harriet unfolded the paper she'd been holding and thrust it forward. "Mother was looking at houses in Portland. Look, here's a newspaper with houses she looked at when she visited me."

Darlene figured she was probably showing the paper everywhere. Olivia's interest in property did suggest another side to the story, but Darlene remained cautious. "I don't believe anyone heard about her plans to move."

"Mother wouldn't have breathed a word until she had a new place signed and sealed. When she was ready to put a For Sale sign on her JumpRope house, then, of course, people would know."

Darlene tilted her head. "The purchase of a new place wouldn't have been contingent on selling her house here?" It was none of her business, but Harriet had brought it up.

"Not at all," Harriet answered, looking proud. "Father left Mother in an extremely fortunate situation, plus she'd made excellent investments. She planned to buy the new property outright, no mortgage."

Darlene had the impression that Olivia was comfortably well off, but not to the extent of making a substantial purchase outright.

Harriet continued speaking, her tone increasingly troubled.

"I came into town last evening, and the first thing I did was go through Mother's home safe for her will, cemetery deed, and other papers. I'm familiar with her finances. She was extremely methodical, but the paperwork for one bank certificate of deposit hadn't been updated for some time. I called the bank this morning and learned she'd cashed it in when it came due two years ago. It was for thirty-two thousand dollars. She never said a word to me. It was unlike her." She looked to her husband for confirmation and he nodded.

"You'll probably find out what happened to it when you have more time to go through her papers," Darlene said, thinking that she had to leave soon for a scheduled inspection. She'd given a landlord two extensions. If he hadn't correctly repaired his exterior stairway to make it safe for his tenants, their next meeting would be before the judge.

"I already searched," Harriet said. "I was up half the night. T I tore the place apart. That money disappeared with no record of how she used it. She had a home safe to keep everything handy, no running to a bank for her. That money is gone, like into thin air. " Harriet clasped her hands and looked toward her husband. "I don't need to tell you how extremely upset I've been."

With a look at Darlene, he nodded tiredly and repeated what must be his wife's favorite word, "Extremely."

Observing the couple, Darlene had two disparate thoughts: first, it was clear that Olivia kept financial secrets from her daughter, but also, Francine had mentioned having trouble finding Sable's financial records. Two deaths and missing financial records in both cases? Was there a connection?

In any case, Darlene felt that Harriet had said enough to at least raise a question about the assumed suicide, so she said, "When you leave my office, why don't you go to the Police Department and tell everything you just told me to the Chief of Police."

Harriet Bunker did not go to the Chief of Police, at least not then. Instead, she went to the county newspaper, the *Melton Monitor*.

The next morning's paper carried the interview under this headline:

DAUGHTER CLAIMS MOTHER MURDERED
Harriet Bunker Johnson, a Maine resident who grew up in JumpRope Township, came back upon learning about the death of her mother, Olivia Bunker. The daughter claims her mother did not commit suicide, as many residents, including the police, apparently believe.

The article continued. Darlene saw it contained almost word for word what Harriet had told her the previous day. Annoyed that the woman hadn't gone to the police as she'd advised, she marched into Slim's office as soon as she arrived for work that morning to straighten him out.

"Did you see this?" She held the paper out to him. "She came to see me yesterday and I told her to go see you. Going to the newspaper was never mentioned."

"Yeah, I saw it. Some reporter asking a question that would sell more papers."

"Do you think murder is possible?" Darlene demanded. "The reporter also mentioned two other deaths that had been ruled accidental. He didn't mention Sable or Rufus by name, but anyone around here would know who he meant. He was raising a question about their deaths as well."

"Trying to sell papers, that's what it's about," Slim said tersely. "If I'd gotten answers about the material I sent to the County, I'd know something. Without that, I'm in the dark as much as anybody else." At least, he thought to himself, the fear-mongering article hadn't been under JJ's byline.

Chapter 17

*A*lexander and Solstice arrived at his mother's house for the weekend. After dinner, they went off to Teddy's for the evening.

Pilar was amused that her brilliant son, who was once uncomfortable in public situations, had cheerfully gone off to a bar that specialized in social atmosphere. Plus, he was looking forward to partnering with Solstice in undercover work on Sunday, when they would attend Senator Fergusson's brunch. Thanks to her grandfather, she'd received an invitation. Fergusson no doubt assumed she represented her grandfather's wealth, with no idea of her true purpose.

Pilar and Max, (he had finally moved in), took the dinner dishes to the kitchen and did the kitchen work together. With the dishwasher humming efficiently, Pilar settled at the cleared dining table to start making dress design sketches.

Max, on his way from the kitchen with a second cup of coffee, paused to look over Pilar's shoulder. He saw a bridal gown pattern and a sketch pad. "So," he said, "while doing interior decoration for the Mather House where Acer stays when he's in town, you've stepped into the wedding business. Looks promising."

Ignoring the meaning behind his comment, she smiled. "The dress is for Toria, This vintage pattern for a princess line gown is perfect, except a different neckline would be better, so I'm designing it. She'll come tomorrow for measurements and we'll discuss fabrics."

Max sighed exaggeratedly. "Since you've broken my heart yet again, I'll leave you to it."

Her gaze followed him as he took his coffee to his favorite chair where his current book waited. He was an easy man to love, but why wasn't her love enough to satisfy him without talk of marriage?

His mention of the Mather House caused her to recall an odd experience when she'd been there.

In the downstairs showroom were framed photos of houses that Acer's company would build. One caught her attention, a woodland mansion overlooking water with a boat and a pier. The house had a high peaked roof, but there had been none of those phantom words about gables and peaks. Still, the photo had given her an eerie sensation, almost like a warning. It made no sense. She dismissed the memory of it and returned to her work.

Alexander and Solstice entered Teddy's crowded bar room and looked for an empty table. As they moved, they greeted and were greeted by others: the chief of police, his officer, Donny, a friend from Alexander's high school and then reporter JJ and a news crew buddy.

A few steps further, they met Chuck Newton and his wife, Amy, coming from the main dining room after dinner.

The men shook hands and then introduced the women to each other. Alexander said to Solstice, "You remember Chuck—he picked us up at the bus when we came from the city before I had my motorcycle."

Chuck grinned. "You looked so young I warned this guy you might be jail bait."

Alexander felt Solstice step back and press against him. He figured the jail bait comment had reminded her of being held prisoner when she was young. Fortunately, Amy gestured to the two men and then to the teddy bear murals, and said to Solstice, "Pay no attention to these fur-faced grizzlies. Hang them on that wall and they'd fit right in Teddy Town."

Solstice laughed and Alexander gratefully saw that Amy's joke had changed Solstice's mood for the better. He said, "Why don't we all find an empty table."

Chuck shook his head. "Sounds good, but our babysitter is expecting us home. One thing I want to ask. You still interested in theater?"

"Yes, I'm directing a little group performing in Ibsen's, *The Wild Duck*. He made himself sound more satisfied with the jab than he was. He didn't want to direct a play; he wanted to write one that would be produced.

"Why don't you two stop at the Methodist Church Hall around three tomorrow?" Chuck suggested. "That's where our theater group practices. Afterward, we go to the Spyglass Inn for something to eat."

Alexander nodded. "Thanks, we'll see. Maybe we can."

After they left, Solstice said, "You want to see that little theater group, don't you?"

"Well, we don't have anything else planned for tomorrow."

"That's true, Smoky. And Amy made me laugh. We'll enjoy seeing them again."

Smoky the Bear, he thought, and smiled "Okay, we'll go."

He'd once believed he'd never enjoy visiting his hometown until he had a Broadway play under his belt. But now, visiting felt good and Solstice had made that possible. He added, "Tomorrow, at the Spyglass, I'll order a Gilbert, the preferred drink of famed playwright Eugene O'Neill."

Solstice gave him a look. "And when Sunday comes ditch the playwrights. We're going there to learn the truth about Fergusson and his stepdaughter. Step into a hit spy film at the brunch, Order a martini, shaken, not stirred, and play James Bond."

Chapter 18

Sunday's weather was perfect. After a pleasant drive with Alexander and Solstice discussing Chuck's theater group and the meal afterward, they reached the long, sweeping approach to Fergusson's estate. Alexander drove his mother's sunburst yellow Mazda Miata. Even with the seat pushed back he felt too big and burly for the sporty vehicle, but he liked it, especially the updated features.

He said to Solstice, "When you park this, it automatically maps the location on your smartphone. You can always find where you left it."

She stared at him. "I never had a car, but if did, I wouldn't park it and forget where it was. That's silly."

Alexander laughed. "Max misunderstood something my mother said. When she says something about finding some wonderful new shop while looking for her car it doesn't mean she lost it. It was her excuse for wandering with no particular purpose. Max talked with Acer Wolfgang, and ended up with automatic locators for this car that would work on his and her phones. My mother acted pleased because she didn't want to hurt Max's feelings. He likes to take care of her."

They rounded a bend and had a full view of Fergusson's impressive country house, a sprawling affair with arched windows, wrought-iron balconies, and sloping slate roofs. Alexander decided that a two-story addition to the left was more recent than the original house. He wondered if the wing was for guests and entertainment, reserving the original structure for Fergusson's private quarters.

"Look!" Solstice pointed. "Way behind the house. There's a helicopter."

"I see. Wonder who zoomed in on that?"

"Maybe we'll find out,'" she said.

The driveway passed through gates that opened to a circular cobblestone parking area filled with elegant automobiles by the two-story addition. Alexander pulled up and got out, handing the keys to a parking attendant and then moving quickly to the passenger side to open Solstice's door before another attendant beat him to it.

He extended an elbow to her as she emerged. She willingly rested her hand on his arm as they made their entrance. Inside, another attendant took their names and led them across a hall and into a huge room with white walls and a white tile floor. Although it looked like two stories from the outside, it was one sky-high space with French doors and tall windows above them, creating a dazzling display of glass sparkling in the sunlight. Although they weren't needed, all the chandeliers were illuminated. Music from a pianist seated before a white baby grand in a far corner softly played familiar show tunes as a well-dressed crowd milled around food and beverage stations.

Alexander thought the space resembled a fabulous stage set as a man came from house left, stage right, and greeted them, introducing himself as Senator Fergusson's secretary, Roy.

"He will be delighted to meet you," Roy said, his focus on Solstice. Alexander noted Roy's earbud and figured he was in communication with the man who had taken their names.

"Lexy," Solstice said to Alexander, calling him by one of her fabricated names. His role that day was to be her faithful assistant.

She stripped the lightweight wrap from her shoulders and casually passed it to him. "Lexy, carry this for me, I might want it later, but please—" her tone became long-suffering, "keep it where you can find it again, will you? Not like you did with my sunglasses in Monaco."

Lexy? Monaco? Alexander grinned inwardly as he accepted the wrap as if were an honor.

Roy escorted them to Fergusson, who stood talking to a dignified woman about his age. She had with Scandinavian coloring, her flaxen hair in a braided coronet. Alexander had seen photos of her in group shots with the Fergusson, gazing at him with respectful admiration, as she did now. The woman reminded him of an actress he'd viewed in classic films, Ingrid Bergman. *Bergman,* that was this blond woman's last name. She was Astrid Bergman, one of the senator's staff members.

Roy spoke to the senator who, after giving Astrid a pat on the arm, shifted his attention to Solstice. With a wide smile blazing like one of the chandeliers, he stepped toward her. "My dear Miss Windsor! What a pleasure!"

"A pleasure to meet you, too," she responded with enthusiasm as if she hadn't noticed the hand he expended in greeting.

Fergusson blinked, then began telling Solstice what a wonderful man her grandfather was. Roy chimed in several times with additional researched details. Fergusson had learned enough to give the impression that he and Solstice's grandfather were cronies, but his patter was as phony as his smile.

Smiling as if in agreement with everything said, Solstice asked, "Is your stepdaughter here? I'd love to meet her."

"Certainly." Fergusson turned and caught the eye of a tall, auburn-haired young woman and signaled her.

Looking annoyed to be drawn from the man she'd been talking with, Leslie walked leisurely toward them. Her eyes flicked over Alexander's bearded face and Solstice's freckled one.

She didn't look interested until she drew near and Fergusson introduced them. With a grudging change of expression, she said, "Solstice Windsor! How delightful!"

Absently patting her stepfather's arm as Roy drew him off to chat up someone else, Leslie eyed Solstice up and down and said too sweetly, "What a marvelous dress. Roberto Cavelli?"

Alexander sensed a trap. Although the horrors of her younger years were unknown to the public, there had been enough media attention to fuel the suspicion that she had been destitute before fate reconnected her with her wealthy grandfather. Not hard to guess that she might not know one designer from another.

Solstice handled the moment with ease. "Cavelli? Goodness, I have no idea. I'm too busy to dither with fashions. I leave it all to my stylist."

Leslie, momentarily taken aback, showed a brittle smile. "You must be terribly busy, then. What is it that you do?"

Solstice smoothly replied, "Charity work."

Alexander gazed at her with admiration. Considering what he knew of her precarious previous life, an acting ability had been necessary for survival. Her skills were well-honed.

As the two women continued to exchange words, he noticed a table of fruits and pastries and a station where a chef made omelets to order. At another station, a chef prepared French toast and waffles with assorted toppings. There were three beverage locations: one for liquor, one for hot beverages, and another for assorted juices.

Roy politely interrupted to ask Leslie a question. She responded with authority.

Alexander touched his beard, thinking it difficult to imagine haughty Leslie as a victim. But the same could be said of Solstice, at least at the moment. He shouldn't judge Leslie so quickly. Hauteur could cover emotional damage. Who knew the truth of her relationship with her stepfather?

He considered his knowledge of the man. Fergusson started his career as a lawyer and then entered politics. On the personal side, he and his first wife divorced. No children. He then married an older woman, a widow with a five-year-old daughter, Leslie. After five years they separated, but never divorced. When the wife died, he took custody of the girl, who was by then thirteen. A third marriage was annulled.

Did the annulment have anything to do with his wife seeing Fergusson's interest in Leslie? By then, she had been fifteen. That was also when the two of them had been spotted on vacation as a couple. Had Fergusson groomed her for the position? His stomach soured at the thought.

Startled at hearing Solstice speak the word *abuse* Alexander then heard her say heatedly, "You're mistaken if you think human trafficking only happens in other countries. Young women are victims in this country, too."

Leslie shrugged. "If you wish, contact my assistant with details about your organization's events." Then, smoothly uttering stock words about being so happy to have met Solstice, Leslie turned to respond to a couple who had drawn near, seeking her attention.

With the two of them alone, Alexander, unable to read Solstice's expression, said, "What did you think of her?"

"She's not what I expected. I have to think."

"Let's get something to eat while you're thinking." Like Solstice, Alexander was always interested in food.

A few minutes later, at the buffet, they overheard an exchange between Fergusson and Leslie, who were further down the table. The man gestured to one of the dishes and asked plaintively, "Do I eat this?"

"There are no onions cooked in anything," Leslie said. "I made that clear to the caterer. Onions are only offered on the side."

Finished filling their plates, Alexander and Solstice moved to sit at one of many small tables. Solstice took a bite of her French toast and then dabbed powdered sugar and cinnamon from her lips. She looked at Alexander, her brows drawn together.

"Leslie couldn't imagine what I meant about human trafficking. It didn't relate to anything she might have suffered. Hearing about a group that helps abused children and teens bored her." Solstice stabbed the air with her fork. "I don't know what her past was, but I can tell you this: she was never hungry, hurt, beaten or terrified. She's in a comfortable situation and cares nothing for anyone else."

Alexander finished his last bite of eggs Benedict. "I didn't like her either, but that doesn't make what happened to her right." He told her what he had been thinking about Leslie being groomed when she was young. "Fergusson's a sick man."

Solstice lifted her eyebrows. "Maybe *she* was grooming *him*."

Alexander stared. "You think *she* made the first move?"

"If she saw an advantage to it. The people who controlled the girls like me, called themselves handlers as if we were animals. Some handlers were women. Out for nobody but themselves. Leslie reminds me of one of them."

Alexander frowned. "Isn't that going too far?"

"No. This venture started because Fergusson seemed unfit for public trust. The photo of him with his stepdaughter at age fifteen proved it. I assumed he was evil and felt sympathy for Leslie. Now, I dislike them both." She mimicked the senator's whine, "*Do I eat that*? It's hard to imagine him taking the initiative in anything, but I believe it of Leslie. Whatever was in the past, she's in charge now."

A glance across the room showed Leslie chatting and laughing with the man she'd been with earlier. Alexander now recognized him from photos: Congressman Birch D. Charles.

"Your mother should have given that photo to the newspaper reporter instead of those club members," Solstice said. "Other than wanting you to get involved in spying, what else has the group done?"

He shrugged. "They thought of putting something on the Internet, but as my mother mentioned, that was too much like what Jessi Spellman might do. They wouldn't stoop to her level even though she hates Fergusson, too."

Solstice cocked her head. "Jessi, the one that showed up at your mother's party months ago, dressed in a harem outfit?"

Alexander laughed. "You called her Cookie Pants."

"I did. What's her grudge against Fergusson?"

"She convinced him that Acer Wolfgang gave her money to win a town election. Fergusson cozied up to her to get to Acer. He made a big fuss over that restaurant she's going to open, but Donny, my friend the cop, said that Jessi was in Town Hall complaining about Fergusson snubbing her. He must have learned she lied to him about Acer."

Solstice frowned. "If I'm right about Leslie, Fergusson might not be a monster, but he's still a pervert. And Leslie is so high and mighty she doesn't care about helping abused children."

"All true, but what should we do about it?"

"Hired help likes to talk. When you're done eating, scout around outside. Find somebody who takes care of the cars, who drives Fergusson and Leslie. See what they have to say. They might have overheard something we can use."

"Good idea," he said and started looking for a table.

There was a sudden commotion near the entrance. Still standing, they turned to look, seeing a small, well-dressed brunette arguing with one of the attendants. Roy stood blocking her from the room.

Fergusson, for once without a smile, hurried toward them.

Surprised, Alexander said, "It's Jessi Spellman!"

At that moment she looked in their direction. Abruptly, she broke Roy's hold and started running toward them.

"Solstice!" Jessi cried in apparent joy.

Solstice and Alexander could only stare as Jessi kept coming, her arms now outstretched.

"Solstice Windsor! Solstice, darling!" Jessi cried. "So wonderful to see you!"

Chapter 19

The senator rushed up behind Jessi. After a pause to catch his breath, he said to Solstice, "Do you know this woman?"

"Of course. She's Jessi Spellman."

"Same small town," Jessi told him, then she said to Solstice, "I had no idea you would be invited, too!" She said it as if she'd received a hand-engraved invite when she couldn't even get a return phone call.

"Oh," the senator said. "I didn't know you two were friends."

Solstice smiled and echoed Jessi's words, "Same small town."

The senator's secretary came up behind him, whispered something into the man's ear and drew him away.

Jessi wanted to toast herself with champagne for being so brilliant. Just as she was about to be tossed out, she'd looked across the room and saw a freckle-faced ragdoll with one shoulder hanging crooked. Her name—something to do with astrology, Solar—no *Solstice*. Solstice Windsor. Jessi had heard enough to know the girl had lived in rotten circumstances until her rich grandfather found her. Now she was an heiress, invited to the brunch because Earl hoped to grab some of her grandfather's green. So, Jessi thought, I took a brilliant chance and ran to Solstice. For some reason, she'd played along, pretending we were friends. But, really Jessi thought, who wouldn't want to be my friend?

"We should talk," she said to Solstice.

"Sure," Solstice said. She angled to look at Alexander. "Go find us a table, James."

So now he was James, not Lexy. He grinned. "Certainly."

Jessi went with the girl across the room to a table where Alexander stood like a big shaggy dog, ready to pull out chairs for them, which he did. He then sat at a nearby table, close enough to take orders, but not close enough to take part in the conversation.

Good dog, thought Jessi. Ragdoll had him whipped.

"So Solstice," Jessi said, leaning forward, elbows on the table, talking as if they'd been pals for ages. "Thanks for the save. I was going to get thrown out, do you believe that?"

"That's how it looked," Solstice said.

Jessi crossed her legs, showing off her little feet in sassy little high heels. There was something she wanted to know, but first, she had to establish that Earl was in the wrong.

"I had no idea Earl would kick up such a fuss when I arrived today," Jessi said, making it up as she told it. "I had to reject him, you see. I thought we were simply friends, both of us in politics, with interests in common. But he wanted to take friendship to what he called 'the next level.' I was stunned." The story was so good Jessi almost believed it herself. "All the same, I had assumed he wouldn't hold a grudge." Jessi opened her big, slouchy purse and pulled out brightly colored business cards. "I thought he'd want to see these. Here—" She passed a card over to Solstice.

Solstice read the words aloud. "The Carousel Restaurant?"

"You bet," Jessi said. "I've got colored flyers in my purse for the grand opening, with all sorts of specials. Until our misunderstanding, he'd been supportive of the restaurant, but now . . ." She shrugged. "Some men just can't take no for an answer." The more she told the story, the better it sounded. "Nobody should trust him."

Solstice frowned. "A politician, out for his own gain? Maybe he was being nice to me because of my grandfather."

"Exactly," Jessi said. "He's sneaky. Uses people." She leaned a bit to one side and elevated her voice to include Alexander. "Do either of you know anything about that women's Hoodoo group?"

Alexander spoke. "You mean the Voodoo Club?"

"Sure, them," Jessi said. "I was interviewing for waiters for my restaurant. This one guy has a wife who works at the Teddy Bear restaurant. That club has meetings there. He told me the women were passing around an old picture of Senator Earl snuggling with a girl on the beach. They were saying the girl was only fifteen years old. Sound kind of young for a grown man, huh?"

"Oh, my goodness sake, yes!" Solstice's tone was shocked. "Outrageous."

"Yeah, what I thought. And you know who the girl was?"

"No." Solstice leaned forward. "Who?"

So the heiress was a gossip, Jessi thought happily. She'd spread the word.

"The girl was his stepdaughter!" Jessi arrowed a finger across the room at Leslie. "Her! Senator Earl's been doing the mattress-boogie with his stepdaughter since she was a kid."

Eyes wide, Solstice said, "She looks so nice!"

"She probably is, or was, before he ruined her," Jessi said with satisfaction. "And believe me, she could do better than Earl. You know who she's talking to?"

Solstice's eyes were wide. "No, who?"

"He's got some kind of a tree name, like pine or oak. Anyway, he's a big shot. A Congressman, from Washington, DC. He flew here in a helicopter. A guy outside told me that."

"Golly, you know everything," Solstice said.

Jessi tapped the corner of one eye. "Make it my business to see and know things." What she saw next, was Leslie leaving the room. Jessi jumped to her feet.

"See you later," she called over her shoulder and she was off.

With her gone, Alexander moved to Solstice's table, and said, "More and more I think you're an actress."

She grinned. "You discovered me."

"Yes, maybe I did." He wanted to touch her hand. Maybe she read it in his eyes because she edged her hand across the table a little closer to his. He dared touch the back of her knuckles with his fingertips

"What do you think Jessi's going to do?" she said.

Alexander shrugged. "Nothing good for Fergusson, that's for sure."

"Time for your next step in our investigation." She reversed her hand so their palms met.

Finding the contact thrilling, he couldn't speak. He finally cleared his throat and said, "Right. The car park." He looked into her eyes, admiring her. "Where did you get the idea to go along and pretend you knew Jessi?"

"Well,'" she said, and then, referring to the man she'd called the Scholar, who had given her an excellent education, "the Scholar once told me about an old proverb. These aren't the exact words, but you'll get the idea: The enemy of my enemy is my friend."

Chapter 20

*J*essi watched as Leslie passed through an archway at one end of the room and entered a wide hallway. Following at a safe distance, Jessi saw her mount a set of marble steps to the left. Ah, she reasoned, the destination must be Fergusson's and Leslie's private quarters.

Exactly what she'd come to find!

With Leslie out of sight, Jessi stepped into the hallway.

A guard appeared.

"Ma'am," he said. "The ladies' restroom is back where you came from. Off at the far end of the big room."

"Okay, thanks," she said as she reversed direction, but she only went far enough toward the party room to glance back and see that the guard had turned away. She slipped into an alcove beside the stairway, invisible to the guard if he looked again.

Months ago, when Earl Fergusson had been playing nice, she and Arnie had been invited to his holiday bash. Their guest bedroom had been on the far end of the party room, not where she was now.

She was still concealed when Leslie descended the steps and returned to the party room, looking neither left nor right. The upstairs was now clear if there was a way to keep the guard from seeing her.

Still concealed, she peeked and saw him against the wall where he'd been when he'd spoken to her. She slipped off her shoes and stowed them into her capacious purse. From her cosmetics pouch, she pulled out a glass bottle of liquid makeup.

Bending, she leaned forward and sailed the bottle as hard as she could down the smooth tiles of the hallway as if it was a bowling alley. The bottle hit the far end wall. Had it made enough of a sound? *Yes.* The guard moved swiftly toward the end of the hall and away from her. Jessi moved to the staircase, her stockinged feet soundless as she bounded up the steps.

Having reached the second floor, she figured a rich old house would have a back stairway for servants. If she found it, she wouldn't have to risk going past the guard after she'd completed her task.

She started opening doors. The first one was a utility closet. The next door opened to a narrow staircase that wound up from the first floor. *Hot damn!* Jessi scurried down and ended at a door. A turn of a bolt unlocked it, giving a view of a porch screened by shrubbery. Jess stepped out and saw a deserted lawn that led away from the end of the building that held the party.

Escape route! Solid proof she was born under a lucky star.

A moment later she up the steps and again on the second floor. She found guest rooms for real friends, not business ones, and then a larger bedroom in use: queen-sized bed, cosmetics on the dressing table, a walk-in closet of fancy clothes, and an adjoining bath with a whirlpool tub. Surely Leslie's, but there was no sign of a male presence. Jessi wanted proof that "family-friendly" meant something unique to Leslie and Earl.

Fingers crossed, she pushed open yet another door. A bedroom with a king-sized bed, tables on either side, each with a lamp and reading materials. An official-looking folder stamped *Fergusson* on one night table, a *Vogue* magazine and a current novel was on the other. A postcard addressed to Leslie was used as a bookmark.

Pay dirt! The step-daddy-stepdaughter love nest.

Jessi tapped her shiny white teeth and smiled.

Eight minutes later she was out of the house and in her car, her only disappointment as she drove away was that she couldn't be a fly on the wall that night when Earl and Leslie went to bed.

It was eleven that evening when Leslie and Earl Fergusson prepared to retire. After being "on" all day, constantly talking and responding, followed by a late-day meeting after his guests had departed,
he was exhausted. He had watched a film in his home theater as he ate
his supper—his favorite foods prepared by his faithful cook. He knew
Leslie would have enjoyed getting out for the evening, maybe going to a
club, but she had seen how dragged out he was. She was always thinking of him. Paying attention to his attire, making his travel plans and
tirelessly attending to what was important.

In the bedroom, with a stomach full of comfort food, he spoke to
her about the feature that had made this day especially satisfying: his
special meeting with Birch D. Charles, a powerful man in Washington.
He remembered how Leslie had met him at a charity concert and persuaded the man to help him in his bid for a congressional seat. Leslie
constantly showed her faith in him despite his secret misgivings. He
loved being a state senator, feeling he had a gift for meeting and greeting. He was making a difference, but did he really have the tempera-
ment to move higher? But it was something Leslie wanted.

She was so young, he reflected, with astounding energy and drive.
Just look at how she had reconfigured their home—it was amazing—it
allowed entertaining on a grand scale, yet protected their precious privacy, which would become increasingly important as they moved into
an ever more public arena. If she wanted it, he had to go along. After all
she'd done for him, he couldn't let her down.

"The meeting with Birch Charles went well," he said as he checked
his hair in the mirror over his dresser. "The smartest thing I ever did
regarding him was to make you his contact person.

""You always do the right thing," Leslie said with a nod.

As she moved toward their bed to arrange it for the night, she recalled a time when she felt Earl was so mature. Of late, he just seemed
old. Birchy, ten years younger than Earl, had so much more confidence

and stamina. Just thinking about him made her smile. Plus, Birchy was light years ahead of Earl politically, but he'd been kind enough to spend a few minutes with Earl that afternoon. And then she and Birchy had enjoyed a few moments of their own. The highlight of her day.

Not that she would ever totally abandon Earl.

Suppressing a sigh, she forced herself to recall the plans she and Earl had made. She could never be the First Lady, which was a disappointment, but as he moved toward the presidency and then achieved it, she, his charming stepdaughter, would perform much the same function, although without the glory. However, considering Earl's aging, she would still be young when he was gone. By then, she would have gained access to incredibly wealthy men, powerful figures who could take her to heights she could only begin to imagine.

So, unless she could think of a better plan, Earl remained the key to her future. And admittedly, she had a soft spot for the old dear. Although it was only a shadow of what it had been, they would continue as secret lovers unless she came up with a better idea that would keep both of them happy

Behind her, she heard Earl sigh contentedly.

"I'm a fortunate man, Leslie. You're so wonderful in every way."

She pulled back the bedspread. For a frozen moment, she stood shocked and rigid. Then she screamed.

"She knows!" Leslie cried, feeling fury bubbling up like lava.

"What?" Fergusson pivoted toward her.

"Look!" she screeched, her hands stiff and arched, like talons seeking their prey.

"What? Who knows what?"

"That stinking glob of filth, Jessi Spellman! She's been in here! In our room, touching, violating . . . she knows about us! Look!"

Scattered over the surface of the bedding and even slyly peeping out from under the pillows were brightly colored Carousel Restaurant business cards and a flyer with a special offering circled in red lipstick:

A Romantic Dinner for Two:
A Carousel Restaurant Special for Lovers.

Below it, carefully printed in black marker:

FOR A COUPLE WHO HAVE BEEN
LOVERS SINCE SHE WAS FIFTEEN.
THERE'S A DATED PHOTO TO PROVE IT.

Chapter 21

*L*ate Monday afternoon, Francine called Pilar and suggested they have dinner at Teddy's. "Bob has a meeting tonight and you said the other day that Max would be off somewhere in his truck."

"I suppose I could go out for dinner," Pilar answered, feeling that Francine had something she wished to discuss.

"Excellent," Francine said. "You come to my house to pick me up and then drop me off after dinner on your way home."

Pilar smiled at Francine's commanding manner. It was probably a flaw to be amused by behavior that others found annoying, but that's the way it was.

In the restaurant, as they followed the hostess to a table, Pilar saw a poster announcing that Mar-see-ah would do readings that night. From her experience with the Voodoo Club, she knew readings were done in an alcove between the private dining rooms and the bar. No chance of running into her that night, thank goodness.

On their way to their table, they paused to greet Shirley DeGarmo and her expanding family: her two sons, Kurt, the tax assessor, with his hugely pregnant wife, and Donny, the police officer with his wife, Bethany, who was due to deliver their first child in June.

After exchanging a few words, they continued following the hostess, greeting and being greeted by a few others along the way. Pilar nodded to herself. Yes, Teddy's certainly did specialize in a social atmosphere.

When they were finally seated, had ordered, and received their meals, Francine said, "Has Alexander, found anything helpful to our group about Fergusson?'

Ah, their vendetta, Pilar thought. "He may have. He and Solstice attended a brunch at Fergusson's home and when he returned my car—that's how they drove there—he told me I'd been right about Fergusson's step-daughter."

Francine drew her head back shrinking her short neck into her shoulders. "You were right about his daughter? How?"

"I thought that regardless of what might have happened with Fergusson when she was in her teens, she's now the one in control."

"Why would you think that? You've never met her, have you?"

"No, but I've seen her with Fergusson on TV. It's something about her manner."

"Nothing you can prove."

"Correct." Pilar put a hand to her dark hair. She'd pinned it up to show off her ear hoops with dangling enameled parrots. They went with her outfit, skinny black pants and a parrot green blouse with floppy sleeves.

When they finished their meal, they stopped off at the lady's room in the lobby. Pilar came out first and jolted to a stop, the parrots on her earrings swinging. Mar-see-ah stood a few steps from the women's room door.

"I was with a client," Mar-see-ah said, "I felt your presence and the fact that you needed me."

Pilar frowned. "I had no such thought."

"Perhaps not," Mar-see-ah said, "at least not specifically, but you've been thinking of certain words that mean something. You have a true gift, one that carries responsibility. Did you have any feeling that what I told you at the women's club meeting connected with what happened later when you discovered the body?"

"I don't see why I should have," Pilar said, although she had recalled Mar-see-ah's words, *Look for the Light,* crossing her mind when she'd seen the light on in Sable's shop and decided to stop in.

Mar-see-ah smiled. "You sense things and call it intuition. Have you always had this ability to see beyond your physical grasp and arrive at a correct conclusion?"

Pilar uttered a small laugh. "God, if only."

Mar-see-ah gently touched Pilar's hand. "The shock of a tragedy could have brought you this gift; creating a powerful desire to make certain that nothing so terrible ever again catches you unawares."

"No!" Pilar jerked her hand away. "Go back to your waiting client."

She pivoted to face the opposite direction as Francine emerged from the restroom.

"Were you talking with Mar-see-ah?" she asked, seeing the woman retreating. "Something about interior decoration, I bet."

"She was passing by and stopped to say a few words," Pilar said, sidestepping a question with an answer that hopefully gave nothing away.

Chapter 22

Thanks to *Monitor* articles, rumors started saying that deaths in JumpRope that had been ruled accidental were now being considered suspicious. Slim, who was in the Melton County Building, answered a panicky call from JJ.

"Listen," she said. "None of the information came from me. What we talked about in your office was said in confidence. I respected that."

Slim glowered. "What the hell are you talking about?"

"I'm not the only one who saw evidence photos showing roses."

"You mean some two-legged rat here at the County?"

"Yes, but I don't know who. I only know that a call went out that there will be a press conference in a half hour on the steps outside the Prosecutor's Office. It mentions you. I'm heading there now. I wanted to give you a heads up and tell you that if there's anything said about roses, it didn't come from me."

Disgusted, Slim went looking for County Detective Isaac Ellis, the only one he trusted there—and that wasn't saying much.

He met Ellis coming down a corridor.

"I've been looking for you," Ellis said. He was a light-skinned black man dressed like a banker, wearing a trim gray suit with a light blue shirt and a darker blue tie.

"Looking for me, why?" Slim asked, although he already knew.

Ellis grinned, "Because a certain person, who shall only be known by his exalted title, *The Melton County Prosecutor*, heard something about your town. He also heard you were here and thought it a perfect excuse—or rather a perfect *reason,* to call a press conference."

"About what," Slim snapped.

"About what he saw in the *Melton Monitor*—that the death of a woman, previously believed to be suicide, and another death considered an accident, were now being viewed as 'suspicious.' The local TV news reported the same."

"There's nothing solid to back that up," Slim said. "If he's so interested, why didn't he light a fire under his lab guys? I've been waiting for reports on evidence that's just sitting. If Mr. Title Only was on the ball, he'd make sure his department didn't allow backlogs, which is the excuse I've been getting."

Ellis grinned, his dark eyes amused. "I don't know anything about that. I've been sent to drag you outside to where the press conference is about to begin. Let's go."

Grumbling to himself, Slim ran a hand through his hair and went along with Ellis.

Opening the press conference, the prosecutor grandly stated that two recent deaths in JumpRope Township had been under investigation from the start and that work was continuing. He then turned to Slim for confirmation. Slim grimly echoed the prosecutor's words, and then added, to the gathered reporters, "I'll have no further information until the results of evidence lab reports have been sent to me."

JJ called out a question to Slim that asked specifically about fingerprints from objects found at two of the death scenes, that of Olivia Bunker and Rufus Neilson.

Slim answered tersely. "I've already stated that without the lab reports, there's nothing to say." He paused, and then, with his jaw tightened and his eyes narrowed he looked at JJ and said, "At this point, the only fingerprints I see are from the inky fingers of *Monitor* reporters."

There were a few chuckles from the gathering and cameras caught Slim's expression as he jabbed at the *Monitor*.

Unfazed, JJ addressed the prosecutor, "Can you please explain the hold-up on the lab reports?"

The prosecutor replied smoothly. "Haste is not warranted in matters of importance. As Chief Parkerson has said, we must wait until the lab studies are complete." With a glance at Slim, he added, "Pressing for results in an investigation of suspicious deaths is pointless. A professional person should be aware of this."

That was when a TV reporter called out, "I've been informed of a connection between two of the deaths and yet another recent death."

"What connection?" someone called.

The TV reporter answered. "The connection is that cards picturing red roses were at the scene of one death and actual red roses at the scene of another." His gaze went from Slim to the prosecutor. "Would either of you two gentlemen care to comment?"

Almost in unison, they said, "The investigation is continuing."

The six o'clock TV news that evening ran a video from the press conference showing Slim's expression as he spoke to JJ. The program's news anchor said: "It seems the question about fingerprints put a finger on a sore point for JumpRope's Chief Parkerson.

The co-anchor jumped in. "Does this mean there's a killer who leaves a red rose as a signature at the crime scenes?

"A Red Rose killer?" the anchor questioned, "We will have to wait and see. For now, in closing, we say to our viewers that the formerly peaceful township of JumpRope, New Jersey, now appears to be skipping through a rose garden to the tune of murder."

Chapter 23

At 6:30 that evening, Holly drove to Toria's house. He had been looking forward to a quiet evening: ordering a take-out dinner and watching an amusing movie. But after watching the news, he was in an uncharacteristically gloomy mood. The month of March had crept into April, but instead of having an April Fools' Day, there had been an April Fools' Week. A sick joke on the entire town. And now the TV reporters label for the other deaths: *Red Rose Killer*.

When he saw an unfamiliar truck parked in Toria's driveway and next to it, a big pile of wood, he thought that someone must have dumped the wood at the wrong address. Then he looked at the truck's license, *Delaware*. Toria's father? Another April Fool's joke.

While she'd been in Texas, he'd looked up her father's address on the Delaware tax records and had driven there. He'd found no one home, but noticed that everything about the property was all spit and polish.

Had Toria's father been like that with his family? Demanding perfection in everything including his wife and child?

The front door opened just as Holly reached it. There was Toria, her smile tense. She seemed to be huddled within herself.

"Hi, honey," Holly greeted as he reached toward her.

She went into his arms as if he were an oasis in the middle of a desert. "My father showed up this afternoon." Her head was tucked down, her words muffled against his collar.

"Good. We should get to know one another."

Before he could say anything more, a male voice from the room behind Toria boomed, "Well, well, what have we here?" As if it was his house, not hers.

Toria drew Holly inside, but she turned to keep herself in front as if protecting him.

"It's okay, hon," he said, moving her aside and stepping out to face the tall, broad-chested figure dominating the center of her living room. This physical confrontation was so different from the full-of-talk issues he'd been dealing with all week that he welcomed it.

Toria's cleanly shaved father stood with his booted feet planted far apart. His muscular body, which was starting to run to fat, strained the fabric of his neat plaid shirt and pressed khaki trousers. The man had an outdoor face, red with broken veins as if he was always facing a harsh wind of grit or cold or heat or any other punishment the elements had to offer that would cause a lesser man to wilt.

"This is my father, Martin Dahlgaard," Toria said as if forcing the words. "Daddy, my fiancé, Holland Kingston,"

He stepped forward and stuck out a muscular right hand in greeting. "Only you're called, Holly, right?" *A girl's name,* said the unspoken jeer. "And you're the mayor of this *tiny* burg?" Dahlgaard's tone held a nasty note as he emphasized the word tiny.

Having taken a quick measure of his challenger, Holly saw the palm-angled-down hand that was surely intended to master his hand by painfully squeezing his knuckles together. Holly led with his left foot as he clasped the extended hand and stepped into Dahlgaard's space, exerting a pressure equal to the larger man's and neutralizing his power. Being mayor might be a desk job, but he was experienced with *let's play who's boss* antics, and he wasn't shy of heavy work. If Martin Dahlgaard thought to establish himself as the top dog, too bad because the handshake ended in a tie.

"Well, well," Dahlgaard said, stepping back.

"Why don't you two sit down while I finish dinner." Toria watched anxiously as both men took their seats as if making sure this wasn't just a one-minute rest period in a boxing match.

Holly flashed Toria a confident smile and after another hesitation, she left. Holly was content with height and the fact that he was strong despite his smaller frame, so peering up at taller, larger men was nothing he couldn't take in stride. He eyed Dahlgaard, seeing a resemblance between him and Toria in the high cheekbones that made their eyes tilt up slightly. It was enchanting on Toria, but not on this character. The man's brown hair was smashed down with some product. If he let it go, would it be as flyaway as hers? Amused, Holly thought of Dahlgaard fighting every morning to cement his electrified hair.

"That wood out there yours?" Holly asked.

"Yeah. Saw it at a nearby garden place. Fellow had cut down trees and sold the wood cheap. Hefty pieces, but I've got a log splitter. His loading crew was out on the road, so I paid him and gave him this address. They were supposed to load it in my truck when they got here, but the chiselers dumped it and ran off." As he sat, he added with a scornful laugh, "You can help me load it before I leave."

Not suggesting that Dahlgaard should have waited until after they'd loaded the wood as agreed, Holly settled into an easy chair and said, "I'll be happy to help you and I'm glad you showed up. It's good we could meet before the wedding."

"Oh, the wedding. Ha! My daughter's doing everything wrong thanks to my ex-wife. She lets herself get screwed up listening to her mother. No backbone of her own."

"Really?" Holly moved forward in his chair, his warning tone as sharp as the creases in Dahlgaard's khakis.

At Holly's glare, the man shrugged. "At least that's how it was."

The two men exchanged a few more comments that were civil enough. Holly suspected Dahlgaard was as leery of the wedding as Toria's mother, neither one knowing how it would be when they were in the same room again.

Toria called them to dinner. As they ate, there continued to be things that irked Holly, including Martin calling Toria "Stringbean." She didn't seem to mind, but she'd told Holly that when she was a teen she'd always felt too tall and skinny. Her father's pet name had to have been hurtful. The man had the sensitivity of a wrecking ball. He kept taking shots at his ex-wife by making critical comments about Toria. Holly had never seen her blush so painfully since they'd gotten to know one another.

The main meal finished, Toria cleared the dinner plates and brought out dessert, an ice cream cake. Even with a sweet taste in his mouth, Dahlgaard kept sniping at his ex-wife, attacking her through criticism of Toria. Holly, knowing Toria's dislike of discord, struggled to rein in his rage over her father's deliberate belittling.

Martin cleaned his dessert plate. "Not half bad, Stringbean, but I saw that one of the dinner items and this dessert were bought frozen. Too bad your mother never taught you better. Getting married—" he flashed Holly a glance, as if expecting his cooperation, "even this guy here will expect home-cooked food and oven baking."

Last straw. Holly pushed his chair back from the table and rose to his feet. He might have no control over possible murderers in his town, but he knew how to handle bullies.

"Mr. Dahlgaard—" Holly's eyes held that steady, withering gaze he awarded to planning board shysters seeking approval for "beneficial town uses" that would only benefit their own pockets. "I'm glad we could meet and have dinner, but it's time for you to say goodbye."

"What?" the man spoke in a tone of disbelief. It took a moment before he stood and moved around the table to confront Holly.

To say the man's face went beet red was no exaggeration, and his nose, with its broken veins, threatened to turn into a Rudolph look-alike. Holly thought it would have been comical if the moment wasn't so strained. He said, "I'm sorry for whatever difficulties you've had with your ex-wife, but I'm sick of hearing you criticize her by finding fault with Toria. Whatever you think your ex-wife did or did not do, Toria's turned out to be the beautiful young woman that I'm in love with and that I intend to take as my wife."

Looming over Holly, Martin Dahlgaard glanced at his daughter. She was still seated, her head down.

With a sound like a swallowed roar, Dahlgaard glared at Holly. "I'll not stay where I'm not welcome." He cast another glance at Toria. Still no help there. He then looked down at Holly with a malicious grin. "You gave me a promise about that wood."

"Correct." Holly bit off the word.

Holly was in the driveway by the woodpile before Dahlgaard got outside. The wood was in the form of logs cut short enough for a wood stove, but a foot or so in thickness. As Dahlgaard had said, they needed splitting.

Temper simmering, Holly observed the white truck. Not a scratch or a speck or a ding on it, hub caps gleaming, the vinyl liner in the truck bed spotless. The man could keep everything perfect except his relationship with his daughter.

Holly saw how it must have been. When Toria's parents had been together, her father had attacked his wife through their child. No wonder Toria thought she'd been the cause of their troubles. She'd been just a kid with no way to understand their blame game. Every time her parents fought, her father's finger pointed at her, making her think it was all her fault, and even now, making her feel uncertain

With revved-up fury giving him extra power, Holly hoisted a log and threw it into the truck. Then another and another. He became aware of the older man's presence. Straightening after throwing in another log, Holly said, "You get up in the truck. Arrange the wood before I toss in more so everything will fit."

The man looked at the pile of remaining wood, then went to the passenger side, punched a button on the key fob, opened a door, and reached in. He came out with two pairs of gloves. "Might find 'em a little big," he quipped as he handed them over.

Holly said nothing as he accepted the gloves.

Together, they loaded three-fourths of the log pile. Together they climbed into the truck bed and shoved logs more compactly. Together, they jumped down again and finished the job.

Straightening, Martin Dahlgaard rubbed his back. "It's getting late. Time I was moving on, other things to do. Going to go tell my daughter goodbye." Turning on his heel, he paused only to open the driver's door and throw in his gloves.

Holly slipped off the borrowed gloves and examined his hands, seeing no real damage from the work he'd done before he'd slipped them on.

When Toria's father returned, Holly handed the gloves back to him and was amused to see that the glop the man had on his hair had dislodged and strands were starting to stick up in cartoon-like clumps.

Dahlgaard threw the gloves into his truck and then turned to look Holly up and down. "Feisty little devil," he muttered. Showing a reluctant smile, he stuck out his hand.

This time, it was a mutual handshake, no power play.

Holly stood in the driveway watching until the truck was gone, and then, he returned to the house and Toria.

She met him at the door with a wild hug. "You made him go home," she said, against his shoulder, her voice tremulous. "Nobody ever tells my father what to do, but you did. You made him go home."

"He is what he is," Holly said, holding her close.

"You were right," she said, leaning back and looking into his face. "What you said about him trying to hurt my mother by using me was right on target. I never saw it until you put it into words, making it obvious." She started to laugh and cry at the same time. "He even insulted the wedding dress he'd never seen, saying I'd probably let my mother browbeat me into something that wasn't feminine. The truth is I let my mother browbeat me into that horrible ruffles and bows dress because she thought he would approve. Right now, I hate everything about both of them."

Holly showed a faint smile. "At least your father and I won't be strangers at the wedding."

"I don't want him there!" Toria cried. "I don't want him to give me away. I don't want my mother there, either."

Man, now she was going overboard. "Sweetheart—we can't cut them out."

She put her fists on his shoulders. "I'd spend my wedding day worrying about trouble from them." She gave his shoulders twin thumps for emphasis. "They can't come. We won't allow it."

"Sweetie, we can't do that. Can't have everybody there except them. My parents will be there, and—"

She cut him off, her voice rising, "I don't want the big June wedding! I want to get married now. This minute. We already have the license, so why not?" She started to laugh. "Yes, that would be perfect. We could run away. Elope."

Holly felt as if his thoughts were spinning. "But we've made all these plans—"

"What plans? For months we haven't made plans. Now we have too many to stop? A judge can marry us. Get the court judge, Judge Fisher. If he can't do it, find someone else." On a roll, she barely paused. "We should cancel the church, but the reception, the flowers? We can still have all that in June. A reception is just a big party. My parents can come to that. There will be a million people around and I won't care what they do."

Her tears all dry now, she giggled. "If they really act up, you can throw them both out."

"But your dress . . ." Did he like the idea of not waiting? Yes! But it was his nature to plan—it seemed too much of a rush.

She ran on, "Pilar doesn't have the fabric for the dress, not yet. But maybe she should go on ahead and make it. I'll wear it at the party. Although . . . " She gave him a sidelong glance, "By that time, wearing pure white will no longer be appropriate."

Holly stared at her realizing the implications of her words. His shy violet? He laughed, looked into her eyes, and hugged her close. "Okay, we'll do it." He couldn't keep combined excitement and longing from his voice. "I'll call Judge Fisher."

Chapter 24

Their plan went more smoothly than either of them could have imagined. While Toria packed, Holly went home to throw his things together, retrieve the license, and make the call to Judge Fisher.

The judge was home. "I'll provide the two witnesses," he said. "Come on over."

Holly drove back to get Toria and soon they were at the judge's house in Melton. The man asked no questions about the hurry-up, but Toria felt obligated to say, "We didn't want to wait any longer and there was a problem with the invitations." She felt guilty because she wasn't telling the whole truth, which was she didn't want to invite her parents, but she couldn't say *that*.

Judge Fisher, a saggy-eyed man who combed his graying black hair away from his horsey, good-humored face, chuckled. "I know of marriages that almost ended before they began because of the guest list."

His comment had Toria feeling better. Maybe he would have understood the whole truth.

The two witnesses were the judge's wife and his next-door neighbor, two dependable people the judge said he always called. Mrs. Fisher put on a CD of wedding music that played in the background during the ceremony. Holly's and Toria's kiss was short and sweet because people were watching, except the neighbor, who said she had a pie baking and kept glancing at the clock to see when her oven timer would go off.

When all was done, the certificate signed and it was just the three of them, the judge said, "How are you two going to let people know they don't have a big June wedding to look forward to?"

Holly hadn't thought that far in advance. A glance at Toria told him it was the same with her. Before either of them could say so, the judge gave them his advice.

"Tell the people who need to know why you're away and let word get around to the rest. If either one of you were sick or hurt, the world would manage without you. No one is indispensable. Give yourselves the gift of a week for just the two of you."

They headed for New York, where they planned to spend their honeymoon: a nice hotel, fancy restaurants, and a Broadway show. Toria said, "Will we do what the judge said and stay a whole week?"

Holly reached over to clasp her hand. "When you get good advice, you should take it. A week it is."

She squeezed his hand and uttered a sound of delight. "I can't believe it. Any of it. We're married!" She glanced over at him. "Do you feel any different?"

"I guess not." He smiled. "It's happened so fast, I can't take it in."

"Me too. I'm in a whirl, but it's a wonderful one."

Holly thought of something. Smile fading and suddenly uneasy, he said, "What the judge said about word getting around . . . people will be looking at you when we get back." He hesitated, and then said, "They will think we rushed into marriage because you're pregnant."

There was silence for a moment. Holly waited tensely.

Unexpectedly, Toria giggled. "By the time we get home again, that may be true."

Holly almost ran the truck off the road.

Since finding a place to stay in the busy city at night might be a hassle, they pulled off the Turnpike when they saw a big hotel.

In their room, Toria told him to use the bathroom first. She said she wanted to look at a brochure she'd picked up in the lobby about the attractions in Manhattan.

After his shower, Holly shaved and rubbed his face to make sure it was smooth. At home, he slept in his underwear, but he'd brought along gift pajamas he'd never worn before. There was tissue paper tucked inside and pins in the top and bottom fastening them together for some insane reason. He had trouble with the pins because his hands didn't seem steady. Why so many pins?

Wearing the pajamas, he came out, gestured toward the bathroom, and said to Toria, "All yours."

"Thanks." Her smile seemed shaky as she passed by him, entered the bathroom, and closed the door.

He saw that she'd pulled back the covers of the king-sized bed invitingly. He gazed at it a moment, then sat in a chair. The new pajama top felt scratchy. Didn't he find all the fool pins? He took off the top and looked. It was a label on an inside seam that was uncomfortable. He liked to wash new stuff before he wore it. He looked at his hands and moved his arms and his back, still surprised that he felt no ill effects from moving all the logs. The room felt too warm. He decided to leave the pajama top off. He didn't want to get all sweaty.

Shower sounds came from the bathroom. How long would she take? Sitting around was driving him crazy. She'd wanted to wait until marriage to make love and he'd agreed because that's what she wanted and he'd wanted to do what she wanted. He was proud of her for sticking to what she felt most comfortable with, proud of both of them because it sure hadn't been easy.

He started thinking that maybe the reason she'd wanted to wait was because she hadn't wanted intimacy as much as he did. Did he believe that? She was a modern woman, but innocent in the old-fashioned way. He realized the responsibility it placed on him. Any new experience was scary no matter how it was longed for. He wanted to make everything perfect for her, but if she was really afraid—

The bathroom door opened. He jumped up from his chair as if it had been attached to the bathroom door by a spring.

"Hi," she said, her smile tremulous. She wore some sort of long white thing that wasn't opaque like he would have expected her to wear. It was like a veil; he could see right through it. She was always surprising him, he thought, wonder combining with desire. Everything about her was more beautiful than anything he could have ever imagined.

As he stepped toward her, not realizing he was trembling, she reached to her left shoulder. That wasn't where he'd been looking, but he saw the gown was fastened at the shoulders with bowed ribbons.

Gazing into his eyes as he approached, she pulled the bow of the ribbon at one shoulder. Any doubts he might have had about her feelings toward him and their love slipped away as surely as that side of her gown slipped to the upper slope of her breast. Her fingers moved the ribbon at her other shoulder, hesitating as she held his gaze.

He stopped a breadth away and found his voice, "Need some help?"

"Yes, could you please help me?"

"Always," he said, and his voice betrayed him, unsteady again as he gently undid the little ribbon.

She spoke his name and lifted her hands to touch his face, the movement allowing the diaphanous gown to slip to the floor.

He felt her warm skin against his bare chest. He drew back a moment so he could look at her, overwhelmed by her beauty.

"My darling, my sweetheart . . ." He drew her close again. "I love you so much," he whispered against her lips as their kiss began, their bodies close, warm and alive against one another.

His arms were strong and steady as he lifted her and carried her to the bed.

Her head resting against the pillow, she looked up at him as he bent over her and she smiled and touched his face again.

"My husband . . ." she whispered.

He smiled. "My wife," he said as he gathered her into his arms.

At long last, the night was theirs.

Chapter 25

A week later, Holly was in Town Hall, being bombarded by staff members with their congratulations. The women, including Darlene, hugged him. Kirk from the tax office, the zoning and construction officials who worked in Darlene's department, the public works team, and whatever cops were in the building all showed up, except Slim.

After Holly finished shaking hands and getting one-armed hugs and shoulder knocks from the guys, he headed for the police department end of the building and met Slim coming from his office.

"Hey, hey, bud—" Slim wore a big grin as he grabbed Holly's hand. "I was just coming to see you. Only one honeymoon week for you and your blushing bride?"

"Wish it could have been more, but it was a great week," Holly said, in answer to Slim's wicked grin.

"Come in for a moment." Slim backed into his office and went around behind his desk, which seemed piled higher than usual with papers and snack food packages. Holly took his customary chair.

"Where are you two going to live?" Slim asked. "I bet your apartment's almost bigger than Toria's entire house."

"It is when you include the attic." Holly had gotten himself a snack and a water bottle from the lounge machine on his way, and now he took a sip. "Her house is a lot more private than an apartment."

"Yeah, with Lillian Brent on the floor below in your place, you'd have to move your bed to the attic." Slim threw a sideways glance, checking for Holly's reaction. "Old gal would have her ear turned to the ceiling every night hoping for some action.

"Yes, sure," Holly said. Over many past months, Slim had made his share of remarks about Toria's Victorian attitudes. Well, what Slim didn't know! "Everything's terrific and Toria is one special lady, okay?" His good-natured tone still managed to say, *enough of this*. He settled back in his chair. "Anything new related to Olivia or Rufus?"

"In a way. Rufus' son, George, had a spell last Thursday. He collapsed at the food market. He stayed overnight at the hospital and came home with new heart medicine."

"Heart trouble rubs in the family?"

"Seems so. I called this morning to see how he was doing." Slim heaved a sigh. "He's not over his father's death, and his family squabbling about him getting the house hasn't helped. As for Olivia Bunker, her daughter, Harriet, is nagging about the lack of progress. I'm thinking she has a right to call it murder even though the country still hasn't made a public statement. You missed seeing her at her mother's funeral and I hope she's gone home to Maine."

"Right. Is Neece Van Doran giving you grief? I thought that TV interview about fingerprints and George's father's drowning sounding suspicious might have gotten under her skin. Maybe it was bothering George, too."

"I doubt they paid attention," Slim said. "Neece's concerned about George and he's concerned about his family's behavior. Now they won't even talk to him. He feels he no longer has a family."

"Tragic. They could have handled it differently."

"Yeah, they ganged up on him, accused him of cheating them." Slim leaned back and looked at Holly. "And speaking of cheating, how come the elopement and cheating me out of being your best man?"

Holly smiled. "All about you, huh? Well, I finally met Toria's father. He's a know-it-all guy and a bully."

Slim raised his brow. "Sounds the opposite of Toria."

"He sure is. Remember when I told you that Toria's mother might be lagging on the wedding plans because she wasn't well?"

"Yeah, what happened with that?"

"Her health is fine, but after her second husband died, she— "

"When did it happen?"

"A while ago, but Toria's mother never told her. A family for secrets. Anyway, she was stalling on wedding plans because she was afraid of seeing Toria's bossy father at the ceremony. Toria got fed up. If the wedding was going to be a hairball, she'd rather elope. We'll have the reception later." Holly grinned. "As best man, you can give the champagne toast at the reception."

After Holly left, Slim picked up a package of cheese snacks and studied the mess on his desk. Stuff piling up, including a bunch of Melton Monitor tear sheets with articles about the troubles in JumpRope, written by JJ Gilbert. He shook his head. She should be strung up by her ponytail to keep her out of traffic.

Then the officer at the cop window called and said there was a lady who needed to see him. Somebody named Harriet Bunker Johnson.

Not back in Maine, Slim thought with a groan, and then said, "Okay, send her in."

A middle-aged woman with curly brown hair walked in. He'd glimpsed her briefly at the funeral. She didn't look like a troublemaker, but then she opened her mouth and started recapping everything that was in her *Monitor* interview and how extremely upset she'd been over the lies about her dead mother. She added, "I saw you on TV and you said my mother's death is still being investigated."

There had been no specific mention of her mother, Slim thought, but this woman only cared about one thing, clearing up any notion that her mother deliberately ended her own life.

As sympathetically as possible, Slim said, "Since you watched the interview, you also heard that there are delays at the county with processing evidence. I won't know anything more to help you until I know more."

They talked a few minutes longer and he said, "I understand your frustration, but if you give me your contact information, this office will give you answers as soon as they come in."

"That would be extremely gracious of you," she said, as she wrote down her cell phone number on the paper he'd handed to her, and then stood. "My mother was so excited about her plans. I'm sure you can understand why this talk of suicide has me extremely upset."

"I do understand," he said, standing and shaking her hand. "I'll be in touch just as soon as I have anything to tell you."

About an hour later, he received two reports from the county prosecutor's office. One was about the cup that had belonged to Rufus.

There were no prints—it had been wiped clean. To Slim, that said he'd been right. Someone had been on the scene, deliberately broken the cup and tossed it before the Colonel arrived. As for who that person had been, he supposed he'd never know.

Olivia Bunker's report also had something about prints.

Yes, she had died from an overdose of sleeping pills. The pill container had an excellent set of fingerprints. The bedside water tumbler had a clear handprint. It was as if the bottle and the tumbler had been wiped clean and then someone had pressed then into Olivia's unresisting hand. Her death, which had appeared to be suicide, now looked like murder. But only the county could pronounce that officially.

That would satisfy the daughter, Slim thought, but it would be trouble for his town. He sank back in his chair and stared bleakly up at the high window in his office, seeing only clouds across the sky, thinking that there was also the theft of Sable's electronic equipment and the missing files.

What was going on? More questions and no answers.

Restless, he went to Holly's office and told him about the fingerprint report and the fact that Olivia's death had gone from suspicious to a possible homicide.

"Nothing's public yet," Slim cautioned.

They talked a bit more about Olivia's death and then Holly said, "I heard something about Jessi Spellman. What did you do, embarrass her again?"

"Embarrass her?" Slim was glad for the change of subject. "She gets caught running the department's color copier out of toner and I'm the bad guy?" He laughed. "Here's the new Jessi caper. This guy, Geno Pena, said he'd been hired to work at Jessi's new restaurant. She ordered him to trap the stray cats that once lived inside that old barn that's going to be the new restaurant's dining hall. The animals are still hanging around. Jessi wants them gone."

Holly grinned. "So she can be the only cat on the property?"

"Yeah, sure, and get this. She ordered Pena to trap the cats and toss them, cages and all, into the retention pond behind her property."

Holly's eyes widened. "Was she serious?

Slim shrugged. "Pena believed she was. I heard she wanted to sell Wolfgang that restaurant property, only he wasn't interested. She's probably holding a grudge, so dead cats in his pond."

Holly looked troubled. "Pena didn't do it, did he?"

"Nah. He's a cat lover. He wanted me to arrest her."

"She'd deny it and, make trouble for him."

"What I told him. He had the cats already trapped, so I called a no-kill shelter, made arrangements, and told Pena to transport them. I heard later that Jessi fired him for insubordination."

"At least he saved the cats," Holly said, "but there's going to be a steep charge if there's a bunch of them. Who's paying for that?"

Slim gave a rueful look. "Pena was trying to do the right thing. The police budget has a line item for animal control."

"I'll support you on it if there's a question." He shoved a freshly opened packet of mustard-flavored pretzels across his desk to Slim. "It would have been a shame to try and wreck that pond. When Acer is finished with his houses, that place should look really good."

"Thanks," Slim said about the support and the pretzels, then added, "That pond is still a drainage basin as far as I'm concerned. Nothing fancy about it."

Holly shrugged. "His development is fancy. Instead of building model homes for people to choose from, he's taking orders for homes to custom-build. Darlene saw what looked like a southern mansion going up and saw pictures of other homes buyers wanted to have. Everything upscale, a credit to the town."

"Uh-huh," Slim said, thinking he still didn't trust Acer, and Darlene was probably too impressed with the guy even though she pretended she wasn't. "That so-called pond is still nothing but a hole dug for run-off water."

"A rose by any other name," Holly said."

"Sure," Slim said, not wanting to hear any mention of roses.

Chapter 26

The rest of Slim's week was neither good nor bad, until Thursday. That's when George Neilson had a heart attack for real and ended up in intensive care. He'd tried to drive himself there but ran himself off the road and into a sidewalk display at Jolly's Yesterday's Treasures. Grumpy Jolly was more upset over a busted array of antique jugs full of spring flowers than anything else, but he at least called emergency help for George.

George's heart attack was bad enough, but then, Claudine Hackamore burst in through Slim's door, followed by Officer Farley. "I'm sorry, Sir," he said. "I couldn't stop her."

"I can imagine," Slim sighed as he waved Farley off.

Claudine looked about the same as she had at Rufus' funeral and bristled with the same outrageous manner.

Hands on her ample hips, she rasped in a belligerent, years-of-too-much-smoking voice, "I'm Neece Van Doran's sister, Claudine Hackamore. When in God's name are you Rent-A-Cops going to catch that killer, who murdered her boyfriend's father!"

She refused to listen about the lack of proof for anything except an accident. She finally stormed out, slamming the door behind her.

That evening, after a visit to George at the hospital, Slim stopped at Teddy's for some relaxation. JJ waved to him and he walked over.

Her latest article said there was still no progress on Olivia Bunker's death, which was now being called a *Red Roses Mystery*.

"Hey," she said with a grin. "I gotta tell you who called me at the newspaper this afternoon. Claudine Hackamore."

Slim scowled. "She saw me too. I finally got rid of her." He gave JJ a hard look. "Don't tell me you're printing something she said."

"How can I not? Plus the photo op. Readers won't be able to able to tear their eyes from the page."

"Are you crazy? She flies up on her broom, set on destroying the town you live in, and you'll give her print space?"

JJ pantomimed using a pencil and pad. "Quote you about the broom?"

Slim's expression turned blacker. "Sean's Pub is getting my drink orders tonight." He turned on his heel and left.

JJ looked after Slim's tall rangy form and decided it was a good thing she hadn't mentioned that Jessi Spellman had called her on another matter, something about State Senator Earl Fergusson. Jessi was a sore subject with Slim, but she was another person who always made good copy.

That same Thursday, Francine called Pilar. "Have you heard any pushback about Holly's elopement?"

"It was a surprise, but push back? What do you mean?"

Francine huffed, "My sister thinks it's just fine and while I don't mean to criticize, if Holly had been *my* stepson instead of hers, he would have known proper protocol, and not run off like he did. A mayor of a small community should have a formal church ceremony, with the entire town welcomed. Now there's going to be gossip about Toria, who is a very decent girl, having a hurry-up wedding. That's not right. Holly must have talked her into it."

Although Pilar knew that Francine was happy with her husband, Bob, she would never forget that the former mayor, Holly Kingston, Sr., had jilted her to marry her sister Peggy.

"I see what you mean," Pilar said. "I think the least said, the better. Why keep it on everyone's mind? Let's just hope they will be happy."

"I knew you would agree with me," Francine said, because in her mind that's what she heard. "Probably everybody feels the same way. " she added. "Disgraceful or not, it's over and done with."

With a free mind, Francine finished her preparation for an impromptu meeting of the ladies from the two organizations planning the sale of Sable's household goods.

When all were assembled, Francine stood at the head of her dining room table after refreshments had been served, and said, "With the help of letters drafted by that fish-nut lawyer, Earnest Cobb, one of his people gave me information from the card companies Sable did business with. "In the past seven years, Sable's greeting card sales earned over sixty thousand dollars, sent directly to an online bank. From that account, Sable sent a cashier's check to a Buckley A Hightower."

Elevating her voice over the surprised exclamations, and question Francine continued. "I checked with Holly's father, who was Sable's accountant. He said Sable reported her earnings and debts including home repairs of twenty-thousand dollars. Hightower's name was not included. That made me suspicious."

Amy frowned, "Who's this Hightower character?"

Toria spoke up. "Francine wanted to know, so we searched on the library computer and couldn't find anyone with that name with an 'A' as the middle initial."

Darlene asked, "Sable also sold paintings. Are the earnings from those sales included in the sixty thousand dollars?"

"Holly's father was Sable's accountant," Francine said. "There's money from paintings in a local bank account. Despite this little mystery about Hightower, we have much to thank Sable for." She paused, then said< 'There's another matter to discuss. Claudine Hackamore is back in town."

"Oh, boy." Amy blew her breath upward, making her long bangs fluff out in all directions. "What's she want now?"

"I have the answer to that," Nancy Lou said. "I talked to Neece in the hospital cafeteria. She's been staying at George's bedside with occasional breaks to walk around. She's still wearing an ankle brace for that sprain and it's not good for her to sit still for long periods. She said that Claudine came trumpeting into George's hospital room saying she was staying in town until the police did their job. Neece said she now dreads going home because it reeks of Claudine's cigarette smoke."

Francine wrinkled her nose. "I ran into JJ at the food market. She said there's going to be a picture of Claudine in tomorrow's paper."

"Too late for April Fool's Day and too early for Halloween," said Amy with a laugh.

"Not funny," scolded Francine. "I'm suspicious about Claudine's reason for coming back. We've advertised the yard sale, and I bet she saw the ads and that's why she's here. She's trying to find a way to make another claim on the estate. Maybe she's rigged up a letter that's supposed to be from Sable and she'll *accidentally* find it."

"Sounds farfetched," retorted Amy, not taking Francine's scolding lying down.

"In any case," Toria said, striving to keep the peace. "If she shows up at the sale, we'd best keep an eye on her."

When Darlene reached home after the meeting, she was in a quandary. She had information she hadn't mentioned at the meeting because she'd decided it was a police matter. When Olivia's daughter had been in her office she said her mother had closed out a substantial bank account leaving no clue as to what she'd done with it. Was it possible that Olivia's money went to this Hightower person? She had to tell the police chief there might be a connection between the two recently dead women having missing money. It was after hours. She would leave a message for Slim to call her at his earliest opportunity.

* * *

The next day, Friday, Slim showed up early for work, thanks to the fact he had currently sworn off women and had no sweet reason to linger in bed. He intended to run over to the hospital to see George, but he wanted to check his messages first.

He found nothing he couldn't put off, including a call from the Empress of Code Enforcement. Darlene's recorded voice sounded tense, but she always sounded tense. He figured she had probably tried nailing Juan Buenaventura for renting rooms again and he'd thumbed his nose at her. He'd return her call later.

At George Neilson's room at the Melton Hospital, Slim found Neece Van Doran by his bedside, her patterned dress rumpled, and her hairstyle gone flat on one side from napping in a chair. George, in bed and hooked up to gadgets, mumbled something without awakening.

So as not to disturb him, Slim and Neece stepped into the hall.

"The doctor said he's stabilized," Neece said wearily. "But if his oxygen level doesn't perk up he'll need a tube down his throat."

With Slim listening politely, Neece spoke at length of the future she and George had planned. "We talked of marriage and retiring somewhere where the weather was warm, maybe Florida. If his family had talked with him, they would have learned about it, and maybe there wouldn't be all this fuss about their father's house."

Slim nodded and then Neece said, "Did you know my sister, Claudine, is in town?"

That holy terror, Slim thought, but he said, "She stopped by."

"She's got a bee in her bonnet about Rufus. Thinking he was murdered and yelling to get somebody arrested." Neece spoke with more feeling than she usually expressed. "She showed up at my house and piled in on me, suitcases and all. Last thing I need."

Despite what she'd just said, Slim considered that Neece might have taken some of the gossip about Rufus and the cup he'd have being treated as evidence, more seriously than she let on. She could have asked her aggressive sister to speak for her. He asked, "Did you ask her to come?"

Pinching her mouth, Neece shook her head. "That's something I'd *never* do. She showed up at George's father's funeral and made a big show of herself. Now she's talking about murder. She's the kind who believes Elvis is still alive and she hunts the sky for flying saucers. People spreading gossip on the news and elsewhere are troublemakers, exactly like Claudine. If she shows up at the police station, feel free to toss her out."

Slim left the hospital wishing he could do exactly that.

Back in his office, he thought that, as unpleasant as Claudine's surprise visit had been, the worst part was the cigarette smoke she'd swirled in the air. The lingering smell had left him wanting to fire up a butt more than any time since he'd given up the weed.

Chapter 27

*S*aturday morning, Slim made his rounds, making sure his town was safe. He swung by Sable's property to see how the second day of the yard sale was going. The April weather sparkled brightly over a line of cars parked along the curb. Shoppers milled around in the yard. He slowed, thinking he had time to stop and say hello to people.

He saw Claudine. She was helping out, her hair whirling like a tornado as she swung a heavy-looking coffee table up into the back of a lady's pickup.

Slim pressed the accelerator, escaping before she saw him.

"That one of your sad-sack coppers running off?" sharp-eyed Claudine asked Amy, waving her freshly lit cigarette in the direction of the disappearing police car. "I tore that chief of yours a good one yesterday. He don't know what hit 'im." Her hacking laugh ended in a ferocious coughing fit.

As promised, Amy was watching Claudine like a hawk but she found the woman interesting, especially some of her verbal expressions. Claudine said she'd been born in New Jersey and had since "flocked around" places like Texas, Louisiana, and now Maryland, which she pronounced like the fish, "Maar-lin." Various men had moved with her from time to time, although she said she was settled in her mobile home, which she raved about, expressing gratitude to Neece for helping her keep it out of foreclosure.

"We're not real close," she said, apparently not knowing what an understatement that was, "but she bailed me out when it counted, paying back rent on my double-wide, the classiest home I ever had."

Amy told herself to remember to tell Chuck about house-proud Francine's facial expression when she overheard Claudine speak of her double-wide mobile home's "fashionable interior."

Continuing to stay with Claudine in case she tried any of the tricks Francine had warned them about, Amy got her talking about Sable.

Claudine said, "I was seeing interesting stuff in Ocean City, near my place and I saw a lady with classy clothes, carry'ng awkward-looking packages into a store, so I helped. Inside the shop, I saw what we brought in was pretty pitchers, all framed and everything. I told her, Sable, she'd told me her name, that I'd never seen anything so pretty. She treated me to lunch and we got to talk'n and I met her again when she came again. She was doing real fine with them painted pictures and we got to be friends.

""So you were going to live together?" Amy said.

"Talki'n' about it." She blinked back tears. "She was coming this summer and we was gonna talk more only we never got a chance."

Customers came to the table where they stood and Claudine pitched in, helping to bag up purchases. Amy didn't quite know what to make of Claudine, but she didn't object to sticking with her.

Around noon, Jessi Spellman stopped by with a stack of flyers for the grand opening of her Carousel Restaurant in May.

Neither asking nor receiving permission from those sponsoring the sale, she breezed along on her four-inch grape-purple platform shoes calling greetings and shoving flyers into hands, introducing herself to everyone as if she was a celebrity bestowing favors She then zipped on to the next group without waiting to see if her animated greetings were returned, which they rarely were.

After she departed, the flyers somehow found their way into a recycling bucket. Everyone was blind as to who had done it.

Around one o'clock, Amy and Claudine joined Francine and Iris for hot dogs, sauerkraut, chips and cool drinks, courtesy of an auxiliary fundraiser. The civic group took charge of the desserts with a bake sale table. Claudine bought three hot dogs, but no sauerkraut on account of, as she announced in colorful language, it gave her gas.

There was talk about the murders. Claudine said, "I knew I'd have to jump-start them po-lice." She kept clicking her lighter after lighting another cigarette. "Had to oil up Neece's cause for justice. She used to be just fine until them mini-strokes drove her to retiring."

Iris said, "I heard she didn't want to learn the new high school computers."

"That's what she told people, not wanting to tell about having strokes." Claudine tucked the lighter in a pocket and started smoothing her hair, which didn't cooperate. "Neece was okay with computers afore she went downhill. She might have even had an online boyfriend. Some kind of mixed family, I guess. A name like he was part A-rab."

Amy cocked her head. "No fooling? Like tall, dark and handsome?"

"Don't know, but I visited Neece afore she gave up on computers and saw his name writ out on the screen. It looked sorta A-rab to me."

Claudine's scattered cigarette ashes blew across Francine's tan and black mid-heel spectator pumps. With a smothered snort, Francine jerked her feet back.

"Sorry, Franny." Claudine flicked more ashes off to one side. A breeze drifted ashes on Francine's purse, which she'd set on the grass.

Deliberately not noticing, Amy asked, "Was this before George?"

Claudine shrugged. "No idea, but George, he never struck me as a feller to stir up a girl. No accounting for taste." She stood and hitched up her pants. "I'm so full I'm about to pop. Dessert later. Work to do. You should have roped more fellas into this job, Franny. People buying stuff need help getting their junk loaded."

Later, still staying with Claudine, they came to Pilar, who said she was looking for vintage fabric.

Claudine, said, "There's funny old cloth in a bedroom in the house. Probably all rotten. I'll show ya."

Amy dutifully trailed along, thinking she'd get a kick out of telling people later about Claudine's calling Francine "Franny," throwing cigarette ashes all around and talking about Neece, who seemed so quiet, but apparently had *two* boyfriends.

When Pilar later approached Francine, who was collecting the money, she happily paid for a purse that looked like a little box, old jewelry, and fabric pieces she called "retro florals."

Francine said to Iris after Pilar left, "Somebody's grandmother's cut up old drapes."

"Wish I was handy with a needle," cheerfully missing Francine's point. "Pilar will make something really pretty out of those fabrics."

"And have the nerve to wear them," Francine answered with a sniff, smoothing her brand new beige name-brand slacks, which coordinated beautifully with her fawn-colored cashmere sweater.

The two women's groups had decided that the original painting in Sable's shop should be taken to the Maryland art gallery that featured her work. Toria volunteered for the job, thinking she and Holly would enjoy the adventure. Any sales, less commission, would go back to the two groups.

While Toria was still at the yard sale, Holly was at Sable's card shop, taking inventory. Around three o'clock, he locked up and went to meet Slim at Sean's Pub for a beer. He was going to Sable's house later to help Toria and the other women clean up after the sale, but for now, he had free time. On his way to Sean's he thought about the term, *free time.*

He loved being married but he was also accustomed to free time. However, his favorite way of using it had been spending it with Toria. She felt the same about him. So did *free time* now mean time *away* from one another? Confusing. They had discussed it and she found it confusing, too. Maybe that was what "adjusting to marriage" meant. Sorting through behaviors that they had never thought about before.

Arriving, Sean met him with two foaming beer mugs held in the fingers of one of his hands.

"This way," he said with a gesture, leading Holly past his booth and through a curtain to a table in a space between the dining room and kitchen. Slim was already there

Setting down the beer, Sean, a bright-eyed, youngish man with receding blond hair, stepped in. "This table behind the curtain is what I "zone of invisibility." He gazed at Slim. "I saw the morning paper and figured invisibility would sound good."

"Got that right," Slim said. "Thanks." He'd seen the newspaper and was still steamed.

After Sean left, Holly gave a devilish grin and revealed his copy of the *Melton Monitor*. The front-page headline, slugged *JumpRope Township, NJ*, bylined JJ Gilbert, screamed:

SISTER CLAIMS POLICE INACTION INCREASING GRIEF

Claudine Hackamore, a Maryland resident, came to JumpRope to comfort her sister, Eunice "Neece" Van Doran, one of many who mourn the loss of the town's beloved octogenarian, Rufus Neilson.

Although there is no proof that Neilson's drowning in the Hitchmile Stream was anything except an accident, rumors of a crime abound. As has been previously reported, police found evidence that indicates an unknown person was on the scene near the time of Neilson's death. A vintage cup Neilson had treasured was found wiped clean of prints and left in the brush a distance from the stream.

It was only due to the diligence of the JumpRope Police Chief, Allen "Slim" Parkerson, that this evidence was located.

Grief-stricken George Neilson, son of the late Rufus Neilson and a friend of Van Doran's, has now suffered a heart attack. Hackamore is protesting the inaction of the JumpRope police in finding the unknown person on the scene who may have heartlessly stood by and watched Rufus Neilson drown.

The article's attention-getter was the oversized photo of Claudine leaning toward the camera, her tousled grey hair filling the frame in a bird's nest of knots, her mouth twisted, her eyes enlarged, the whites showing all around.

Holly said, "Guess the picture had no room for the caldron, the cat, and the pointed black hat. And I guess I'm supposed to put this paper in the trash." His eyes twinkled. "Don't know why I even brought it in."

Slim snarled, "Because you're such a good buddy, that's why."

Holly grinned. "Kidding around aside, JJ did manage to say something nice about your investigative abilities."

"Yeah, throw the poor dog a bone." Slim had been on the job too long to take shots at law enforcement personally, but seeing JJ's byline on the article made it sting more than it should.

Holly said, "Who was on the scene when Rufus drowned will probably never be known and the other details are still up in the air, but you'll be the hero when Olivia's killer is caught."

Slim slouched back against his seat. "Darlene Gage came up with something good, but I don't see where it fits." He wrinkled his nose when he talked about Darlene. "At one of the women's meetings about Sable's bequest, Darlene learned from Francine that Sable had her card sale earnings sent to an online bank. From that account, she'd sent a cashier's check for twenty grand to a Buckley A. Hightower. Francine knew your father was Sable's accountant," he said, and then told Holly about Sable listing the twenty-thousand as home repairs instead of a check to Hightower. He added. "Her house showed no signs of recent repairs."

"Hiding something," Holly said. "Never heard of Hightower."

"I hadn't either until now. Darlene said that Olivia's daughter said her mother had cashed out a certificate of deposit for thirty-two thousand, but there was no clue as to who received the money. I called up to Maine and asked her daughter to confirm. Harriet wasn't cooperative at first, but when I mentioned Hightower's name, she loosened up and said her mother had mentioned the Hightower name in connection with financial advice."

"About buying a house near her daughter?"

"Harriet didn't know, but since Sable's files are gone Hightower might have gotten even more money than we know."

Holly drank some of his beer and then said, "Did you know Sable was saving to buy a house in Maryland?"

Slim frowned. "I could have thrown that into the mix when I was with two other cops last night. Officer Alfonso and Detective Isaac Ellis, are pals. They hauled me to a dive with great food near Trenton. They wanted to see if a guy with a face like white bread could handle an endless refills plate night."

"Could you?"

"Alfonso said he wasn't too embarrassed to have me as his chief. But the point is—" Slim waved a corn chip. "We were knocking around what the two deaths had in common and struck out. There were drugs involved in the deaths of Rufus and Olivia, but his was an accident and her's was murder, and while Olivia has money missing, Rufus had no money left to miss. So there was nothing in common between them. And while Sable had missing money, her death wasn't murder."

"Or so we've been assuming," Holly said.

"Bite your tongue!" Slim growled.

"Okay, okay, Sable's death was an accident, but if Hightower is a realtor, Sable and Olivia could have both been talking with him about arranging for money to buy a house. That's a connection, although I can't see why either of these two savvy women would have given him so much money ahead of time to make the arrangements."

"Would if he was a con man," Slim said.

"Sable and Olivia wouldn't have fallen for that."

"Why not? This Hightower guy could have sweet-talked each woman into thinking she had a future with him. That would explain them handing over money and also keeping it hush-hush. He would have given them what sounded like a good reason and secrecy might have made it seem more romantic."

"And Olivia got suspicious, so Hightower killed her?"

"Maybe," Slim said. "I looked for him in the records and found nothing. Whoever he is, he's kept under the radar."

The two men sipped beer in silence. Slim reached for more corn chips and cursed Claudine once again for making him wish he had a cigarette.

Chapter 28

After the yard sale, Pilar reached home to find Max had started supper. He was making chili, corn bread and a salad. He added, "I'm also doing barbecued ribs. How does that sound?"

"Very good! " She looked at his neatly compact frame that belied his appetite. Max favored hearty food and also liked to cook. A prize of a man, she thought. "I'll help after I show off my purchases," she told him. "Look! She showed him a purse.

"It looks like a lunch box for a party," He was puzzled yet pleased to see her pleasure.

"It's made of Lucite. We saw one in an old Doris Day movie." They both enjoyed old movies.

"Well," he said, not knowing what else to say. He had a few days off. He had chores lined up at Pilar's house. That evening, the kids, Alexander and Solstice, were coming for supper and bringing a cheesecake. He didn't know how a cheesecake would fare on a motorcycle.

"Glittery treasures," he remarked as Pilar proudly displayed beads that needed restringing and a brooch with missing rhinestones. "What's that all wrapped up?"

"Remnants of bark cloth fabric." She unrolled the bundle. "Aren't these floral designs wonderful? I think I'll make placemats for the table on the patio. They will look perfect with my Fiestaware.

So colorful."

"It will be that," Max said. Smiling, he went out to fire up the grill. He loved everything about Pilar, but there were some things he'd never understand.

The meal wasn't quite ready when Alexander and Solstice arrived. After their greetings, they handed Max the cheesecake, which had survived the ride just fine.

Pilar, who was setting the table, suggested that while the light was still good, they go look at the rosebushes Max had put in.

Outside, Alexander and Solstice admired the newly planted roses and then strolled around the yard, enjoying the balmy late afternoon. Solstice didn't know the names of most of the plants. Her youth had been mostly spent in southwestern terrains and later, in Florida. She liked touching flower petals and tree blossoms. She kept poking her snub nose into petals to inhale their fragrance.

"You have pollen on your nose," Alexander said after she'd sniffed apple blossoms. He gestured toward her face with his finger.

She scrubbed her nose, looked at her fingers and laughed. "Looks like I've smudged off some freckles."

"Don't ever do that. I love your freckles." He still couldn't get over the marvel of having a girlfriend. And to think she was someone so terrific!

She grinned at his words, then became somber as pointed to a place in the yard where azaleas bloomed. "Is that where the swimming pond used to be?"

"Yes," he said quietly, remembering the tears that had come into her eyes when he'd told her about his father's death.

Equally as quiet, she said, "Do you think your mother really might have drowned herself if the pool hadn't been filled in?"

Alexander shrugged. His mother's annual sad periods were a part of his life. He tried not to worry about them. "When I was old enough she told me that caring for me was what kept her going."

Solstice grinned. "Trolling for compliments, Rumpelstiltskin? Okay, I'll say it. You're special."

"Thanks.' He returned her grin. "I'm hoping my mother will do better this year when the anniversary comes around."

"When she hides for a week? Why would it be different this year?"

"Because of Max. You only met her a few times before she and Max more or less settled together. Before him, the men she had weren't supposed to stay. They were all broken and grief-stricken over something and she provided—" He broke off.

"Comfort with benefits?"

"I guess." Having her spell it out embarrassed him.

"Max is nice." Solstice had stepped closer, looking up at Alexander.

He was aware of how fragile and waif-like she was compared with his bearded bulk. At five-foot-eleven, he had about twenty pounds of pudginess that he couldn't seem to work off, but she seemed to think he was okay and he was *never* going to shave off his beard as long as she liked it.

She touched his hand. "I like your mother and him together."

"I do, too," he said, thrilling to her touch but afraid to show it because it might make her scared. But he did dare one thing. Looking into her eyes, so large and such a lovely brown, he lowered his voice and said, "I like us together, too."

She stared at him, then gave a lopsided little shrug. "We're okay, Romeo." She gave his hand a squeeze, then backed off a little.

Together, not touching again, but still side by side, they returned to the house for dinner.

Max's dinner was excellent as was the cheesecake. During it, Pilar mentioned Claudine. "She said Neece quit her job at the school because of strokes."

"I remember her," Alexander said. "Old lady Van Doran in the business office. If you lost the combination for your locker, you went to her in the office for a new one."

Looking at her son, Pilar thought that if he was like his father, by age twenty-five he would have had another growth spurt, top six feet, lose the last of his baby fat, and become quite a fine-looking young man.

As the main meal finished, Pilar continued to talk about the yard sale, remarking about the Internet boyfriend with the foreign name that Claudine claimed Neece used to have. As she heard herself speaking Claudine's words, it seemed an easy transition to what she wanted to discuss. After leaving the table to get the cheesecake and sitting down again to serve it, she said, "Remember I said I was told I might be psychic?"

Max gave her a fond smile. "I told you I had no trouble with the concept."

"Neither do I," Alexander said with a grin.

The men's comments and her answering laughter set the correct mood, making it clear she wasn't taking the subject seriously.

"There are these words that keep jumping into my head," she said. "*Gable* and *peak* and such. It happened again today at the sale. I was talking with Amy about the murders and all of a sudden the words came, almost as if someone was speaking them. I have to admit it was weird."

She lifted her fork over her dessert. "Mar-see-ah, the psychic who works at Teddy's Restaurant, says the words have to mean something. Only what?" She looked brightly around the table, and said, "If anyone has any ideas, let me know."

Chapter 29

*G*eorge Neilson was dead!

The news was a shock. Only a little more than a month after his elderly father was laid to rest, arrangements were now being made for his son's funeral.

JJ's article in the *Melton Monitor* contained an interview with George's cardiac specialist, who said that a great deal of damage had been done by the heart attack that had put George in the hospital in the first place. There had been no way to predict or prevent his second, fatal attack.

As to George's last few hours, his friend, Eunice "Neece" Van Doran, was reported as saying that he appeared to be sleeping when she went to the hospital cafeteria to get a cup of tea; when she came back with it, she couldn't hear him breathing. She had immediately screamed for help, but all heroic efforts had failed.

His daughter, Wanda, was quoted as saying, "Daddy never got over grandpa's death. The fact that he dropped his father off that day at the Hitchmile and then drove away troubled his mind something terrible. He felt like he'd left him to a murderer." Over the photo of the daughter's tear-stained face, the headline read:

HE DELIVERED GRANDPA INTO A KILLER'S ARMS.

The rest of the article recapped the incompetence of the local police and a possible killer's signature red roses left in two other recent deaths.

"Where do they come up with that stuff?" Slim said in disgust when he'd stopped in to see Holly in his mayor's office Thursday morning and saw a copy of the morning's *Monitor* on the desk. "The red roses were a coincidence and I learned that the daughter never said anything about George delivering Rufus to the killer."

Holly hadn't liked the article either. He'd been getting calls on the subject.

Nodding, he said, "You're getting it from all sides."

"Got that right, bud." Slim folded his rangy, uniformed figure into his usual chair. He was going to have to talk with JJ Gilbert for several reasons, but he didn't want to think about it. He said, "Even got another call from Neece's sister, Claudine. She had nothing to say except to repeat the garbage from that lousy article. And now, she's saying I'm responsible for George's death because I couldn't find out all the facts about his father's death."

"Claudine's trying to support her sister."

Slim muttered something unprintable. "She's making things worse. Neece can't stand her. The woman's a steamroller in a fright wig."

"Hmmm." Holly touched his necktie—it depicted Greek temples, one of a set Toria had bought for him in New York that showed ancient wonders of the world. "You're quoted with the usual statements that the investigation is ongoing and leads are being followed up. There's nothing more that you can say at this point. JJ has played more than fair with us before. Have you talked with her about the con man theory? If she knows you're working on something specific, she may be willing to ease up."

Chapter 30

Slim entered Teddy's barroom. He was taking Holly's advice about telling JJ about the con man theory and was going to do it over dinner at Teddy's. Not the usual quick bar fare, where people stopped by to chat, but while they were in the dining room, out in public they were seated where they could speak privately.

The two people Slim had always been able to discuss things with were Holly and JJ. Even though he still thought of her as a kid he had known forever, she was quick and smart and had resources and contacts. Plus, she respected things said to her confidentially, even though she had blind-sided him on occasion. And after the yellow journalism job the Monitor had done, blaming him for George's death, he wasn't feeling so friendly. Still, he wanted to talk with her.

She stood at a table that held other *Monitor* news rats. She wore slacks and a soft-looking blouse and held a cranberry-pink cocktail.

He forced a smile as he approached. She returned that cheeky look that she'd always had when he'd hung out with her brothers.

At his nod, Teddy who'd seen him come in, moved to escort them to their table, pausing while she finished signing off with the newspaper crew. Slim could see that she was liked and respected by her news team. And one guy was giving her the eye. She did look good, her hair in the usual ponytail, but it was fluffed out around her slender face and her eyes were sparkly. And evil.

Teddy had seen them plenty at the bar together but this was the first time it was a table in the dining room. An out-of-the-way corner was what Slim asked for and that's what Teddy led them to. JJ smelled nice, like oranges. Slim thought maybe it was the drink she'd brought with her. They were seated and Teddy left them with menus, saying a server would be right over.

Frowning, Slim asked JJ, "What's that you're drinking?"

"A Cosmo with lime for a cosmopolitan evening with you." She fluttered her lashes like a swooning heroine.

"Sure," Slim said.

The server came. Slim ordered a dark beer. He thought he could still smell orange. Maybe it was her shampoo. That explained why her hair was looking fluffed out.

Not talking, they looked at their menus, studying them as if preparing for their doctorates. Slim put in her order for calamari and for him, hot wings with hot sauce, the hotter the better. They also both knew what they wanted to eat, so those orders went in, too.

"So what's this about," she asked, leaning forward after the server left. "An elaborate ruse to drug my drink and seduce me—would you give me a red rose first!" She mock-gulped and put up a hand to cover her mouth. "Touchy subject. Shouldn't mention roses."

"Jeez!" He slumped back in his chair and thrust his feet out. Her legs were right there, his feet sliding next to them. He jerked his feet back.

He said, "Look, there's stuff you don't know. Off the record."

"Isn't it always with you, Tall Boy?"

"Not always and you damned well know it." He hadn't been called Tall Boy since he shot up past her brothers in grade school. Was she remembering that? He shifted his mind back on topic. "I like to keep it quiet when things are still developing."

"Developing?" JJ narrowed her green-brown eyes that had dark circles around the iris. In the dim light, they looked all brown.

The server brought their appetizers. After he left, she reached for a piece of calamari. Slim reached out before she got there and turned her hand over.

"What?" she asked.

"Just checking your thumb. Figure it's all blistered from leafing through an online thesaurus, searching for words to describe a police chief. *Ineffective. Incompetent. Inept. Incapable.*"

"*Impotent?*" She added, grinning, slipping her fingers free.

Exasperated, he looked at her mischievous face and that mysteriously enticing gap-toothed grin and felt an unbidden surge that told him how far off the mark that last word of hers was.

"Come on," he growled, shifting his position in his chair. He rubbed his fingers. It was like he could still feel her warm skin against his. Why had she said stuff earlier about him seducing her? Last thought he'd have. "Come on," he repeated. "This is serious."

"*What's* serious?" Her eyes had gone narrow and intent. "And yes," she said, "it's off the record."

Slim knew if she made a promise to keep it off the record, she would honor it. He'd had this idea running in the background of his head ever since his talk with Darlene, an idea he didn't want to think about so he'd kept denying it. He'd done the same thing when he'd talked with Holly.

He lowered his voice "I can't prove it, but I suspect Sable was also a murder victim."

JJ's eyes widened. "You've got to be kidding."

"Unfortunately not."

They broke off as the server brought their food. Alone again, Slim explained how it could fit together. "There are three things Sable and Olivia had in common, large cash withdrawals from their banks and the money can't be found, a desire to buy a house, and knowing a man named Buckley Hightower."

Slim leaned back further. "Let's start with Sable. With her, it's more than the mysterious withdrawals. Her computer, laptop, cell phone and paper records have all disappeared. Probably to keep those records hidden. What the thief didn't know was that Holly's father was her accountant. He found checks in Sable's files from a previous year when she'd endorsed them over to a Buckley A. Hightower."

"Who is he?"

"Don't know yet. It's not a local name, no police record, nothing on the Internet. Olivia Bunker also drew out a large cash amount. Her daughter, Harriet, can't find out what she did with the money because Olivia's financial records are missing. However, she does recall her mother mentioning someone named Hightower."

Expression intent, JJ said, "So, you're thinking that Hightower, posing as a realtor, conned the two women, only they got wise?" She wrinkled her nose. "Two single women? He probably romanced them only something went wrong and he not only killed them, he removed all records pertaining to their dealings."

"Head of the class, kiddo."

"Kind of far-fetched that both women caught on at the same time?"

"Look at it this way," he said. "Olivia got wise and he killed her. Then he worried about Sable and decided she too was a risk. Sable's body was found first, but she was killed second. Olivia was dead in her house when people thought she was still in Maine."

JJ cocked her head. "And since Olivia didn't answer her phone, her worried neighbors would have tried to call her daughter, but with Harriet on a camping trip, they couldn't reach her." She frowned. "Are you sure that's what she was really doing? Maybe she wasn't willing to wait for her mother's natural death."

Slim forked up a cut of his prime rib. After chewing and swallowing, he said, "You're not the only one with a suspicious mind. I checked and learned Harriet and hubby were on a long-planned church camping retreat. It all checked out." He shrugged. "Routine, boring police work. Not the sort of information that runs under your rumor-rat byline."

"Okay, okay." JJ's expression was momentarily sheepish, but she defended herself. "I write the articles and arrange for the photos but not the headlines and captions."

"Yeah, I know that."

"Okay." She finished buttering a roll and then looked up. "So, both Sable and Olivia had money missing and were interested in real estate, plus they had a connection to a possible con man named Hightower. On that basis, you've decided Sable was possibly murdered and that her stepladder fall was engineered." She looked thoughtful. "If I recall, Sable suffered a head wound but her death was asphyxiation caused by a broken neck. The killer's lucky break? Pun intended. Or did the killer break her neck after the fall?"

"I talked to the medical examiner," Slim said. "A broken or torn spinal cord leads lead to instant death. But if the cervical vertebrae are broken and the spinal cord is unharmed, the bones can heal."

"But if someone moved her after the fall, that could have caused fatal damage." She winced. "That's why you're never supposed to move an accident victim."

"Right, and the examiner said he had no way of telling if the damage occurred from the fall or a moment or two later."

"So there's no way to prove anything." JJ made a face. "Funerals every time you turn around."

Slim narrowed his eyes. "There's something that Neece said in the hospital the other day. She said she and George had intended to eventually retire to a warmer climate, maybe Florida."

JJ blinked, then leaned forward. "You think George started looking into real estate and *he* was the one who attracted Hightower's attention? Maybe it wasn't a lovelorn scam. It could have been a real estate con, a pitch that sounded like a terrific deal."

Slim nodded. "I'm planning to talk again with Neece. See if she recognizes the Hightower name. But right now, she's visiting with some family from out of state that she likes a lot better than her sister, and who wouldn't? She'll be back for the funeral on Monday and I'll see her then." He looked thoughtful. "She might not know the Hightower name if George went house hunting without telling her."

"He wanted to surprise her?"

"Could be." He thought JJ should wear her hair the way she had it now more often. Keep the ponytail, but fluff the sides around her face. He winced at how he was thinking. Sure, Slim, the hairstylist. Something to fall back on if he ever got canned as a cop.

JJ said, "George always appeared so dull and drab. Totally colorless. And Neece, with her funny print dresses and old-fashioned hairstyle." She grinned. "But when they were together, I bet they felt like Anthony and Cleopatra."

Slim grinned back at her. "Bogart and Bacall."

"Romeo and Juliet."

"Bonnie and Clyde."

They burst out laughing.

Slim looked down and realized that their hands on the table were touching, his fingers slightly over hers. They each noticed and each eased away.

JJ was silent for a moment and then said, "If George never said anything to Neece, how can you learn if Hightower contacted George? If George had money missing, it would be a good lead."

He grinned. "Good thinking, kiddo. I would have gotten there eventually. I'll ask George's daughter if she ever heard him mention Hightower. Also, find out looking through his financial records."

She gave him a sideways look. "More boring police work?"

"That's what makes me so scintillating."

"Scintillating, huh?"

"You're not the only one who knows words."

"Maybe not." She studied him for a moment and then said, "A con man will make a good story if we ever get to the bottom of it. He slips undetected into Olivia's house and then into Sable's card shop." She paused and teased, "Next you'll find he was at the Hitchmile when Rufus drowned."

"Yeah, sure," Slim said. "You're already thinking of the headline."

"Told you I don't write them."

"Yeah, right," he said, wondering why he enjoyed talking with a person who was so annoying, and yes, sometimes cute. Cute enough to be appealing.

Chapter 31

*M*ourners milled impatiently around the Sycamore Shade Cemetery. They had traveled from George Neilson's funeral service at the Methodist Church to his grave site expecting a reverential, yet speedy dispatch. A few tears, comforting words and flowers to place on the casket. Then off to a funeral repast. However, the minister had not yet arrived. But what was a few more minutes? Tell that to George's daughter, who was having a hard time keeping her two kids in line. The youngest kept asking when Pawpaw was coming out of the big box.

"Like he's going to pop out like a rabbit from a hat," Francine said with a critical sniff. "She should have kept those children home." She smoothed the lapel of her stylish two-button blazer, worn with silk slacks and low-heeled pumps, and arrowed a look at Pilar, whose black jacket had 1940s-style wide padded shoulders.

With another sniff, Francine asked, "Is it true you've been over to see Jessi's new restaurant?"

Pilar nodded pleasantly. "Jessi's artistic touch is too amazing to ignore. Her restaurant's grand opening will be a stylish production. You should be there."

"I will be." Francine showed a cat-that-ate-the-canary smile. "I've received an invitation from State Senator Fergusson's stepdaughter, Leslie."

"That's very nice," Pilar said.

"It certainly is. Leslie sent me a letter on behalf of her stepfather. She said a misunderstanding regarding the community of JumpRope had come to the attention of State Senator Fergusson. She said the senator is fully committed to the town. He's attending the opening of the Carousel Restaurant and is inviting both women's groups as his guests to demonstrate his commitment." Francine uttered a sound of smug satisfaction. "It's obvious the senator realizes how important we are and is trying to make it up to us."

Pilar nodded, but she knew it was Alexander and Solstice who worked the real magic. Solstice played nice with Jessi and learned how angry she was with Fergusson. Solstice also learned that Jessi knew about that old photo that showed Leslie and Fergusson on the beach together. Pilar was willing to bet that Jessi used the photo to blackmail Leslie into persuading the senator to support the restaurant's grand opening, hence his invitations to the women.

Over in another section of the waiting crowd were several members of the Ladies' Civic Group.

Iris said to Amy Newton, "Why hasn't George's family asked the two women's groups to help with the funeral luncheon at Neece's? We did that when Rufus died."

Amy laughed. "Chuck was with the funeral director at the Neilson house with the family. Claudine exploded in. When she told them that Neece would have the luncheon at her house, one of George's sisters, said Neece had no right. She was only a girlfriend. Claudine flashed back that none of them had acted like blood kin. They'd hounded George and pushed him into his grave so they could have the house."

Iris, her eyes large, said, "What happened next?"

"The nasty sister told the director, Mr. Snow, that they would arrange George's funeral, but if somebody else wanted to make a party over their beloved brother's death, they'd have nothing to do with it. So, Claudine put herself in charge of the funeral luncheon at her sister's house, making it a catered affair. She said if any of the Neilson family members wanted to come, they had better be on their best behavior."

At that point, there was stirring through the crowd. The minister had arrived and the funeral service began.

Slim Parkerson's official vehicle stood in front of Neece's house, waiting for the funeral procession. The women's groups that would normally be present weren't there. An empty house during a funeral could be a temptation to thieves. Slim wasn't leaving anything to chance.

The property was located on Winesap, the last apple variety named street in the 1940s era development. When Neece's late husband had returned from Vietnam, he'd made the property a showplace, with terraces, a goldfish pool, a fountain, and fancy gardens. Behind the house was a vacant field where Slim and other kids had flown kites. Further on loomed the multiple roofs of the DeGroot mansion.

The caterers appeared. Claudine opened the door. Slim cursed. He hadn't been protecting an empty house. He'd been guarding that Baba Yaga look-alike.

The funeral procession appeared. Two black limousines came down the street with flags fluttering. Like massive trained seals they floated over to the curb and parked. A line of vehicles pulled up behind them. Slim saw George's family members emerge from the first limo. Neece and others came from the second one. Slim joined the people moving toward the house.

Inside, the mourners greeted and offered sympathy to Neece, who sat in a corner of the dining room looking lost. They filled their plates from the buffet table and moved to the living room. Neece remained silent and vacant-eyed in her own little corner of gloom.

Claudine, whose snarly gray hair aimed for all points of the compass, fixed a plate and encouraged her sister to eat.

Slim talked to people in the living room, then returned to the dining room and told Claudine he needed to have a few words with her sister.

"Can't stop you, lawman," Claudine rasped, puffing clouds from her cigarette. "Lord knows what you're gonna get. Neece's all tore up about George and spaced out on pills from the local sawbones." With her cigarette, she pointed toward the living room. "Considering the hard feelings in George's family, I didn't think any of them would show up, but it's the last thing they could do for George. The event to die for, right?" Claudine laughed so hard at her joke that she started coughing.

"I'll swing back later," Slim said, edging away. Returning to the living room, he paused by Holly and Toria.

"On the job?" Holly asked.

"Yeah, asked members of the Neilson family if anyone heard of Hightower. So far, nothing. On the chance that Rufus overheard something, I asked a couple of Old Geezers. The name didn't ring a bell with them, either."

"Toria and I have had better luck. Claudine told us the name of the Maryland art gallery that displays Sable's work. If he's interested in the paintings that are still in her shop, we'll deliver them to be sold on consignment on behalf of the two women's groups."

"Good," Slim said absently. After a few more words, he retraced his steps to the dining room where Claudine was still fussing with Neece, who sat in her private gloom. Her heavy-breasted figure, garbed in a black-on-black silk print, slumped like a holiday balloon leaking air.

Slim sighed. Nothing in the manual told a cop to deal with a pair of sisters like them. He glanced to the window where Pilar stood, apparently watching the kids playing outside.

Pilar hadn't noticed the children. Her gaze was lifted to the multi-roofed DeGroot mansion. Gables. Peaks. The phantom words were frightfully clear. From behind her, she heard Slim say, "Those kids playing outside look like they're having fun."

Startled, Pilar turned and looked up into Slim's face. *Kites*. The word sounded in her mind. Before she could stop herself, the word came to her lips. "Kites," she said aloud, then was stricken. Slim would think she had a screw loose.

"Yeah," he agreed, "it would be great if they had kites and could run in the DeGroot field." Pilar mentioning kites had surprised him. Hadn't he just been remembering playing with kites as a kid? It was as if she'd snatched the word from his mind. Conversations with Pilar could be odd, but he guessed the coincidence made sense with the kids running around outside and the wind blowing.

Pilar nodded, relieved that Slim had found logic in what she'd said. She wished she could. Max was away. Thank goodness Alexander had come with her to the funeral. The words peaks and gables were so constant they'd become old friends. The word kites was a stranger.

Abruptly, it came to her that peaks, gables and old-fashioned kites all had triangular tops. It still made no sense, but at least there was a relationship. She couldn't help but smile. It also explained why she'd caught herself compelled to arrange objects, like turning her square coasters on a corner so it they had pointed tops. The why of it was still lost to her, but at least there was something they had in common: the tops reminded her of triangles.

Slim glanced from Pilar to Neece, who looked worse than George had in his casket. He recalled how drab the two of them appeared when seen separately, but at the diner, they had talked and smiled with animation. Neece must be devastated by his loss. Loss could be hell. Like Pilar, still suffering bouts of grief because of her dead husband.

That's when Slim got his idea. He wanted to talk with Neece, but having her smoke-breathing dragon of a sister at her elbow was a discouragement. If Pilar would sit with him, he would have the sympathetic influence of another woman there for his interview. That might soften Claudine's belligerence.

Pilar agreed. Slim pulled up a chair for her next to Neece and grabbed one for himself. Neece seemed to have sunk into a semi-comatose state. To expect her to aid in the murder case was like expecting a drunk driver to walk a straight line.

"So what are you callin' this?" challenged Claudine from Neece's side, glaring at Slim and Pilar. "Good cop, bad cop?"

"I'm from Internal Affairs," Pilar said, "watching for police misconduct."

"Good one, Pilar!" Claudine rasped and took a drag on her cigarette.

Pilar, who didn't often joke, liked Claudine despite her rough edges. She knew that the members of the Voodoo Club didn't trust her, but she had been helpful at the yard sale by finding items for her, and she showed sincere concern for her sister.

Smiling gently, Pilar said to Neece, "I wanted to say again how sorry I am."

"Thank you." Neece's voice was a near whisper.

Quietly, Slim asked, "Did you ever hear George or his father speak of anyone named Buckley Hightower?"

Neece blinked. "I'm sorry . . . I'm so tired."

Slim repeated the name, "Buckley A. Hightower to be exact."

Neece shook her head. "I don't think—".

"That's that A-rab guy," Claudine said.

"Arab?" Slim asked, puzzled.

"Sure. His name was like what you said, English-like, but he signed it with a foreign name, like Aram or something." She pointed her cigarette at her sister. "He was that online boyfriend, remember? I saw his name on your email computer screen."

"Oh . . ." Neece covered her face. "I wanted to forget about that."

"Hold on," Slim said. "He was someone you communicated with?"

"Only for a short while. A long time ago." Uncovering her face, Neece shook her head, looking miserable. "I used email to keep up with old friends. One day Mr. Hightower was just there, saying hello."

Claudine snorted. "Keep up with your friends, not your relatives."

Ignoring Claudine, Slim encouraged Neece to continue.

She said, "We talked back and forth, the way you do online. He had questions about me and the town. He seemed so nice. I sort of enjoyed it, but I felt I was betraying George." She covered her face again and started rocking. She spoke through her fingers. "I stopped answering and erased everything. Poor George. I could never tell him about it."

"You said he asked you about the town." Slim felt he was on to something. "Could he have been a realtor?" If so, that would match what he believed about the man who had communicated with Olivia and Sable. Also, the angle of his playing up to women.

"He never said. Remembering makes me feel guilty all over again."

Pilar was distressed for her. She knew from her own experience how corrosive guilt could be. It could eat you alive. She wished Slim would stop, but he kept right on.

"Look," Slim said. "We're trying to track this man. I'm sorry if this makes you feel bad, but you told me you and George had plans to move. Were you two looking at property? Did Hightower ask you about that?"

"No, I wouldn't have said anything about that to Mr. Hightower. That . . . that would have been betraying George even more." She looked close to tears.

Slim was thinking that realtors have multiple listings. If Neece had explored property on the Internet, it could have led Hightower to her. And to George too, for that matter. He asked, "Did George use a computer?"

"Just me. I used to email a while ago, like I told you."

Pilar couldn't stand it. Slim should never have picked the day of the funeral for this *inquisition*. A thought came to her. Impulsively, she turned to Slim. "That foreign name Claudine mentioned like Aram begins with the letter A. That's the middle initial in Hightower's name—Buckley A. Hightower. Making it sound like a foreign name means something special to him."

Slim stared at her. "You know the guy?"

Pilar looked confused. "No, it just sounded right."

Alexander stepped into the room and moved to the table for another helping of food. Holly was behind him.

"So how do you know it's special to him?" Claudine demanded of Pilar. "You got that whadaya call it, triple sight?"

'Triple what?" Slim said. Things were going nuts around him.

Alexander, who couldn't help overhearing the conversation, said in that pretentious tone he rarely used anymore, "It's second sight, not triple. It's a paranormal ability to see what most people can't see with their normal range of senses."

"Okay, okay," Slim said. People were coming into the dining room for buffet refills. If he had more questions, he would see Neece alone. Time to shut this down.

But nothing was going to stop Claudine, who continued staring at Pilar. "One of the gals at the yard sale said you had a pow-wow with a psychic. You got something like that going on?"

"No," Pilar said. She was rarely flustered, but she was now. She knew she was going off the rails and couldn't regain control. She heard herself mumble about triangles and the words that she'd been trying to figure out. "Roofs, gables, corner shapes . . ." She noticed Holly's necktie, which showed black and white scenes of the wonders of ancient Egypt. "Pyramids," Pilar said, and then looked desperately at Alexander. "You said earlier you were about ready to leave?"

"Sure did." It wasn't true, but he moved to the rescue. He didn't know what was wrong, but he figured it was his fault. He'd spouted stuff like he was an encyclopedia, all stuffy and uppity, the way he used to carry on before he'd met Solstice. He'd embarrassed his mother.

As Pilar rose, Claudine demanded, "So what did the crystal ball gazer tell you?"

"Nothing much." Pilar felt calmer now that she was on her feet and Alexander stood so solid and reassuring beside her. "Mar-see-ah said that the words were important and what they meant would eventually come to me."

Chapter 32

A few days later, Pilar was home after spending time in New York City shopping for a client who was redecorating her home near Princeton. She wondered if she'd find interesting clients close by, such as the people ordering custom homes from Acer. Mather Woods would be an extremely high scale. Would the residents mingle with the d community or keep to themselves? She'd have to wait and see.

Max was away so she had the house to herself, which was fine, but it did feel a trifle empty. Except for yard work and general maintenance, he spent almost no time at his former home. They were a couple, no question, and he wanted marriage. She couldn't envision a more perfect match, and that was a dilemma. Would her refusals eventually drive him away?

Not wanting to dwell on that question, she gathered the needed materials and descended to her lower-level workroom. After an hour she was almost finished with a presentation board for decorating the bedrooms of the Mather House. When in town, Acer stayed in the private second-story level. He could also offer that space to select visitors since the town offered no other such accommodations. She remembered he had once done so and it had turned into a disaster, putting Solstice's life in danger.

The phone rang. It was Francine.

"Did you go outside in Neece's backyard at the funeral luncheon yesterday?" Francine asked without preliminary. Not waiting for a reply, Francine ran on. "I'd never been there before and from what I knew of Neece, I'd had no interest, but her backyard is fabulous! I guess it was the inspiration of her late husband, but she's maintained it over the years. The inside of her home surprised me, too. Much better quality than I expected from someone so drab. And with such a sister! That's why I walked around outside—to escape the cigarette smoke."

Francine came to the point of her call. "Neece's yard made me realize that while the inside of my home is perfect, my landscaping has been the same for years. Will you take a look at my yard and make suggestions? Maybe this coming Monday?"

"I'm not sure I'll be free," Pilar said, the phone in her hand again. "I'll let you know as soon as I'm sure of Max's schedule."

"Good," Francine said. "And you may have another job coming. Did you know Neece plans to sell her house? Claudine told me that Neece and George intended to move. Now, even though he's gone, she's going to follow through. Claudine says she needs a play-actor for her house, to fix it up so it looks better than it is."

"A home stager?"

"That's what I said! Oh, I forgot to tell you, Senator Fergusson's stepdaughter, Leslie telephoned me personally." Pride blossomed in her voice. "She wanted to know how many Women's Club members would be attending Jessi's restaurant's grand opening. She's arranging the guest reservations. I wouldn't normally support that polecat, Jessi, but with the senator's interest, I'll make an exception. I included you and Max in the count, plus Alexander and his girlfriend. After all, they did go to that brunch. Guess who else will attend? Congressman Birch D. Charles! Leslie let that slip. He's from an aristocratic family and pictured at charity events with fashionable socialites. If anyone has the presidency in his future, it should be someone elegant like him, not some piddling state senator like Fergusson, who's nothing but teeth and hair. But you know what I can't figure out?"

"I can't imagine," Pilar said.

"Well, since Jessi learned about that old photo, is she holding it over Leslie's head? From what you've said, though, Leslie doesn't sound like a pushover. Is Jessi being her usual tricky self? Or is it Leslie who's up to something?"

"I guess we wait and see,"

After Francine finally hung up, Pilar tucked the work away. Thinking ahead to the restaurant opening, she put in a call to Alexander and left a message.

By eight-thirty, she was in her kitchen preparing her dinner when Alexander called. "What's this about Jessi's restaurant?"

Pilar explained that he and Solstice and she and Max were invited to the grand opening. "Apparently we're guests of the state senator."

"I don't know if we can make it. Solstice had the greatest thing happen." The pleased excitement in his voice lifted his baritone tone a notch, making him sound younger. He said, "Remember hearing about that little dog she loved so much? Toodles?"

"Yes, I remember." She'd learned from him that in addition to other horrors in Solstice's young life, she'd suffered enforced domestic labor. Her only joy in that life had been a fuzzy little dog. When Solstice had escaped, she'd taken the dog with her, but it had since died.

"She found a lost puppy that looks like him. It's a female, so she named her Toodle-Lou."

Alexander laughed, clearly charmed by the puppy. "It's all white and not quite four pounds, with a soft, curly coat and a funny little stiff-haired tail. Solstice found it in the vestibule of her apartment house. There was a long rope knotted around its neck and tangled around an exposed pipe. It was starving and filthy, the pads of its little feet raw. There's no collar, no identification, no chip, or tattoo. Solstice has asked around and nobody knows anything. The vet said it should recover and thrive with good care. Solstice takes it with her to work and everyone is fine with it. Toodle-Lou is sweet-tempered and quiet. It's easy to see why Solstice is in love with it."

And Solstice isn't the only one, Pilar thought with a smile, hearing the affection in her son's voice as he spoke of the animal. "Okay," she said. "Solstice won't go anywhere without the puppy, but you may be missing an interesting evening. Francine expects fireworks at the opening of Jessi's restaurant. I haven't published a *JumpRope Jive* for a while. The evening may present possibilities."

"What does Max think about the newsletter?"

"You think I should discuss another issue with him first?"

"Well . . . yes," he admitted.

"You like him, don't you."

"I do. Solstice does too. I think he's good for you. You're happier when he's around."

"Unlike I was yesterday at Neece's, right?" Pilar sighed. "I already told you. It was nothing you said that embarrassed me." Alexander was always so quick to blame himself. "Those crazy words that I told you about had me rattled. The only good thing is that I realize they all represent the shape of triangles, but it still makes no sense."

"Here's another thing that makes no sense," Alexander said. "Before I butted in with that second-sight business, I'd overheard that Neece's sister talked about an online boyfriend with a name like Aram. Then you said something about pyramids. There's an Arabic word, *Ahram*." He spelled it out. "That could have been what Claudine was trying to say. I couldn't match it to a person, but there's an Egyptian newspaper called *Al Ahram*. Translated, it means *The Pyramids*. It seems a weird coincidence. Does that mean anything to you?"

"No." Pilar smiled. "I should have a crystal ball."

Alexander chuckled. "I'll get you one for Christmas."

"No thanks, but thanks." She recalled that Mar-see-ah at Teddy's had told her she had a *gift* brought on because of a tragedy.

After hanging up her phone, Pilar wrapped her untouched dinner and put it into the refrigerator. She wasn't hungry. She'd had a long day and was weary.

By nine-thirty, she was bathed, in her nightdress and tucked into her wide, four-poster bed. Although she had turned off the lamp, there was enough ambient light through the windows from the starry sky to create faint shadows in the room. She could see the edge of the bed canopy and the charm of the vintage handkerchiefs she had hand-sewn together to fashion the canopy border. Over the years, under this canopy, she had offered comfort in brief relationships with men who had been wounded by tragedy. Now there was Max, who needed none of that. He met her as an equal, believing she was whole and strong and suited to be his companion. She was not. Desolate, she stretched out a hand to his empty side of the bed. A side that should remain empty. She didn't deserve a man like Max. She loved him deeply, but he offered a life she had no right to claim.

Bleakly, she stared into shadows that held no answer.

She slept, but at some point she roused. Unbidden came memories that she usually held at bay except for that one week each year when she allowed herself to relive the misery of that long-ago day when she had failed her young husband.

She had been eighteen when she and Vincent married and twenty-two when he drowned in the icy pool behind their house. That afternoon she had been all unawares, happily working in the kitchen, preparing a special dessert for his birthday. Dear God, if she had special powers why hadn't she paid attention when three-year-old Alexander had come running in, his cheeks all rosy from the cold, saying, "Daddy flew away."

In her mind's eye, she saw him standing in his blue snowsuit, his eyes wide and imploring. She knew that Vince had taken Alexander outside to play with a toy silver airplane that spun in circles at the end of a long string. She'd said she would be out in a few minutes. It was only after Alexander dashed back a second time to say his father was gone that she, faintly annoyed, had washed her hands (oh, yes, taking time for that!), put on her coat and boots (taking time for that), and trailed Alexander outside where horrified, she'd seen the gaping hole in the ice. After rushing out onto the ice herself, and then finding that Alexander was trying to follow, she grabbed the child and ran back through the snow to the house to call 911.

It was all a blur after that.

It was others who pieced it out later and explained what must have happened. The holder with a snapped string was found in the snow and the toy plane was found underwater. It must have broken loose and landed on the icy pond. Vincent had gone to fetch it. The weather had been below freezing for several days and the ice appeared safe. What Vincent hadn't realized was that one section hadn't frozen as solid as the rest. That's where the toy must have landed. Once the ice gave way to the deep water beneath. She'd been told his head showed a slight bruise. From one of the of the rocks surrounding the pool? If so, that, plus his heavy winter clothing had left him helpless.

Pilar had been too late to save him.

Young Alexander had been convinced that his plane had flown away and his father was with it. For a time afterward, when Alexander saw an airplane flying overhead, he would wave and call to his father.

Pilar thought it was her sanity that had flown. Guilt had nearly destroyed her. She was the only one who could have saved Vincent and she had failed. If she had been capable of the love Vincent trusted she held for him, she would have *known*. She would have *known* he needed her, *known* he was desperately calling for her in his mind. If she had responded to Alexander immediately, she was certain she would have found Vincent still clinging to the edge of broken ice. She could have found something to reach out to save him. There were so many things she could have done. She had reviewed them all a thousand times.

The things she could have done . . . *should* have done.

If only . . .

Pilar Fanshawe, most always outwardly composed and unruffled by all things big or small, wrapped her arms tightly about herself, turned on her side and wept unremittingly until sleep finally saved her from the further torture of agonizing regret.

Chapter 33

On Thursday, close to four o'clock in the afternoon, Slim was reaching for his jacket getting ready to leave when JJ whipped into his office looking like a million bucks. Her hair was fluffed and waving on her shoulders and her cheeks were pink. Flushed with excitement? Maybe, but it sure wasn't for him. Whenever they met, she didn't dress like this. Silky dress with a short skirt, glittery necklace and sparkly high heels with ankle chains.

"Trying to keep those shoes from falling off your feet?"

"Ha, ha, Tall Boy. These chains are a fashion statement."

The words he was thinking were, *Who* are you dressed up for? What he said aloud was, *"What* are you dressed up for?"

She flipped a sassy little purse on his desk and sat. "Cocktails on Philadelphia's Main Line, then a concert at the Kimmel Center, followed by a divine little supper in a divine little spot."

"Demoted to fashion news?" He figured her going out was personal. That bag was too small for her on-the-job note pad.

She grinned. "Maybe demoted to police work."

"What's that mean?" If a gap between two front teeth was a flaw, how come her smile was a turn-on? *Almost* a turn-on, he mentally corrected. "Your police work always has me getting the worst of it."

"Touchy, touchy," she said. "Want to hear that the dead Mr. Buckley Alfred Hightower was last seen alive in a homeless shelter in Melton, New Jersey?"

Slim straightened. "Now, you're talking."

She perched on his desk and leaned forward. "I found out more from a Hightower Family website. The family is on the West Coast. I managed to contact a ninety-year-old second cousin of Buckley's who likes to chat. We spoke on the phone."

Slim noticed JJ's dress neckline had a "V" shape, but it didn't show much. Not that there would be much to see. Women should be curvier, not so straight up and down. He made an impatient winding motion with his hand, "Keep moving, what's the story?"

"According to this relative, Buckley was an aimless drifter who eventually drifted to the East Coast, where he died in a drunk-driving accident. The relative looked up his death notice—she keeps a family scrapbook—he was pronounced dead at the Melton County Hospital."

"Our neck of the woods," Slim muttered.

"Right, I learned he worked for a time for a janitorial company that did jobs for public buildings. Mostly mopping floors. He never lasted long because of drinking. His relative didn't know where he worked last, but I figure that each time he got a job, employers had his social security number. Maybe our killer is a county cop who hunted for a usable SS number for his scam. Buckley's was perfect. A dead guy with no real connection here, who died twenty years ago."

Her tone became teasing, "Then again, it seems that the fake Buckley A. is swift enough to pose as a realtor who can sweet-talk women out of their retirement funds. Swift thinking and clever sweet-talking? Doesn't sound like a cop to me."

When Slim gave her a stone face, she laughed. "Francine got the name of the bank where Sable's check was deposited from Holly's father and she gave it to me."

"Yeah, then what?" he said, sounding bored, but he wasn't. JJ's work, compared with that of the prosecutor's office, was impressive.

She tilted her head. "With the name of bank, it was easy to find out it's in North Carolina. The bank manager said he'd opened the account for the man presenting himself as Hightower. He said—"

Slim interrupted. "Why in hell was he spilling stuff to you?"

"I'm irrepressibly charming. Of course—" She elaborately examined her fingernails and then looked up again. "I *just might* have created the impression I was calling on my Police Chief's behalf." She cleared her throat. "Moving on, I found out it wasn't a new account opened with Sable's checks. Our guy, under the name of Hightower, opened the account *six* years ago, so he's been at this game for a while. I doubted the manager would remember him after so long, but he did—at least the fact that he wore huge horn-rimmed glasses and a red cap." She tilted her head, making her hair swing. "What do you make of that?"

"If a person wears something noticeable, that's all people recall."

"Exactly, and here's another thing. Hightower didn't close out the account after Sable's murder. He closed it a week before. Was he already planning her death? The bank manager balked when I wanted Hightower's SS, but after he spoke with an official at Sable's bank to confirm the investigation, he said he'd send it to you. Now, the ball's in your court. If the imposter got the SS from Hightower's old personnel records, he could be someone working in the county. Old files might be stored in some building's basement. Find out where and who could have had access and you'll narrow your range of possible suspects."

She crossed her legs and swung one foot. "More details. Horn Rims opened his account six years ago with forty thousand dollars. By the time he closed it out this April with the cashier's check, the amount was less than ten thousand. Nine thousand forty-five hundred, to be exact."

"So he's been spending it. Wonder what happened to Olivia's unaccounted-for thirty grand." Slim grinned and added, "Thirty-two thousand—to be exact"

"You'll figure it out," JJ said.

"You think?" Her confident tone when she said he'd eventually figure it out made him feel good, not that he was letting on. Continuing, he said, "Our man made a mistake. The small amount left in his account indicates he used that bank primarily to cash checks."

JJ frowned. "Where's his mistake?"

"You said he closed out the account with a cashier's check. He won't hold it forever. Whatever he does with it, cashes it or deposits it someplace new, that North Carolina bank will have a record that will tell us where he was most recently."

"Okay, I get it," JJ said. "I emailed you the North Carolina bank information. Contact the manager. He said he will notify you as soon as the check comes in."

She started to turn away and then whirled back. "Pick me up at six next Saturday for the bash at Jessi's restaurant. It starts with cocktails at six-thirty and I don't want to miss a thing." Giving him a finger wave, she disappeared out the door.

Telling him what to do, huh? Slim thought, shaking his head as he reviewed his mixed feelings about Joyce Jane Gilbert.

Chapter 34

*S*aturday evening, State Senator Earl Smythe Fergusson stood alone in the bedroom of his spacious master suite. Wearing silk pajamas and a robe, he stared with fretful desolation at the empty king-sized bed. Leslie was busy with their guest list for the opening of that obscene Spellman woman's restaurant. He didn't understand it. When he asked, all she would say was, "You'll see." But it made no sense! Inviting a crowd to the restaurant would only put money into that woman's pocket. Why would Leslie do that? Didn't they hate Jessi Spellman?

He pressed a hand to his midsection and bit his lip. His stomach hurt. Distress always did that. In the bathroom, he fumbled around until he found anti-acid tablets to chew and swallow. If they didn't work, he couldn't call Leslie because she was busy and would be annoyed. He would call Astrid. Just listening to Astrid's voice soothed him.

Realizing his stomach was settling, he returned to the bedroom.

Once again, the sight of the empty bed depressed him. He was lonely and a little frightened, aware that circumstances were drifting too far from his control. He could do with some comfort. Not necessarily anything intimate. Soothing words and reassurances were all he needed at the moment. Leslie hadn't wanted to share their bed since they had found those advertising cards for Jessi's restaurant and the scrawled message about "lovers." Leslie said he could come to her room as long as he informed her ahead of time. Having to make an appointment was wrong. Nothing had been right since Jessi Spellman trespassed in their room.

Leslie had been furious and he had been petrified about the public learning of their relationship. She finally solved the problem by having Astrid ask questions in Jessi's town. Astrid learned that there indeed was a photo of him and Leslie when she was young. Those pushy women who were always hounding him to show interest in their town—*they* were the ones who had the photo. Leslie said not to worry. Now that she had the facts, she'd make sure the photo never surfaced. He knew he could count on Leslie.

He thought back to the start of his political career. As a lawyer employed in his family insurance company, he became a solicitor in one of New Jersey's insanely small communities. Although public service had been outside his radar, when the neighboring community, where he'd been a resident, asked him to serve on the town's council, he agreed and won the election. He had a legal mind and what came off the top of his head impressed his fellow committee members. They admired him. He didn't mind being in front of a crowd. He adored public speaking as long as he had the backing of his group.

His stint as a committee member was successful, yet he had no intention of running again when his term ended, not even when begged to do so. Despite his outward confidence, when his first wife divorced him, saying he was all surface and no substance, he was deeply wounded, mostly because he suspected it might be true. His second wife had been a widow with a child, Leslie. After she left him, taking the child, he was more certain of his inadequacy. Then she died and his stepdaughter, thirteen-year-old flame-haired Leslie, came to live with him. He married again. Soon after, his third wife walked out saying she wasn't sharing her house with another woman. She sought an annulment on the grounds that their brief marriage had never been consummated. An insulting lie that he didn't fight because that was only publicize her charge and it left him feeling like a fool.

When Leslie learned he'd been asked to run for a second term on town council, she'd been so eager for his success, she persuaded him to run again. A top student in a private day school, she distributed flyers, made calls, and worked the Internet. So young, but with such drive! She came by it honestly. Her late father had been an aide to the governor of some western state and her late mother had filled her head with the excitement of politics. When he won a four-year committee term by a landslide, he gained attention from his party. With their help, and Leslie's, he then won a highly contested race against an incumbent state senator and kept that seat this past November.

The next step in the plan, outlined by Leslie, was a run for Congress. But now, all he could think of was that once he won a congressional seat (and with Leslie behind him, he surely would) he would have to run again every two years to hold his position. After that, the next part of her plan was him becoming his party's candidate for president. That meant constant meetings, interviews, never-ending publicity, keeping on the good side of his party, and the grueling, unending hustling to keep the coffers filled.

What had seemed so exhilarating when the goal was born now seemed exhausting. Becoming a United States President was truly scary. So many duties and responsibilities! And a president couldn't simply depend on others—he had to think on his feet and stand out there alone.

Fergusson hated being alone.

He *liked* being a state senator. He had sponsored any number of excellent bills and worked with other senators on theirs. He'd responded to the needs of his constituents. That's why he'd been re-elected. Couldn't he just stay where he was? Yet, how could he disappoint Leslie when life in the White House was her long-held dream?

He sat on the edge of the big bed wondering when the downward spiral had started. It hadn't really been all that long ago. When was it?

He thought back.

JumpRope. That deceptively pretty town, where, if newspapers could be believed, residents were currently dropping like flies.

That's where his downspin had begun.

How was he to know the townspeople believed their Memorial Day event was so special that he should show up again? He'd gone once during a previous campaign. Once was enough. But last June his office started getting letters of recrimination over his failure to appear to hang a wreath on a veteran's monument. The president of the JumpRope women's auxiliary had actually questioned his patriotism.

Astrid had been disturbed, but Leslie said JumpRope was a waste of time. "Common people. Nobodies."

"Veterans," Astrid had said.

"But none with power or influence," Leslie shot back.

"Common people have the same vote as everyone else," Astrid said.

Leslie hadn't bothered to reply.

Just thinking of Astrid's dependable warmth was like a balm to Fergusson. She had been with him all his life, starting with a childhood friendship and then secretary with this family's company. She had seemed like a sister, comforting him, encouraging him, supporting him in every way. When he became a state senator, she became his assistant, working along with Leslie, of course. He was always proud to be seen with Astrid. She set him off so well. While always beautifully dressed, there with nothing flashy to distract from him, although her flaxen hair in a braided coronet was remarkable in an old-fashioned way.

It was her shoulder he had cried on when his first wife had divorced him, and again when his second wife walked off. "What's wrong with me?" he had sobbed. "They failed to appreciate you," she had said, her quiet manner calming him. Astrid would do anything for him. She was dependable, like a comfy old shoe.

He wished he had asked her advice about JumpRope after Jessi Spellman came sashaying into the New Jersey Statehouse in Trenton during a break last November. There she was, an adorable doll-sized woman in an eye-catching red suit and high-high heels. She'd caught the eye of every man in the room, but she'd made a beeline straight for him. What else could he do except invite her for a drink?

She sat primly in a booth at a nearby bar, so fetching with her jet-black wings of hair and tilted green eyes. How could a man fail to be charmed? She congratulated him on his re-election and told him of her battle to win a seat on the JumpRope Town Committee that had been bankrolled by none other than the renowned businessman, engineer, and financial genius, Acer Wolfgang. Fergusson immediately saw that if Wolfgang had supported Jessi, then by showing interest in Jessi, Wolfgang would view him favorably. Fergusson could confidently tap Wolfgang as a big contributor for his coming congressional run.

How was he to know everything Jessi had told him was a lie?

It wasn't until Astrid, who felt Leslie was wrong in dismissing the town, paid a visit. While visiting various little shops she chatted with people and learned that Jessi was viewed by the established citizenry as a troublemaker who had won the election through scandal-mongering and lies. Acer Wolfgang had nothing to do with it.

From that moment on, he refused all of Jessi's calls, and when she barged in, uninvited, at the Sunday brunch, he tried to have her escorted right back out again. Only then, Solstice Windsor, heiress to an impressive fortune, turned out to be Jessi's friend. What could he do? It wasn't fair to blame him for letting Jessi stay—except that she had contaminated the bed he shared with Leslie with the droppings of her restaurant cards and the horrible flyer.

Leslie had been beside herself with rage. Yet now, for reasons he couldn't begin to fathom, she was inviting the trouble-making townspeople to the opening of Jessi's new restaurant.

Crossing the room to the liquor cabinet, he poured himself half a tumbler of scotch and moved to sit in the chair next to the gas fire, which he had switched on with the remote because feeling bewildered and lonely left him chilled to the bone.

His thoughts whirling, he took a sip of the soothing amber liquid. He had to trust Leslie, didn't he? If there was ever a woman who knew exactly what she was doing, it was she. From the start, she had known what she wanted and how he fitted into it. Of course, he hadn't realized that at the beginning.

Thoughts still in the past, he remembered that after he had won his second term on the Town Committee he asked Leslie how he could reward her for her work on his campaign and to celebrate her upcoming fifteenth birthday. She said she wanted to go with her girlfriend, Cathy, on a resort vacation. Since they were too young to go alone, Fergusson should take them. If that's what she wanted, that's what he'd do. When the girls were off doing whatever girls that age did, he might find an appealing, unattached lady who was on vacation, too.

After an exchange of communications with her friend, Cathy's parents, who were paying separately for their daughter's expenses, all was arranged. Fergusson would fly with Leslie, but Cathy would leave from an airport convenient to her grandparents, where she had been staying during her parents' visit to Europe.

After he and Leslie had arrived at the resort and were settling in, she came to his room to say that Cathy was taking a later flight than planned because of a problem with her grandparents.

"But that's good," she said, perching on his bed. "It gives us time alone. There's something I want to talk about." That was when she began to lay out ambitious future political plans for him. Fergusson had listened but thought that although her continued interest in his career was flattering, it was pointless.

"You're a lawyer so you'll fit in anywhere, especially with the Washington crowd," she'd said. Then she revealed that he should eventually run for president.

"All you'll need is the right people around you," she said. "We'll find them when it's time and I'm out of school." Her late father had attended Princeton and she would too, thanks to top grades and a trust fund from her grandparents. Her intended major, no surprise, would be political science.

She then returned to her room to check her phone to see if she'd heard from Cathy, who was supposed to call as soon as she landed.

She'd run back quickly, crying, "Cathy's not coming! Her grandfather died! Her parents are flying home from Europe. My vacation is ruined!"

What a child she is, he'd thought as wailing, she threw herself into his arms, threatening his balance. He'd sunk back on the bed with her weight against him.

"That's all right," he said, trying to think of how to comfort her. He wasn't good at it and it was awkward. She was a child, but she felt like a woman. He patted her shoulder, suddenly realizing that her hand had somehow gotten inside his shirt and against his bare skin.

"It's so awful," she sobbed.

"There, there," he said.

Her fingers were cool, moving as if in a caress, but he knew that couldn't be true. His gasp was involuntary. He hadn't realized those twin puckers on a man's chest could be so sensitive.

"I feel so awful. I'll be so lonely," she said, lifting her face up to his.

He didn't exactly understand how it happened, but he was kissing her and she was responding. Feeling as if matches were being struck along his nerves, he tried to restrain himself, but once Leslie embarked on a path there was no holding her back.

"Don't worry," she'd said as she wriggled them both out of their clothing. "You're not my first, although I wish you were. Oh, I wish my first could have been you."

What was a man to do?

Afterward, he'd been appalled by his behavior. She only smiled and caressed him, her fingers still cool. "No one will know," she whispered. "It will be our secret." She pointed out that the resort was on an island and that made it apart from everything at home. They had hardly done anything wrong. It wasn't as if they were related. She reasoned that if she'd been an island native, by age fifteen she would already be married and have children. Kissing him, stirring him up again, she whispered that what they shared was just for this magical place.

For the rest of the trip, he was bewitched. He could think of nothing but Leslie. Even when he saw another vacationer that he barely recalled from somewhere, it made little impact, although, after that, Leslie made sure to keep her distinctive red hair covered. Another thing she did during their stay was to assure his comfort. If the air conditioning didn't work properly, it was she who called hotel service, if they wanted their outside lounge chairs shifted, it was she who alerted the pool boy. It was she who snapped her fingers for drink refills and she who called the café waiter to send back Fergusson's overcooked fish.

It was wonderful. By the end of that week, Fergusson felt so cosseted, so special, he didn't know how he was going to manage without her.

He didn't have to.

Once they were home, what they had shared at the resort continued. Discreetly, of course. And sporadically. "Our own little island," she would whisper. "Our own little world." He never knew when it would happen or when it wouldn't. Days would go by and then she would once again take him to that magical place. Uncertainty kept him in a state of aroused delirium. He never gave a thought to other women. There was only Leslie.

But even without that, she was always there to talk with him. He never had to be alone.

It wasn't until she was eighteen and attending Princeton, that she confessed that the whole business with Cathy had been a sham.

He had been astounded. "How did you get her to go along with it?"

She laughed. "There is no Cathy."

"But there were letters from her parents?"

"Electronic messages. It's not like I had to fake handwriting."

"But the scheme was so elaborate!" He was baffled by her audacity, yet oddly thrilled that she had gone to such lengths to steal time alone with him.

She brushed back the flames of her hair with a careless hand. "Elaborate schemes entertain me." She tilted her head in that way he found irresistible. "I enjoy manipulation."

He was still astounded but equally fascinated. Feeling suave, he leaned toward her. "You can manipulate me anytime you want, any way you want."

She smiled and opened her arms to him.

And somehow, her ambitious plans for him started to make sense as she continued to weave the dream about him. They would be together in the White House. Although she would be publicly recognized as First Daughter, privately, she would share his bed. Voters liked a president to be married, so some agreeable woman would be found to stand in as First Lady. That woman would be Astrid because she would do anything for him. How fantastic his life would be with the two most important women in his life caring for him. How blissful it had all sounded.

Her plans for his political career had progressed as Leslie had predicted. And now, the preparations for his congressional run as the party's favorite were progressing smoothly as well, the money already pouring in.

As to the Oval Office . . .

His stomach clenched. He didn't want to think about that. His thoughts wheeled back to the present and his lonely bedroom.

Here he was, years after that charmingly bogus "Cathy" scheme, and he was wondering yet again what Leslie wasn't revealing to him, especially about these invitations to that repellent Spellman woman's restaurant opening.

What did Leslie have in mind?

All he knew was that it would be to his benefit.

Was Leslie toying with Jessi Spellman?

From all he had heard, that would be a major mistake.

Clutching what was left of his drink, he shuddered and moved closer to the fire.

He didn't know how much later it was when he was startled awake by Leslie's hand on his shoulder and her voice in his ear. "Poor darling," she said. "You've gone to sleep in your chair." She picked up his empty scotch tumbler that had slipped from his fingers to the floor.

He looked at her, feeling befuddled, and he said the first thing that came into his head. "I didn't know where you were."

"Silly, I told you I've been working." She studied him. "You don't understand, of course. I've been mean to you, haven't I? You must have felt anxious."

"I was lonely," he said.

"Of course you were." He was still only half-awake as she assisted him to his feet. "Come on, now," she said, "and I'll tuck you in for the night. No, not that way—" she corrected when he started for their king-sized bed. "You know I won't sleep there anymore."

She steered him through the connecting door, opened her bed, helped him off with his robe and slippers, eased him between the covers, and tucked him in.

Her bed was so comfy, but what was really comfy was having her there.

"I was scared," he whispered, so very sleepy, but there were things he wanted to say. "You were working, but not explaining. I don't like that."

"Of course not," she said, smoothing his hair. "But you know I always do what's best for you, don't you? Tomorrow, we'll talk. I'll explain everything."

Leslie watched him close his eyes and drift into sleep.

She smiled, thinking of the triumph that lay ahead.

Chapter 35

Pilar was dressing in the late morning on Sunday when Max called, saying, "I've been checking the road home. It looks like there may be problems on the road ahead that's causing a traffic jam. I may end up taking a detour. It's a longer route, but I'd rather keep moving than sit stalled. I don't want you to worry if I'm several hours late."

She thanked him and added, "No matter which route, be careful."

They spoke a bit more before the call was over.

Talking with Max always left her feeling more peaceful and in control. Checking her appearance when she finished, she saw in her mirror a woman in a long, ruffled skirt, slim red blouse, and tinkling bracelets. She smiled, thinking how Max was entertained by her theatrical attire. He called this one her Carmen outfit.

She spent most of her day sorting through garden catalogs, thinking of what might strike the right note with Francine. Then Neece called. She spoke of her plan to sell her house and how she wanted it to make a nice presentation when it went on the market.

Pilar listened as if it was all news to her, always the wisest approach.

Neece said she had seen shows on TV that advised that a makeover could guarantee a higher selling price or at least a quicker sale.

"Very true," Pilar agreed. TV makeover shows emphasized the value of decorators, for which she was grateful.

"Can you come later this afternoon?" Neece asked.

"Yes. I could,"

"Good. My sister Claudine's off somewhere, but she'll be back here later in the evening." Voice sharpening, Neece added, "She'll want to put her two cents in." She brightened. "But you come early so we can have time together. I'll give you supper at four-thirty."

Supper. Four-thirty? Like early-bird hour at Krupple's Diner? Pilar figured Neece was lonely without George, but best to keep it businesslike. She begged off, saying she would be elsewhere for supper but could be there later. She had no idea when Max would be home, except it would be later than he originally planned.

Having time before meeting Neece, Pilar turned her attention to the vintage fabric she'd bought at Sable's sale. She hand-laundered it and lay it flat to dry. That done, she decided to have a meal ready when Max arrived--one that could be heated up because she expected him to be quite late. Lasagna would do the job. While the main course baked, she prepared ingredients for a salad. When she had everything ready, and the kitchen clean, it was time to see Neece.

When Neece opened her door, Pilar saw a vast improvement from the last time since she'd last seen her. At the dining table where Neece led her, she saw coffee and a dish of cookies. It was clear that although Neece's frame of mind had improved, she was lonely and needed company. It would have been rude to refuse.

Pilar soon found that the coffee tasted over-brewed and the cookies were stale. She wondered if they were leftover from the funeral luncheon.

As they sat, Neece rambled about her reasons for moving, which made no difference to Pilar. What she wanted to do was go through the house and give the woman advice on how to make the house look its best for prospective buyers. Thinking to hurry her into the tour Pilar asked, "When is Claudine coming?"

"She'll show up when she shows up. Never reliable, not since she started running off." Neece poured more coffee and started reminiscing about how upset George had been about his father's death. Then she said she never believed Rufus was murdered, no matter what nasty gossip said. Her topic shifted to George in the hospital and how she'd been annoyed when Claudine barged in and tried to take over.

"I always sent her home," Neece said. "I couldn't trust her not to defy the rules and sneak a cigarette despite George being on oxygen. I set my chair near the door so I could watch him and be ready at the same time to call down the hall for help if something went wrong." Neece trembled. "To think when he really needed me, that was when I'd stepped out to the cafeteria."

She looked at Pilar, her watery-looking eyes searching. "But I couldn't stay with him every minute, don't you see?"

That seemed a habit of Neece's, saying something and then pausing as if she expected a comment and then running on. Pilar found it unnerving.

Neece then started on how guilty she felt when she corresponded by email with the stranger interested in JumpRope. "I admit he seemed a bit what you'd call dashing. I guess that's why I never mentioned him to George, who was wonderful, but not dashing. But then, look at me. Plain as dishwater, right? And then, at the funeral luncheon, it seemed you spoke about the man's name meaning something, as if you knew him! That was so odd. Claudine said the police chief gave you quite a look, didn't he?"

Finally, Neece gave her a chance to reply. "I didn't know him, but my son says the man's middle name is the same as an Egyptian newspaper. In English, it's called The Pyramids."

"Your son seems so bright. You must be proud." Neece sighed. "My only children were the ones where I worked in Melton County Regional School office. Of course, the kids from here called it JRope High. Everybody has their own name for things. It can be confusing."

Tired of it, and thankfully finished with the coffee, Pilar suggested they start going through the house. To her relief, Neece agreed, muttering something about getting it done before Claudine arrived.

Pilar discovered that as Francine had said, everything Neece owned was of quality. On the day of the luncheon, Pilar had been too preoccupied with the crazy three-corner-top images to notice much. Now, taking notes, she saw that the style all through the house was English Manor and quite new, with paint, draperies, and rugs coordinated beautifully. The only problem was it all looked like show rooms, not a place where a real person lived.

"Did you have a decorator help you?" she asked.

"The one at the furniture store. I bought all this after I retired from my job at the school. I figured everything would be outdated by now."

"No, tradition never goes out of style."

The upstairs furnishings were lovely, too, but with the same stage-set feeling: beautiful, yet boring. Pilar stifled a yawn. She should have stayed home and taken a nap. There was nothing personal in the entire house to lend any sparks. No photos, no trinkets. Not even books or magazines. She pushed open a closed door and found an English manor-style home office where, if one had them, computers, printers, and fax machines would be completely hidden from sight.

"All for the show," Neece said, seeming annoyed for some reason as if she'd gotten pushed into buying something. "I gave up on all that electronic stuff when I retired. Writing notes seems more polite anyway, but the store decorator said every house must have an office."

Pilar nodded. Every room had the same type of furniture, the same style, and colors, and interchangeable wall paintings. That's what happened when a decorator's purpose was to sell out the store she worked for rather than reflecting the client's personality.

After smothering another yawn, Pilar said, "I don't think you'll need changes in the main rooms except for a fresh flower. Your decorator handled the traditional style with a modern, light touch. Soigné." (A French word was always smart.) "The bathrooms and the kitchen are where you should update. That's what will count with buyers."

They returned downstairs. Neece wanted them to sit in the dining room and visit some more, but despite feeling sympathy for the lonely woman, Pilar was tired of it.

The visit took a turn when Neece announced she wanted a look at Mather's Woods. She wanted to see the houses being built and the water feature before she went new house shopping in Florida, where she and George had once planned to move.

"But aren't you expecting your sister?" Pilar asked.

Neece's face took on a defiant expression. "It will serve her right to come and find me not here. She knows my car's not working so I'm stuck. It will be a good joke on her if we take a run out to the development and leave her to wait around and wonder."

This was the most animated Pilar had seen Neece all evening and it was a way to gracefully escape the dreary atmosphere. Besides, she hadn't yet seen what Neece called the water feature.

"All right," she said, knowing that with Max due home later, she had the time. Taking her keys from her purse, she said, "Let's go."

Chapter 36

*M*ather's Woods was not a great distance but to Pilar, with Neece beside her in the passenger seat, the drive seemed longer. Clouds had blown in, concealing what light remained on the western horizon, lending the sky an uneven glow that transformed the scene into shifting shadows. The eerie sky seemed to distort everything, including time.

Following Neece's directions, they entered Mather's Woods where the lights of Pilar's Mazda showed a single-track roadway. The brilliant car lamps were ones that Max had recently installed, thinking them superior to what she'd had before. He made certain her vehicle had all the latest features and gadgets that men adored and women ignored, but at the moment, she was thinking an ejection seat might come in handy. She wondered why Neece kept giving her sidelong glances. Was she having second thoughts about the trick on Claudine? It was a dirty trick. Pilar told herself she should have refused Neece's suggestion and gone home. Now she was stuck.

She smothered another yawn. When they'd left the house the night air had perked her up, but tiredness had again folded around her like a smothering drapery. She'd been feeling dragged out lately anyway. She knew her problem was her indecision about Max. If she told him the full truth of how she had failed Vincent, she was sure it wouldn't go well. But continuing to fend off Max's wish to marry would also eventually go wrong. Indecision was like a whirlpool, spinning her around and around, pulling her ever deeper into a place where she didn't want to be. She was relieved when the car lights swept across the expanse of a nice-sized pond.

Neece said, "My new house will have a water feature that's bigger than the one I have at my house now. Stop here, I want to look."

Pilar obediently drew to a stop. The pond was probably built for drainage and the spring rains made sure it was full, but there was nothing yet to make it attractive. There was no landscaping and the orange safety fence encircling the water was studded with signs reading *danger* and *no trespassing*. She lifted her gaze to the dark silhouettes of newly planted evergreens on the far side of the water.

She'd heard that the purpose was to screen the view of Jessi's restaurant. Pilar's lips quirked. Jessi had made enemies in town, but she could be brilliant when it came to impressing strangers. If she planned to depend on locals to keep her restaurant full, she'd be smart to stay home and leave the business to Arnie.

"Might as well turn off the engine," Neece said, opening her door. "I want to look around."

Pilar did as requested. "You want me to come with you?" She figured the purpose of this exercise was to kill time and make Claudine wait. Walking around might wake her up a little. This time, she didn't try to hide her yawn.

"No," Neece said. "I just want to take a look. You stay here."

Alone, Pilar leaned back against the headrest. How weary she was of Neece's company. During the ride, the woman unwrapped candy and shoved a piece at her. She'd accepted it and then was sorry. Stale chocolate. She definitely should have gone home. But what would she have done there except brood about her future with or without Max.

Pilar didn't realize she had fallen asleep until she felt Neece jostling her, pulling her arm. With the door open, the interior car light had come on. In the light, Pilar saw that Neece's shawl had come open, revealing a dark dress printed with red roses. Like Neece's lovely gardens, Pilar thought drowsily.

"You must help!" Neece cried in a frantic voice. "A duckling is trapped in a drain. It's going to drown!"

"Drown?" It was the only word that Pilar registered. She felt so dull and sluggish. How long had she been asleep?

"We have to save it." Neece struggled to haul Pilar from the car.

Finally standing, Pilar blinked, confused, and too sleepy to be sure of exactly where she was. "Drowning . . . so horrible." She could barely get the words out. Her body felt weighted.

"Nobody will be surprised," Neece said. "Everybody knows you've been haunted for years."

Pilar heard Neece's words, but they made no sense. Her legs tangled in her full skirt. She would have fallen if Neece hadn't held her up. Neece was stronger than she looked. Pilar was glad to lean against her doughy bulk.

"Didn't need that duckling story," Neece said. "You'll go along with anything, won't you? That candy did the trick."

Pilar heard her say more about coffee, candy and pills. Pilar thought she must be dreaming, except that her arm hurt where her bracelets dug into her arm where Neece held her. Was that part of the dream?

"Walk!" Neece commanded. "I can't carry you. I've still got a bum ankle from Sable's stupid stepladder falling on me."

Pilar couldn't think clearly. She didn't know why Neece was talking about Sable. Something about her ankle? But she was having problems too, just putting one foot in front of the other took all of her concentration. She couldn't do it without Neece's help. She was grateful to Neece. She stumbled. Her skirt kept tangling.

"Wore your gypsy outfit as a message?" Neece asked. "Too bad you forgot your crystal ball, but you already figured out enough about me."

Neece rambled on about how people looked at her and never expected much. How easy that made everything. She talked about home office equipment that she'd made everyone think she was too dumb to use.

"We had it all figured out," Neece said. "No one would ever look at the two of us." She went on, talking about things Pilar didn't think made sense, but Neece kept on talking. "People would have never guessed, and then you discovered our scheme" She gave Pilar's arm a punishing shake. "You even saw our little joke about giving Hightower a foreign middle name that means pyramids. I saw the look the police chief gave you. It got him thinking, I could tell. Too dangerous, that's what you are."

"Three corners," Pilar said, the word *pyramid* having struck a bell in her head somewhere. "Pyramids have three corners."

"Your head is a mishmash," Neece observed with a laugh. She paused, momentarily out of breath, and rubbed her ankle. "That psychic stuff must have come in dribs and drabs. Bit by bit, that's how it comes to you. Eventually, you would have spoiled our game."

Pilar thought Neece sounded like a character in one of Alexander's failed play scripts. Dialogue that only made sense to the author.

"Claudine," Pilar mumbled, remembering they were playing a trick on Claudine. What was she walking on? It had been bare earth, but now it felt like planks. Were they on a pier? She remembered a picture of a house with a pier. Where had she seen it? Was she there now? Her mind felt fuzzy; she couldn't think.

Neece jerked her arm, getting her moving again.

"Claudine . . ." Pilar wanted to say it was mean to trick her, but before she could get the words out, Neece hooted with laughter. "Still working it out? What a loser of a psychic you are."

Neece paused again to rub at her ankle. Pilar leaned against her. It sounded almost as if Neece was talking to herself. "I retired and we started testing our scheme. We planned to eventually go after even bigger money. It worked fine until Sable wanted her investment back, including the fake interest, to buy a house. Then Olivia wanted to buy a house in Maine and asked for all her investment back, too. We had to do something about them, so we did. But then there was only one problem after another, starting with Rufus, but right now, the problem is *you!*"

With that, she gave Pilar a hard shove. Pilar fell, her cheek pressed against wood. Off to one side was the gleam of water.

Grunting with effort, Neece rolled Pilar's body over so she looked upward. It relieved the pressure on her cheek and she was thankful for Neece's help, but now Neece was rolling her again. She felt the edge of something under one shoulder. Was it the edge of the pier?

"No!" She wanted to explain she was being rolled to where the water spread out, but Neece didn't understand. There was another hard shove. Pilar tumbled face forward into cold water and got a mouthful. She went under, her full skirt pulling her down. Her feet touched the bottom as the water closed over her head. Choking, she came up, shivering from cold and shock. The water was too deep for her to stand. She had to dog paddle to keep her head up, water from her drenched hair spilling cold around her shoulders. Sputtering, she saw Neece crouched on the pier above her.

With no breath to ask for help, Pilar pushed through the water to the pier and grabbed the edge. Something smacked her hand. Then there was pressure on the top of her head, fingers tangling in her hair, pushing her down.

She heard Neece say, "Bye, little duckling!"

Pilar's face was under the water again. Pressure on her head kept her down. She knew Neece was mad at her. Because of the trick on Claudine? She wanted to escape. She grabbed onto a post under the pier. It didn't help because Neece put another hand on her shoulder, holding on, forcing her down.

Pilar felt herself running out of air. She was going to drown. Her thoughts grew even more confused.

Somehow it all seemed right.

Seemed fair that she would drown. Drown like Vincent. It seemed like just punishment.

All she needed to do was relax.

Could she do it?

Just relax and let go.

"Pilar?" called a man's voice. "Pilar, is that you?"

Shocked, Neece's head turned. She saw a car parked behind Pilar's.

Max Osterhagen stood in its headlights. Neece had been so intent on finishing the job with Pilar, she hadn't heard him drive up.

What had Max seen?

Neece pulled back from the water, the murky light catching the ripples caused by the removal of her hands. The ripples smoothed. Neece smiled. Pilar Fanshawe was gone.

Max called again, panic edging into his voice.

Neece scrambled to her feet, prepared to act panicked herself. Not entirely feigned, but really, who would expect anything bad from her? Dowdy Neece, with her flowered dresses and mini-strokes. So boring, and dumb. That's what people saw and that's what she gave them. It served them right and she made it work for her.

"Max!" Stumbling, thanks to her bad ankle, Neece lurched toward him, making a big show of distress as she left the pier and reached him where he stood by Pilar's car. "I couldn't stop her. I tried to, but she jumped. There was nothing I could do to stop her!"

Neece looked back at the pier, deliberately looking on the wrong side. Why make it easy? "She jumped in and disappeared! She never came up!"

Max ducked his head inside the Mazda for a moment, his delay confusing Neece. She understood as he ducked out again with a big flashlight in his hand. She stepped back as he pushed past her and ran out on the pier, casting the beam of light into the water on the wrong side.

Chasing a lost cause, Neece said to herself and smiled with satisfaction.

Chapter 37

$\mathcal{F}$rantic, Max looked into the water where Neece had indicated. He saw nothing. He then searched on the other side, thinking Neece had been mistaken. Still nothing. His heart was beating so hard it rattled his chest, thundered in his ears. It must have just happened or Neece would have been running for help. He played the flashlight over the dark water, his thoughts spinning in frenzied prayers. Please, don't let me be too late. Don't let the seconds it took to find the flashlight and blurt a 911 message make the difference between life and death.

Desperately scanning with the light, Max took another step on the pier. Tense, he leaned forward as he saw the light pick up something in the water. He beamed in closer and realized he was seeing fabric drifting under the surface. Was it Pilar's skirt?

Without hesitation, he dropped the flashlight, took a breath and jumped, went under, and almost immediately surfaced. He could touch the bottom. The water was to his chin. He flailed, located the fabric, and tried to follow it. Almost at once, he was against the side of the pier. He was positive that he'd found Pilar's skirt. She must be caught under the pier. He couldn't say, *her body*, as if she were dead. He couldn't even allow himself to think it. He went under again.

Reached out.

Found her!

Still underwater, he felt around. Pilar's arm seemed wrapped around a post, a pier support. He tried to move her arm. She resisted; tried to fight him off. She was alive! And, by God, he was going to keep her that way. He went under and surfaced beneath the pier. And there she was. He could just make out the blurred shape of her face in front of him. She had been able to breathe because of the space between the water and the pier's underside, where they both were now. The water was too deep for her, but the post allowed her to hold on and keep her face high enough to breathe.

She tried to tell him something, but she was shivering so hard he couldn't understand her. She was freezing, her teeth chattering and she was probably halfway into shock. Only now was he aware of the low temperature of the water.

He tried to draw her close and had trouble getting her arm loose.

"Let go," he said. "Let's get warm and dry." At that, she managed to come to him.

Although there was clearance directly under the pier, the underside of the support beams ran only a few inches above the water. To move out, they would have to momentarily submerge. He was afraid she would panic. He was shivering himself, but he managed to make his voice sound calm and soothing.

"We'll have to go beneath the water to get out. Take a deep breath and hold it. Put your head down. I'll count to three. We'll be under for just a moment."

Without a sound, trusting him, Pilar bent her head and followed instructions. He placed a hand on the back of her head and held her face against his neck as he counted to three, submerged them both, and kicked powerfully. Seconds later they were in the water outside the pier, their faces above the surface.

"There," he murmured holding her close.

BAM*!*

Max didn't know what hit him. He only knew that a searing, star-making pain had exploded above his right eyebrow. He uttered some sound of outraged befuddlement, instantly blinded in one eye by a gush of blood.

A second swing went past his ear. By then he could make out his assailant.

Neece Van Doran, wielding his dropped flashlight like a club.

Still holding Pilar close, all Max needed to do to evade the next blow was to push back in the water and away from Neece's reach. With a cry of frustration, she heaved the flashlight. It sank harmlessly into the water with a splash.

As the sound of the splash died away, Max heard sirens.

Not knowing what was going on or what Neece might do next, he yelled, "I called 911!"

What Neece did was run, thumping up the short length of the pier to where Max had left his Chevy Malibu behind Pilar's car, the motor still running.

Neece jumped in Max's car, put it in gear, and lurched ahead, almost crashing into Pilar's Mazda. She backed, spun the Chevy around, and sped over the bumpy ground only to be blocked on the narrow road by a police car, an ambulance, and a fire emergency vehicle.

There were screeching brakes, shouts, a commotion from officers and EMS crew members, and a wailing sound from Neece. She threw herself out of Max's car, crying, "Thank the Lord! I was going for help." Wavering, she held a hand to her heart.

Recognizing her as Neece Van Doran, two squad members rushed to steady her.

She failed to respond to their questions about someone drowning.

"Heart," she cried, gasping, clutching her breast, and moaning.

She was swiftly assisted to the emergency vehicle where she was given oxygen and an EMT began assessing vital signs.

Alfonso, a dark-skinned, sharp-eyed officer, left the drama to the EMTs as he caught sight of what looked like movement in the water. He started to run. Others followed, reaching the water's edge as Max, with Pilar in his arms, began struggling toward shore. Assistance rushed to them. It was rapidly determined that there was only a near-drowning and the fire rescue boat wouldn't be needed.

Max and Pilar were brought to the ambulance, their sodden clothing quickly and impersonally stripped from their shivering bodies and they were enveloped in blankets. Both were conscious, although Pilar wasn't making sense. She was assessed as being in the worst condition of the two, suffering from cold and exhaustion, her temperature and blood pressure nearing critically low levels. Instant heat packs were tucked in under the blankets and around her upper body. There were no physical injuries found except Max's head wound, which received prompt attention to staunch the bleeding.

The emergency vehicle containing Neece had already left by the time the ambulance with Pilar and Max sped behind it to the Melton County Hospital.

Slim, who had gotten word of the incident befalling three residents, was waiting outside the hospital emergency room entrance when the first emergency vehicle arrived. As Neece was being brought out on a stretcher she saw him and her voice quavered out, "Chief Parkerson, thank goodness!"

The ambulance with Max and Pilar soon pulled up.

Neece called Slim's name again.

"Under control here," said an EMT coming from the ambulance.

Slim halted until they carried the stretcher on through the hospital's emergency door and then, followed.

Chapter 38

$\mathcal{I}$nside the hospital, EMTs were busy with Max and Pilar. Slim waited and then decided to see if he could speak with Neece since she'd been worked on first. He found her in a cubicle where a nurse was crooning, "There, there the doctor's done, I'll take care of you now."

The nurse, a saucy-looking strawberry blond, glanced up. Seeing Slim, she said to Neece, "You have a visitor, Mrs. Van Doran." The nurse's gaze moved back to him. She smiled and added, "Someone tall, blond, and good-looking."

Neece giggled, "That's our police chief," she said, and giggled again.

Neece Van Doran with the giggles? wondered Slim. The miracle of drugs. Slim gave the nurse an easy smile. She wore a gold band on the third finger of her left hand. Always a day late and a dollar short, that was him, he thought, amused at himself.

"I'll get you that extra pillow Mrs. Van Doran," the nurse said. With another smile at Slim, she left the cubicle.

Slim shifted his attention to Neece. She was now gnawing her lip and looking agitated. Dressed in a hospital gown, she lay on a narrow examining table, propped up with a pillow behind her shoulders. The light blanket over her lumpy form was drawn up to her armpits, like a protection against all that had happened to her.

"Do you know where my purse is?" she said anxiously. "The nurse can't find it."

"I'll have somebody check on it," he said."

"Thank you," she said and then she wailed, "Oh, it was all so terrible!" She reached toward him. "I'll tell you everything that happened," she said, "but I'm so shaky. Could you please hold my hand?"

"Sure." He noticed how she went from giggles to agitation. Shock? He took her hand. It was chilled but it seemed steady enough.

"Take it easy," he said. "Nothing to be worried about. Start with how you and Pilar got together today."

She frowned. "I was thinking about selling my house. I asked Pilar to come and discuss improvements, but something about her seemed odd. Like she couldn't get her thoughts together."

Slim nodded as he recalled Pilar's rambling nonsense at George's funeral luncheon, her words unraveling like a coil of crime scene tape in a windstorm.

"I'm not sure when we started discussing the new housing development, but she was curious to see it." Neece gave Slim an earnest look. "I was curious about it, too, but I don't like driving anymore. I thought it would be nice to go with someone and let them do the driving like George used to do." She broke off, looking ready to cry, but then she continued. "We went and stopped by some water, a pond, I guess. I had no idea the development had a pond. What a surprise!"

Slim had heard that a series of mini-strokes had wrecked Neece's short-term memory, but she seemed to be managing now. He'd thought it had been Pilar's idea to go to the pond because they'd gone in her car. It was good to have it confirmed.

"She wanted to walk out on the pier and just started to go."

"It must have been dark or almost dark when you got there," Slim said. "Did she have a reason for wanting to go out there?"

"No, she just started walking, leaving me behind. I hobbled beside her. It wasn't easy because of my bad ankle but I had a bad feeling. The way she was all dressed up, like somebody in a play. And with all that jewelry. All dressed up to see me? It didn't make sense."

She gripped Slim's hand harder. He was surprised by her strength.

"She was still ahead of me, about halfway out when she stopped and crouched. I realized she was going to jump in. I tried to run and got there in time to grab her arm. She whirled, fought me off, tore free, and jumped. There was a splash and she—she was just gone!"

Neece broke off, pulled her hand from Slim, and used both hands to cover her face. "It was so horrible," she wailed.

Slim said, "When did you call 911?"

Neece looked at him, her eyes running tears. "I don't know. It was all a blur after that. I couldn't get my breath and my heart felt like it was popping out of my chest. I didn't know where I was or what. I don't know how I got off the pier. They told me I was driving Max's car to try and get help but I don't remember. Next thing I knew, I was in the hospital. I didn't even know Pilar had been saved until I heard it here. Thank the Lord for that." She covered her face again. "I was so frightened and confused."

The same nurse as before came into the room. "Oh, Mrs. Van Doran! We can't have you getting all upset again." The look she gave Slim didn't make her look cute anymore. "Your guest had better leave."

"I'm leaving," Slim said. As he walked out, he heard the nurse say, "Mrs. Van Doran, I brought you that second pillow you asked for. Let's get you settled all warm and cozy."

Outside in the hall, Slim thought about Neece and the way her mood seemed to switch around. He guessed the circumstances and hospital drugs explained that. Before he'd gone in to talk with her, the doctor told him her symptoms seemed a nervous reaction rather than a heart attack. An EKG and blood test showed no signs of damage even though she'd kept complaining. In the doctor's opinion, she enjoyed the attention but to be certain, he was keeping her for the night and planned further tests the next day.

Slim couldn't blame Neece for liking the way the nurse fussed over her. Things had been rough for her and then a person tried to deep-six themselves right in front of her. No surprise about that. Pilar was as weird as a three-dollar bill. She'd probably been building up to it for years, although you'd think she wouldn't pull something like that when she had Max, somebody stable. But weird is weird.

Figuring he had Neece's story straight in his mind, it was time for a talk with Max and Pilar. Moving past the bustle of technicians and doctors at the centrally placed command station, he came to another row of examining cubicles.

There was Donny, standing at military attention, his red hair a bright splash against a drab off-white drapery closing the cubicle. Donny had come to the hospital earlier and found Slim when he was waiting for the EKG on Neece to be finished. Slim had instructed him to find out where Max and Pilar had been taken and to make sure they stayed put until he had talked with them.

"They're in there together, Sir," Donny said, gesturing to the cubicle behind him. "The doctor with Mrs. Fanshawe said she's suffering extreme cold from the immersion. The best medicine is body heat."

Slim didn't know what Donny meant until he entered the space and found Max seated in a chair, his shoulder bare above the blanket as he cuddled Pilar against what had to be his bare chest. Yeah, body heat as treatment, Slim thought. Pilar appeared to be asleep and Max had a bandaged head wound. The room smelled of blood and disinfectants.

"We're okay," Max said with a tired smile. "Pilar has hot packs tucked around her and she's got me. She still has the shivers but she's out of danger."

Slim nodded and leaned his rump against the end of the high examining table. A glance at Pilar told him she'd be useless, which was pretty much what he thought anyway, so he addressed Max. "Tell me what happened tonight from the time you arrived at the lake."

"I saw a figure on the pier and recognized Neece. She was shouting that Pilar was in the water. I jumped in and, thank God, I found Pilar. The water was deep, over her head, but she didn't drown because she was under the pier holding onto a piling to keep her face high enough to breathe."

Slim said, "Neece told me that Pilar jumped in on purpose."

Max scowled. "She told me that but I don't believe it. Something else must have happened." Leaning down he put his face next to Pilar's. "Love, tell me what happened at the lake."

She roused, mumbled about a trick on Claudine and then drifted off again.

"She said that before," Max said. "I don't know what she means. What did Neece tell you?"

"She said Pilar drove them to the pond and then she went out on the pier. Neece followed and realized Pilar intended to jump. She tried to stop her. I noticed bandages and brown disinfectant stains on one of Neece's arms. It looked like she'd been scratched. She said Pilar got free and jumped in."

"That's all she said?"

Slim frowned at Max's incredulous tone. "Yeah. Neece said she was confused and didn't remember calling 911."

"I did that. I made the call and grabbed a flashlight. The water was all black but my light showed Pilar's skirt just under the surface. That's when I jumped in and found her under the pier, like I told you. I was bringing her out in open water and when I looked up and I saw Neece holding the flashlight I'd dropped. She bent down, to help, I thought. Instead, she swung the flashlight and clubbed me a good one." He gestured to his bandaged forehead.

Slim's eyes narrowed. "*That's* how you were hurt?"

"Yes. How does Neece explain it?"

"She didn't. I didn't know to ask." Slim didn't know what to think. Did Neece tell two stories out of confusion, or was she mixing herself up in a lie? Maybe that was part of Neece's off manner. She didn't want to admit she'd struck Max. Except, why had she done it?

He left the cubicle and told Donny to stay at his post. Before returning to Neece, he located the doctor who'd treated Max and Pilar. He was a youngish man with a pleasant face.

"I'm getting confusing stories," Slim said.

The doctor said, "If you're referring to Mrs. Fanshawe, her vital signs have stabilized, but she seems more confused than an otherwise good recovery from cold water immersion should warrant. When I had

asked if she had ingested anything unusual, she said 'nasty chocolate.'"
The doctor shrugged. "I don't know the woman, but if she ingested
medication, it might have been too much. To be on the safe side, I drew
blood to test."

Slim nodded. From what he'd seen of Pilar recently, he agreed with
the doctor that a test was a good idea."

Leaving the doctor, he accepted the fact that he was stuck at the
hospital. Nothing like that was ever on police recruiting posters, he
thought with an inward smile. When he was on his way to talk with
Neece again, Donny caught up with him.

"I'm supposed to go off duty and Alfonso's on the job. I'll stay here
if you need me."

Figuring Max and Pilar were set for a while, he gestured to Donny.
"I'm talking to Mrs. Van Doran again and then taking a second crack at
the other two. Conflicting stories. Tag along if you want."

As Donny fell into step with him, Slim glanced sideways and was
unable to resist asking, "You carry a purse now, Officer?"

Donny had forgotten he held Neece's purse. He flushed to the roots
of his coppery hair. "No, sir," he said and explained that after Neece,
Max and Pilar were taken to the hospital, he had made sure the two vehicles were secure. He returned the keys and Pilar's purse, which he'd
found in Pilar's vehicle, to Max. Neece's purse had been there as well.
"I'm taking it to her now." Importantly, Donny added, "I saw a video
about what can happen when officers aren't thorough, so I checked
to make sure there were no concealed weapons." He flipped open
Neece's purse to demonstrate.

Resisting rolling his eyes about the concealed weapons talk, Slim
said to Donny, "Good job with the vehicles." He meant it. Unfortunately, Donny could be earnest to a fault and frequently misapplied training lessons. When Slim saw Donny and the doctors were still busy,
Donny had given an opinion that Neece and Pilar had been engaged in
nothing more than a catfight; wisdom gleaned from a seminar about
officer conduct with middle school disturbances involving pre-pubes-
cent females.

Glancing into Neece's purse as Donny held it open, Slim did a double-take. "Hey wait." He took the purse, reached in, and retrieved a plastic bag.

"Chocolate candies, sir," Donny said.

Slim remembered the doctor wondering if Pilar might have taken some kind of medicine and Pilar mentioning 'nasty chocolate.' Candy from Neece's purse? To Donny, he said, "I'm going to talk with Mrs. Van Doran again. Tag this chocolate as possible evidence and you're off duty."

"Yes, Sir!" Donny practically clicked his heels together before he departed.

Slim found Neece sitting up straighter on the table thanks to the addition of the second pillow. She was busy with a bottle of antiseptic hand gel and paper towels, poking under her fingernails with a tissue. "Everybody's sick in a hospital," she complained. "Can't be too careful."

She thanked Slim for her purse and immediately hid it under the blanket. "This situation has me terribly upset." Her newly spotless hands fluttered like ailing butterflies. "I can go home soon, can't I? They say they want to keep me, but my regular medicine is at home. I asked them for something cold to drink. If I have to wait, I should at least be comfortable."

"I think they feel they should play it safe by keeping you," Slim said. "As for me, I have a couple more questions." He leaned against the wall. "What's this about you taking a swing at Max with his flashlight?"

Neece didn't hesitate to admit it. "I was afraid," she wailed, putting her hands to her cheeks in a display of remembered horror. "Max insisted I could have stopped Pilar from jumping. He turned into a crazy person. You should have seen him. He kept yelling and screaming at me, waving his arms. I've never been so frightened! I had to protect myself."

"He was in the water when all this happened?"

"Yes, he . . ." She paused, looking flustered. "Maybe it was before."

"When he first arrived?"

"I think so. It's all a blur." Wailing, she again covered her face with her hands.

Slim didn't press, but he was thinking that if Max was in the water, he couldn't have been much of a threat. It made no sense for Neece to bash him when she could simply walk away. And if it happened before Max entered the water, it meant he'd spent time berating Neece instead of going after Pilar. Nothing was making sense.

He said, "Max says Pilar's been talking about a trick on Claudine."

Neece's mouth dropped open. "Claudine is in Maryland! Did Pilar *really* say such a silly thing? If you doubt my word, you call Claudine, but I'll have to get her number from home." More helpless hand fluttering. "I can't remember numbers." She gestured toward her head.

Slim thanked her, and then went down the corridor to speak again to Max. Along the way, he thought about Neece. She was being dramatic to gain attention, but it seemed more than that. Why did she take a swing at Max? He found himself thinking there was something sneaky about Neece—a notion that had never before crossed his mind.

He headed for his other two charges no wiser about Neece than he had been before, but further convinced than ever that something was off. He found that Max and Pilar had been moved to a corridor outside the emergency room. Pilar was sleeping on a bench, her head on a pillow, a blanket drawn up over her shoulders. She and Max wore hospital scrubs, V-neck tops, and drawstring pants. Slim thought they looked like prisoners except the outfits were blue, not orange.

Max, who was on his feet, adjusted Pilar's blanket.

Slim said to Max, "I still don't know what in the hell is going on. You seem to be the only one of this trio who tells what sounds like a straight story."

Pilar stirred. Opening her eyes a crack, she looked at Slim and said in a fanciful way, "Does a trio have three corners like a pyramid?"

"Shush, now, love. Everything's okay now," Max said to her, bending to smooth her hair, usually so carefully groomed but now matted about her shoulders.

Defensively, he said to Slim, "She's been restless. She wakes up and says a few words that might make sense or they might be nonsense. The doctor is concerned and drew blood to test."

"Yeah, I heard something about that," Slim said. A few cans short of a six-pack, that was Pilar. But then again, what about the chocolates in Neece's purse?

With Pilar looking settled again, Max left for the restroom, which was on the other side of the hallway. Slim flopped in a chair near the bench where Pilar was sleeping. His thoughts returned to Neece. In the examination room, he saw the bandages on her arms, from the scratches made by Pilar's fingernails, surely. He glanced at Pilar. He could see one of her hands, saw neat fingernails, no colored lacquer, the tips rounded and whitened. Would scraping under her nails show Neece's skin? Or could Neece's scratches be self-inflicted? Was he now thinking that Neece, who'd always seemed on the dull side, was cunning enough to make up a story and to clean under guilty fingernails?

Irritably, he changed position in the chair, slumping back on his spine, sprawling out his long legs. Too damn many inconsistencies.

Pilar stirred again and lifted herself to one elbow. "She was mad at me," she said as if continuing a conversation.

"Who? Neece?" Slim didn't bother to lean forward. He didn't expect anything coherent.

Sounding more awake but still vague, she said, "Neece has nice furniture. A home office with everything hidden. She didn't like me seeing the office."

"That's why she was mad?" He could talk nonsense with the best of them.

"That and because of the man's name."

"Uh-huh. What man?"

Pilar seemed to think a long time before she spoke again. "The man with the Arab middle name. A-rab, Claudine called it." Pilar suddenly seemed less vague. "Neece didn't like it because she thought I knew about him, only I really didn't. It was the day of the funeral luncheon. Neece was angry when I said *pyramid*. It made her afraid. She thought I guessed about their scheme."

"Scheme?" Sitting up, Slim started to listen. Listen and play back what Pilar had said, at the luncheon, words he'd paid little attention to at the time. He leaned forward. "A pyramid scheme? You mean like with money."

"I guess." Pilar nodded. "With that man, her partner. She said everybody got to be a nuisance. George's father, Olivia and Sable. She hurt her ankle on the stepladder."

"What stepladder?"

"Sable's I think. When it fell."

Hearing that, Slim's thoughts turned in new directions.

Chapter 39

Sometime later, when Max returned from the restroom, Slim was no longer there. Pilar was asleep again, looking more relaxed than earlier. Weary, he sat on the bench and lifted Pilar so her head was in his lap. With one arm draped across her shoulders, he went to sleep himself.

It was past six in the morning when a different doctor came by and said they could leave but that Pilar should make an appointment with her regular doctor; her hospital test results would be sent to him for her records.

A JumpRope officer came into the hospital and also told them they could leave.

"Has something happened?" Max asked.

The officer shook his head. "I only know you can go."

Max nodded. He wondered what was happening with nutsy Neece, but decided he didn't care. Let the cops figure her out. Pilar, who had just awakened, seemed subdued but reasonably alert. He'd been awake for far longer than she. Cramped and stiff from his hours on the hard bench, he'd felt like he'd been dragged cross country behind an eighteen-wheeler. Trying to work out the kinks, he'd walked around while calling a couple of friends for a favor—come for his keys, go fetch his car from where he'd left it at the pond, and leave it in the hospital parking lot. Another friend took Pilar's keys and would drop off her vehicle at her house. Good friends, who soon returned with both sets of keys. Max smiled in anticipation of getting Pilar home to a real bed. Then he could get some real sleep.

Pilar saw daylight breaking in the east as Max helped her into his car. She was beginning to figure everything out, including the fact that Neece was a killer who had tried to add her to the list. But she didn't want to think about that. The only subject that mattered was Max.

Turning to him, she said, "You saved my life."

The key was in the ignition, but he hadn't started the engine. He smiled. "Yes, I suppose I did."

She nodded. Max had passed the test that she had failed with Vincent. Max had not only proved his love, he had also proved what she had always believed—when you were truly capable of loving someone, you *knew* when they were in need.

She said, "You loved me enough to know I needed you, that I would die without your help."

"At the end, yes," he said, looking faintly puzzled. "I suppose you could say that."

"I can say that because it's true." Fighting back tears, her tone was fierce as she repeated her long-held private thoughts out loud. "You passed the test that I failed with Vincent. I truly believed I loved him, but I didn't love him enough because I just wasn't capable. On that terrible day, I had no idea he was in trouble. He could have been on another planet for all I knew. He was calling out to me, he had to have been, but I was deaf to his pleas. I didn't recognize his terrible danger until it was too late. There was no way I could have reached him in time because of my limitations. But you proved what I always knew. When you truly love someone with all your heart, you *know* when they are in need."

Max listened to her long speech with the realization that her words must be ones she had repeated to herself in the past, but her thinking was so foreign to him that it left him confused. His frown deepened. "You mean when I found you in the water?"

"Yes, I couldn't have held on forever. I would have drowned, just as Vincent did. But that didn't happen. I didn't drown because you sensed that I needed you. You *knew*."

Finally understanding, Max stared at her with gentle eyes. "Pilar, I love you with all my heart." He reached toward her, caressing her cheek. "No, now don't nod your head like you're in agreement with what I'm saying because you don't know what I'm about to say." He gazed into her eyes. "I love you with all my heart and soul, with every fiber of my being. I would protect you from any harm and die in the attempt if it became necessary. If I hadn't been able to find you under that water, I might have kept hunting until my air ran out. But, love—" He paused, shaking his head. "Despite all my love for you, I'm only a mortal man. *I cannot read your mind.*"

The glow in her eyes remained undiminished. "You came for me."

"Yes." He smiled softly. "It is with some risk that I'll explain how it came about. The traffic problem I discussed with you cleared so I returned home without taking a detour. When I arrived home earlier than I'd originally thought, I saw you'd prepared what looked like dinner in the refrigerator. I waited a bit, then decided to find out where you were. The location that came up on my phone seemed strange. I didn't know what had attracted you to drive to Mather's Woods. I went to join you and find out. Thank God, I went immediately." His voice constricted. "And thank God for that GPS tracker on your car."

Pilar stared at him. "You came for me because of a GPS tracker?"

"Yes, we can check each other's car locations through our cell phones." He paused and searched her face. "I know that's not what you thought happened. You thought it was something more . . . more magical."

She started to laugh and cry at the same time. Max found her because of a GPS. Did that mean he didn't love her enough? Of course not. She couldn't doubt it, not with Max. They loved each other. Maybe that was all the magic any couple should expect. She felt suddenly adrift, unmoored from convictions that had bound her, yet had kept her secure in what she had believed was well-deserved shame. The years of pain and tortured thinking seemed to whirl around her in a crazy kaleidoscope: all those years of blaming herself, the dreadful guilt . . .

"Max, I love you." She reached out and went gladly into his arms where it was warm, where she was safe, where t she was loved.

She had a lot of thinking to do, a lot of sorting out the confusion of the past. It might not be easy but one thing she knew for sure. She no longer would have to do it alone.

Chapter 40

It was four days after the announcement that Neece Van Doran had been arrested for a series of murders in JumpRope.

The media screamed:

**KILLER CAPTURED! UNNAMED PARTNER
IN CRIME STILL FREE!
WILL HE OR SHE STRIKE AGAIN?**

Nonsense, thought Jessi Spellman. The opening night of the Carousel Restaurant was the only thing worth thinking about.

Jessi, Jessi, Jessi . . . In her imagination, she heard the crowd in the main dining room of the restaurant excitedly chanting her name. The fantasy voices echoed up to the exposed rafters of the magnificently transformed old building. Maybe even through to the roof, where the illuminated revolving carousel with its six ponies and costumed figures could be seen for miles.

Opening night! Reservations had come in like crazy. Jessi knew how eager the patrons were to see her. To praise her. To thank her.

To behold her.

Of course, they weren't all there yet, but that's what it would be like when the room was filled to the brim. She giggled and hugged herself as the arena of her mind filled with her imagined accolades.

The wonderment, the delighted awe.

Had there ever been a more spectacular, more elegant restaurant?

Never. And *she* was the mastermind.

She stood concealed behind a curtain on the balcony that formed a horseshoe shape over the elaborate velvet and gold-trimmed Gay Nineties dining room. It was a classy, open space of white-clothed tables and glittering candle-lit, floral centerpieces. The ground floor room could hold seventy-five people and at least half that number were already present, mostly in business dress, some even in formal dress, as Jessi was herself. The balcony, which could seat another twenty or so, was presently empty of tables. Since the members of the crowd had preselected their main courses, Arnie wanted them seated on a single level for the waiters to efficiently serve the meals. *She* wanted the diners on one level to make certain she had their focused attention for the promised surprise announcement.

But first, there was the hour of open bar and appetizers that had begun as soon as the first diners entered the door. The waitstaff, uniformed in sharp-looking black and striped grey, had immediately sped into action. The appetizers were small samples of house specialties that were not on the menu that evening, astounding culinary creations from Arnie's kitchen. At some point, she'd have him step out to be introduced, looking magnificent in a tall black chef's hat. The chubby chef who ran Teddy's Restaurant, her chief rival, wore a white hat that was ordinary and common. Jessi was nobody's copycat.

Filled with a sense of rapture, Jessi reviewed her pre-planning and how magnificently it had gone, including a soft opening, in which Arnie's family and friends had dined for free so he could work out any kinks. (Her family was unavailable, having for some reason all moved to a distant location as soon as Jessi was out of the house.) Everything now worked to perfection. There was an expert who set up the lights so that she could control everything with a subtle flick of her fingers: the lights up, lights down, spotlight here, spotlight there, so fierce and fabulous.

And then there were the advertisements in the *Melton Monitor*. The biggest ad had been a full-page color job with photos of the Gay Nineties dining room and balcony, the Roaring Twenties bar with its tall bistro tables and intimate corners, and the "Rock Around the Clock" Fifties-style snack shop.

This splashy ad ran on Tuesday and it *should* have been the center of the reader's attention. Remembering, Jessi scowled. Disastrously, that was the same day the front page headlined some killer arrested, with more coverage inside about the JumpRope police solving the murders of some old people.

Jessi had been furious. The crimes were over and done with and the person arrested was another old bag. So what if her cohort was still on the loose? The news might distract readers from her restaurant ad, which was crucial—the last call for opening night reservations. She had tried to get Pilar to rush out a flyer, but Pilar, who'd somehow ended up getting half-drowned in the murder mess, said she was taking it easy and couldn't do it.

Jessi had been dumbfounded. She knew Pilar could be independent, but the refusal was just plain selfish. If a friend wouldn't help a friend with something that really mattered, how much of a friend could they be?

It was a snub Jessi wouldn't forget.

Resentment fled from her mind at the arrival of her special guests: A really big name, Congressman Birch D. Charles, who accompanied State Senator Earl Smythe Fergusson and his stepdaughter, Leslie, plus another couple, all of them dressed to the teeth. Considering the scandalous information Jessi had on Fergusson and Leslie, she could count on them singing the praises of the restaurant far and wide.

Plus, there was a thrilling surprise that Leslie had promised.

Francine Smithers, who'd been present when the doors opened, looked around from her favored position, presiding over the table she'd arranged for Voodoo Club members. She glanced across the room and saw with relief that irritating Amy was sitting elsewhere. She then caught sight of Fergusson and his stepdaughter, Leslie, being seated.

The arrival of the dignitaries instantly overrode any chit-chat about the murders, a topic that had kept tongues busy for the past four days.

Francine's focus had moved from the crimes to the welfare of the community and how she could continue to be the prime mover and shaker in making good things happen.

Leslie had personally assured Francine that whatever choices Fergusson made with his career, he would maintain a prime interest in the community of JumpRope. In return for Fergusson's interest, Francine promised that the provocative photo of Fergusson canoodling with fifteen-year-old Leslie would never surface. Francine had been only too delighted to agree. Leslie had also warned that if the photo ever surfaced, she had experts prepared to prove it was a fake and the resulting lawsuits would destroy the town.

That satisfied Francine as well as the rest of the club members so the threat held no meaning. What wasn't satisfying was that Leslie had said she would make an exciting public announcement before dessert was served, but she refused to tell Francine what it was. Being denied information chaffed Francine like poor-fitting support hose. Not that anyone had to know. Pasting on a smug smile as if she always had the inside track, she gazed about the table. Her eyes caught on Darlene. She had wondered if Acer would accompany her, but when she asked, Darlene said he was visiting business friends in London.

The table conversation returned to the murders and the fact that the killer of Sable and Olivia was Neece Van Doran. Who would have thought that drab pudding had it in her? It also meant the royalties from Sable's artwork, previously diverted by Neece, would now be forwarded to the two women's organizations. They had unanimously agreed to institute an annual Sable Kilgallen scholarship for a graduating JumpRope student who planned to further his or her education in an artistic field. The only detail left hanging was that Neece hadn't committed her crimes alone. Her partner was a crooked con artist named Buckley Alfred Hightower, but he hadn't yet been apprehended. Thank goodness he wasn't a resident and the newspaper fed readers the usual *the investigation is continuing.*

Francine took another look around, disappointed that not everyone she had invited to her table had accepted. Toria was with Holly, sharing a corner location with the police chief, that *Monitor* reporter, Joyce Jane Gilbert and Amy and Chuck Newton. Pilar, although not a club member, had been invited, only she sat with Max Osterhagen, her son, Alexander, and that spindly little girl with the big eyes and freckles that her son was dating. It was probably the money the girl would inherit from her grandfather that had attracted him. Lord knew it couldn't be anything else. And if Alexander persisted in allowing his whiskers to run wild, he wasn't such a prize, either.

With a sniff, Francine returned attention to her own table where her usually taciturn husband, Bob, had cheerfully made sure everyone had their drinks, including himself, and he was clearly on his way to becoming the life of the party. Francine, most always sure about everything, was never quite sure how she should react to her husband's party mood.

At her table, Pilar was smiling at Alexander, delighted that his concern about her near-drowning had prompted him and Solstice to attend the restaurant opening despite the new puppy. But what was this about Solstice taking up cigarettes? A ridiculous yarn. Solstice and Alexander had arrived at the restaurant at the same time as she and Max. Pilar had been suspicious the moment she saw they had rented a car instead of traveling on his motorcycle.

"Where's the new puppy?" she had asked with deliberate innocence.

Alexander, his eyes not meeting his mother's, mumbled something about a friend watching little Toodle-Lou. Pilar pretended to believe him, but she was willing to bet that the animal was tucked inside their rented car. Now, in the restaurant, Solstice had already gone outside once because she was "dying for a smoke." It now looked as if she was getting itchy again. Pilar figured she didn't need second sight to recognize an oncoming excuse to again check on the welfare of the new dog. When she returned, not smelling of cigarettes, she carried an extremely large purse, which she carefully set on her lap.

Well now, Pilar thought, what in the world could Solstice have that needed such a large purse? She bet she could guess. She thought that Max had guessed too, something about his smile. As for Alexander, he was looking carefully in the opposite direction.

Pilar gazed at Max, thinking how much she loved him. He returned her look and placed his hand on hers under the table. She still hadn't yet told him she would marry him. There was one more thing she had to discuss with him first, but she was feeling relaxed about it. Now, she just wanted to enjoy the rest of the evening.

An evening she felt would be interesting, but now she had a feeling that it would be even more interesting than she could imagine.

Chapter 41

At his table, Slim sat with his back to the wall so he could view the room. People were coming up and congratulating him for solving the murders and pressing in vain to learn more about Neece's partner in crime. He told them there would be no public news until it was released by the county.

People were also busy lauding JJ for her print coverage of the crime.

She was thanking people and smiling, but her mind was elsewhere. What was Leslie's big surprise? Jessi had whispered it was something wonderful in her honor. Possible? JJ shrugged. Politicians adored getting their names in the news no matter how idiotic the reason.

The applauders finally drifted away and Slim could relax with his dinner companions and be more open about his part in the murder investigation. Those at his table could be trusted to keep their mouths shut until the official news was released: Holly and Toria and Amy and Chuck and even that newshound, JJ, his "date" for the evening.

"Are we finally getting the dirt?" Amy demanded.

As members of the Voodoo Club, she and Toria had early knowledge of some of the facts but not how they fit with the whole picture. Amy could be impulsive, but when it mattered, she could be counted on to keep her mouth shut. As for her grave-digger husband, Chuck, he joked he kept secrets buried deep. Even Holly didn't know everything. Except for Slim, they mostly knew only what had appeared in the news, which kept Neece's motive murky and her partner undisclosed.

A beer in hand, Slim explained that after comparing Neece's story with what Max had to say, plus a few words from Pilar, he had enough to get the county prosecutor's office to wake up and pay attention. They tapped Judge Fisher for a search warrant to enter Neece's home, where they found sophisticated computer equipment and financial records bearing the names of Sable Kilgallen and Olivia Bunker. Sedatives were also found, the same as that used to kill Olivia and drug the chocolates Neece gave to Pilar.

In an unexpected turn, once Neece realized she was truly caught, all she wanted to do was brag. She took pride in having tricked the entire community into thinking she was a zero when she had the brains to become a billionaire. She was convinced she would have succeeded if only some home decorator, who should be hanged as a witch for mind-reading, hadn't bollixed the works.

Slim said, "Neece acted like being read her Miranda Rights was an invitation to spill everything. The prosecutor's office plans a big media announcement on Monday, so I'm not jumping the gun too much."

He explained how Neece, who'd been a church treasurer, had chortled over having embezzled small, but regular, amounts, especially when they had big fund-raisers.

"From her high school job," he said, "she copied personal information and Social Security numbers from contracted workers, including Buckley Alfred Hightower, part of the crew hired for janitorial work in county systems years back." There was a pause when Slim took a swallow of his beer and then continued.

"Next," he said, "Neece dreamed up that mini-strokes stuff, claiming a wrecked memory and not being able to work with computers, all to cover up her scheme. She persuaded her partner to open a bank account in another state using the Hightower identity. The first deposit was from the stash she'd embezzled from the church. The two of them put their heads together and came up with the idea of an investment scam."

"A small-scale pyramid scheme," JJ said.

Slim nodded. "That's what got Pilar into trouble. She said she has no idea why words like *peaks* and *gables*, which have the same three corner shapes of a pyramid, kept coming to her. In fact, the word *pyramid* wasn't even in her head until she saw your necktie, Holly, the one with Egyptian wonders. As an inside joke, Neece and her partner had decided Hightower's middle initial A stood for Aram, an Egyptian word for pyramids. Psychic crap makes no sense to me, but at George's funeral lunch, Neece heard Pilar say the word *pyramid* and there was some mention that Pilar was psychic. That's when she decided it was time for Pilar's life to be ended."

JJ chimed in, "Pilar denies the supernatural angle, which is disappointing, but Neece is spilling everything. She sent me a long letter." JJ wrinkled her nose. "She wants to meet me as a journalist and have me work a book deal. She wants me to write it for her."

"One Nobel Prize coming up," Slim said with a grin, thinking JJ was looking all soft and girly, long hair fluffed and wearing one of those wrap dresses with a peek-a-boo top that kept him peeking. She might not be top-heavy, but she sure wasn't flat. Why had he thought that?

Amy said, "You keep talking about Neece's partner. Why are you holding back about who it is? Has the person been caught?"

"We want everything straight before the media starts chewing it up for the ratings. There are family members to consider. We want to be sure they fully understand the guilt and the evidence so we don't have TV people sticking microphones in their mouths and them saying their beloved relative is being railroaded by law enforcement."

"But who is it?" Toria said.

"I bet I can guess," Amy said. "Even though I like her, it's Neece's sister, Claudine. Those two worked so hard to make everybody think they were sworn enemies, but I bet they were really in cahoots. Claudine pretended to be a man, that Hightower guy, right?" She looked triumphantly at Slim. "That's why she's not here tonight, right? You've had her arrested."

Slim laughed. "Claudine's not here because she's with Jolly Kaminski. They met when he was haggling over leftovers from the yard sale and they hooked up. They can't be here because they only like eating in clouds of cigarette smoke."

"If it isn't Claudine," objected Amy, impatiently. "Who *is* it?"

JJ jumped in before Slim could reply. "It is, or rather was, Neece's boyfriend, George Neilson."

There were shocked gasps from around the table at the news. At Slim's sharp look at her for revealing it, JJ laughed. "Got to let me get my scoop somehow. Go on, Tall Boy, give them the details."

"Big thanks," Slim cracked, but he didn't mind her stepping on his lines. "Yeah," he said, "it was George. Neece told me that she and George each felt life had cheated them, so cheating other people was getting even. They felt they were treated like nobodies. Neece decided that being nonentities was a lucky charm for criminals. Nobody looked their way." Pausing to help himself to the appetizers they'd brought to the table, Slim continued to describe how Neece and George had worked the scheme.

"Neece had a computer setup that produced impressive-looking earnings statements for a phantom investment company. She and George selected their victims, Sable and Olivia, carefully—two single women living alone with family at a distance, and in Sable's case, no family at all. They approached each woman separately with their fake high rate of returns. They raved about their investment counselor, Buckley A. Hightower, who had put them in a fund specializing in high-ticket real estate. They told the women it was all hush-hush because Hightower was committed to only make offerings to his New York pals. But he had included George as a favor and George had told Neece. They said if word got around, Hightower would be in trouble and anyone not in their exclusive crowd would be shut out."

Slim took a break for another snack and JJ took over. "Sable sent her art checks to an address George had set up, where he banked the money as Hightower. Olivia's money went there too. Neece and George enjoyed a few trips and Neece bought expensive furniture. They thought of their game with Sable and Olivia as training for the high-style pyramid scheme they would start once they moved to Florida. They regularly and individually met with their victims to review their impressively faked financial statements, which supposedly came through George, the only person reclusive 'Hightower' supposedly trusted."

Allowing his anger to show for the first time, Slim said, "Neece sat there in lock-up looking like somebody's cookie-baking grandma, calmly explaining to me that when Olivia unexpectedly wanted her assets to buy the perfect house, Neece had no choice but to kill her. As soon as Olivia came home from Maine and before anybody else knew she was there, Neece dashed over with fake withdrawal papers to sign. She drugged Olivia during their tea time and sat around waiting for her to kick off. She then cleaned out anything in her house that related to the Hightower scheme."

Expression pained, Holly asked, "Why did they have to kill Sable?"

JJ leaned her elbows on the table. "As bad luck would have it," she said, "before Olivia's body was found, Sable also wanted her investment money for a house in Maryland near the art gallery that featured her work. It was also where she and Claudine could live together. Neece wants an entire chapter devoted to how betrayed she felt when she learned Sable wanted to withdraw her funds to live with the sister Neece despised. In her view, Sable's death was her own fault."

Nodding, Slim said, "Fortunately for Neece—her view—when she and George arrived at Sable's shop to supposedly discuss withdrawing the money, they found Sable on a ladder. Neece called the situation 'fate', and simply knocked the ladder over."

"Served her right when it landed on her ankle," JJ said.

Slim shrugged, "The fall must have broken Sable's neck because Neece said she gave her head a twist and Sable stopped breathing. She and George gathered Sable's paperwork, plus her computers and cell phone and took it to Neece's house. They couldn't risk leaving anything because of Sable's careless ways., which answered my questions about things I found missing.

JJ chimed in again, "With Sable gone, Neece figured she and George could head for a sunset village with no one the wiser, but then, Neece realized she had another problem. She wants this to be a huge section of the book. About the problem with George's father."

"Rufus invested in the deal, too?" Holly said. "I thought he didn't have any money?"

"No, this was worse," Slim said.

"*Worse?*" echoed Toria, clearly upset by what she was hearing.

"Neece convinced George their plans would never work if his father was still alive. How could they take their pyramid scheme to the big time if he was still responsible for his father's care? Since Rufus' mind was failing anyhow, Neece pointed out it would be a kindness to let him sleep away. She told him her plan and George fell for it. When he dropped his father off at the Hitchmile to fish, Neece was waiting to give him a big overdose of his own sleeping medicine. It would look as if he had mistakenly taken it himself. She then rinsed out the memorabilia cup and tossed it on rocks in the brush and it broke."

"A mistake," JJ said with a glance at Slim. "One that a lot of people wouldn't have been sharp enough to notice and view as a valuable clue."

"And not everybody would have been sharp enough to catch me noticing it," Slim shot back, remembering the time the two of them were together at the scene.

JJ gave him her saucy grin.

Distracted, Slim took a moment to get back in gear, and then said, "Neece expected Rufus to conk out on dry land and painlessly sleep away after she left. When George learned that his father drowned instead, he couldn't get over it. That's what led to the heart problems that landed him in the hospital."

"Here's something I don't get," Holly said. "Not to sound insulting, but Neece doesn't seem like anyone special. I can see the appeal of money to George, but killing people? Especially his own father? Why would he listen to Neece about that? How could she get him to do it?"

"You're missing something, bud," Slim said, shifting his long legs, bumping into JJ's legs and leaving them there. "I'm only a small-town cop, but I've seen enough to know women like Neece who can convince a man to commit crimes. Not glamour girls, but women they feel comfortable with, often plain-looking females who have cleverly wormed their way into the man's world to the point where he can't imagine risking that relationship. George would have done *anything* for her."

JJ said, "Although George might have done anything for Neece, her prime concern was herself. When George's guilt over his part in his father's death and his heart attack put him in the hospital in serious condition, she feared he might be driven to confess, or even reveal too much during a hallucination. That's when she decided he had to die as well."

Holly's eyes widened. "*A fourth murder*? Neece killed George? Boy, you sure held that back. How could she pull that stunt in a hospital?"

As he spoke, he glanced to find Toria. She had quietly left the table because she didn't enjoy hearing how Neece had persuaded George to agree to the death of his father. He saw her chatting with Pearl, a waitress at Teddy's. Satisfied that Toria was okay, he returned his attention to Slim's reply to his question about the hospital.

"Neece got loyalty points for sitting near the door of George's hospital room so she could call for help if needed. But she said she was actually there to make sure nobody was coming down the hallway before she started crimping George's air tube or fiddling with his machines."

"But aren't the machines hooked up to central monitoring?"

"Sure, but George was in bad shape. Who could tell if the disturbances in his vital signs were natural or deliberately caused? Neece said she would try something and then run for the nurses if she thought she might get caught, or if he started looking worse afterward, she would leave the room to be away if he died. She said the last time was the charm. He was already dead by the time she came back."

"She's one sick lady," JJ said.

"Might make a great book," Amy said, "Would you write it?"

JJ frowned thoughtfully. "Maybe yes, maybe no. To tell the truth, I don't think I'd want to spend that much time with her."

Tired of the rehash, Slim was happy when there was a musical fanfare over a loudspeaker and Jessi Spellman stepped into the spotlight on the far side of the room.

Jessi's voice carried well through a lavaliere mic clipped to one shoulder, ringing out as she welcomed everyone and said she hoped the Carousel Restaurant was living up to her guests' excited expectations.

As she spoke, Jessi believed that everyone present was a dear friend, except maybe that fat waitress from Teddy's, who was probably a spy.

Speaking to those still milling about the room, she encouraged them to return to their tables so dinner could be served. As that was happening, she presented the third restaurant partner, an old coot of a sharpie realtor called Pastor—thanks to an ordination certificate issued online—who had bankrolled the restaurant operation. She then introduced the other partner, her husband, Arnie, the chef.

Jessi beamed as the crowd applauded Pastor and Arnie. With a brisk motion Jessi sent Arnie scooting back to the kitchen where he belonged, and Pastor back to the table.

Glowing, Jessi promised more exciting announcements to come between dinner and dessert and then withdrew as the waiters laden with trays began serving.

"Quick exit for Jessi," Chuck said in his gravelly voice.

"She'll probably make up for it with her announcement before dessert," Slim said, his eyes on JJ. As soft as she looked that evening, he was thinking she had a tough and practical side. He liked that. Were they going to do anything together after they left the restaurant? It wouldn't be all that late. He sneaked a glance back at her and then away again. For too long he could only see her as somebody's kid sister, but any fool could plainly see she was now all grown up.

He turned back to the table conversation to hear Amy and Chuck talking about whether or not the restaurant opening celebration would top the fiasco that happened when one of Jessi's previous schemes had backfired, ending with her looking like a flour-faced clown.

When dinner was over and the tables cleared, it was time for dessert. The lights dimmed until the only illumination was the candlelight on the tables. A warm spotlight suddenly appeared.

"Ta-da!" exclaimed Amy. "Here we go!"

Jessi stepped into the spotlight.

Chapter 42

With the attention of the entire dining room upon her, Jessi Spellman stood garbed in a floor-length, hot pink gown. The neckline was scalloped, directing attention to Jessi's pretty little triangular face and dramatic coloring—her pale skin, jet-black wings of hair, and vivid green eyes. Her doll-sized evening slippers with their five-inch heels were also pink, the tiny toes tapering to points.

Taking an anticipatory breath, Jessi prepared to introduce her special guests to her huge and adoring crowd. Leslie, Jessi's new best friend, had told her that reporters and photographers were eagerly coming to the restaurant opening.

Jessi knew why the media had gathered. After Leslie introduced Fergusson, he would give her and the Carousel Restaurant an impressive award from the New Jersey State House. Photos and coverage of her receiving the award from the senator would be splashed all over newspapers and news channels and go viral on the Internet.

A subtle signal from Jessi and a second spotlight, not as bright as hers, illuminated a prime front table. Bypassing the JumpRope mayor and police chief as well as anyone else who would only be recognized by the hometown crowd, Jessi enthusiastically introduced State Senator Earl Smythe Fergusson, his stepdaughter, Leslie, and Congressman, Birch D. Charles. There was also a sturdy, middle-aged blonde woman with a braid across her head seated next to Fergusson. Jessi shrugged her off. She couldn't have been important or Leslie would have told her.

Jessi was so excited she could barely breathe as Leslie, who had also been outfitted with a mic, stood. For once, it was okay with Jessi to have her own spotlight grow dim. She would dial it up again when Fergusson stepped forward with her award and the media rushed to capture her stellar moment.

When Leslie started speaking, her auburn hair softly aglow, Jessi paid no attention because whatever Leslie prattled was a preface to what mattered.

She tuned into Leslie's words as Fergusson rose to his feet, his pompadour of perfect hair giving him at least three inches more height. But he wasn't looking at Jessi to give her an award, he was extending a hand to the blonde woman with the braid.

Fergusson spoke. "As your State Senator, I would like you to meet the lovely Astrid Bergman, who has done me the honor of accepting my proposal of marriage."

What? Jessi's eyes goggled. Fergusson was announcing his engagement? *This* was the big announcement Leslie talked about? Her step-father presenting his future bride? Jessi couldn't believe Fergusson's nerve. Trying to transform her restaurant opening into *his* engagement party! Jessi stood frozen, stunned by the gall, the incredible poor manners.

Leslie was speaking again, this time extending her hand to U.S. Congressman Birch D. Charles, as she announced *her* engagement to *him*!

Fingernails digging into her palms, Jessi couldn't believe what was happening. And then, to top it all, Leslie extended an effusive thanks to the Carousel Restaurant for graciously inviting her and the senator to announce their engagements in this truly unique venue. Leslie then beckoned her fellow diners to applaud the restaurant, and so they did, the two brides-to-be flashing engagement diamonds as big as doorknobs.

Jessi could only smile and grit her teeth. It now appeared that Leslie's and Fergusson's barging into Jessi's opening night event had been agreed upon ahead of time. How could she now protest and scream, *"It's a lie, it's a dirty scummy lie!"*?

Truly skunked, Jessi could only stand helplessly as Leslie's revolting performance rolled on, with the Congressman saying how Washington, D.C. was going to be a much brighter and better place with Leslie at his side. Then the photographers and reporters pressed even closer as Fergusson, who also had a shoulder mic, explained he had realized his heart belonged in his beloved district in New Jersey and there was no better place to announce his engagement to Astrid, his longtime friend and secretary, than in the little, quaint, and heart-filled town of JumpRope.

As the crowd applauded again, Jessi soothed herself, thinking that the crowd hadn't seen anything yet! The evening's grand finale would put attention back on her where it belonged.

Fergusson's gaze lingered on the face of Francine Smithers, feared leader of influential women's groups, sending her rays of reassurance that he was trading special treatment in exchange for her deep-sixing that old racy snapshot of him and Leslie. He sighed, happy and contented. It had worked out so well. He could remain state senator and Leslie could follow The Congressman to Washington and hopefully to her dream of becoming First Lady. If there was any gossip about him and Leslie, it would appear ridiculous. Plus, as he also had recently discovered, Astrid had loved him for years and was perfect for him in the intimate after-hours department, and far less demanding than Leslie, who could be sooo assertive. How wonderful when he could go home and snuggle with Astrid and know he'd never feel lonely again.

But before that could happen—he had to suppress a giggle—there would be Leslie's final revenge on that nasty vermin, Jessi Spellman, for violating their bed with her repulsive restaurant advertisement.

From his place in the corner, Slim, amused by the events, idly surveyed the room. He noticed a man in a grey suit who looked familiar. But before he could examine that impression further, he saw Leslie drifting toward the lobby. Something about her movements struck him as furtive.

He waited until she was out of sight, then he excused himself from the table and moved to enter the lobby. Leslie stood in an alcove, her back to him as she spoke on her phone. He couldn't hear what she said, but her tone was what he'd heard in meetings when a leader was emphasizing planned points of action.

It could be anything, he thought. She was a woman with official duties, but to see this behavior now that the event had become a party for a double engagement, made him think more might be going on.

He walked back into the big dining room and headed toward the men's room but went on past it. Familiar with the layout of the structure, having toured when it was under construction, he arrived at a rear exit. He opened the door and propped it open so it wouldn't lock behind him.

Voices came from behind the building. Moving cautiously, he reached the rear corner and peered around. He saw a panel truck, boxes on a dolly, and four men talking together, two of them wearing aprons. Kitchen help? Another man was listening to his cell phone. He put the phone away and said something to the other men. Two of them got into the truck and left.

One aproned man started dragging the dolly behind the back of the building. From what Slim recalled of the layout, it seemed they were heading for the kitchen. A late delivery? It didn't make sense, but the next sound was that of a door opening and the sounds of the moving dolly. Then a door slammed and all was quiet.

Slim thought a moment and then reentered the building, fixing the door so it would close and lock behind him.

This time he did enter the men's room.

After making certain he was alone, he called the station. When the new rookie answered, this one a female, he told her to get hold of Ed, who was on patrol with Donny. "Tell them to come to Jessi's new restaurant, park, and wait until I call. Something bad may be going down."

At her question, he laughed and said, "So you've heard about Jessi. I don't think this is one of her tricks. She may have met her match this time. Just tell Ed to be ready until I give a holler."

As he reclaimed his seat, JJ gave him a questioning look, her eyebrows raised. He shrugged and saw that Leslie was back in her seat. If nothing happened, after this extravaganza was done with, maybe he and JJ could go to Sean's Pub, sit someplace private, and chew over the stupid evening.

The room lights once again dimmed. And then, one bright light appeared.

Amy said excitedly, "Jessi's spotlight has come on! There she is!"

Chapter 43

*T*he light surrounded Jessi like a mother's warm kiss. She knew how glamorously appealing she appeared bathed in that glow. A total package of *Wow*. Leslie might think she had pulled a fast one, but someday, Jessi would get even with her. *Just you wait*. But right now, she had an extravaganza to produce. When she gave the signal, the spectacular dessert table that had been silently positioned behind a screen would be rolled out in the grandest light show this town had ever seen.

Pure theater. That was Jessi Spellman. And best of all, the reporters and photographers were still present. Leslie might have had media for *her* news, but they stuck around because the Carousel Restaurant was the *real* story, the deal to remember long after those engagement rings were nothing but tarnish marks.

Centered in the spotlight, Jessi prattled excitedly, pumping up the crowd. She gave the signal for the dessert table. Out of the corner of an eye, Jessi thought Leslie made some motion as well.

With a musical fanfare, the dessert table appeared as if by magic, attended by waitstaff garbed in black to look invisible. The diners gasped in wonder as the room filled with slashing strobes, colored sparkles and spinning rainbows; and then, there was a musical change to a fast waltz version of a song Jessi felt best described the way her many admirers thought about her: *Let Me Call You Sweetheart!*

As the big room filled with the soaring sounds, Jessi began dancing, her tiny feet moving, her pink dress swirling, her eyes bright as she simpered and pranced and spun, the colored lights flashing like a thousand suns as Jessi stepped and whirled.

"Let me call you sweetheart
I'm in love with you,
Let me hear you whisper . . ."

Sudden silence.

What happened to the music?

Forgetting that the spotlight revealed every nuance, an expression of rage transformed Jessi's face.

What was lousing up her big moment?

And then, in that sudden, stunned silence came a gasp, then a cry, then a scream . . . Then from Leslie, who lifted her still-live mic from the table, came a theatrically terrified screech that soared above all the other sounds:

"RATS!"

And as Jessi took a confused step backward, she heard other women shriek and men shouting and stomping.

As if from nowhere the lights came on full as a befuddled Jessi stared. Rats, mice—lord knows what—*rodents,* dozens of them, scampering all through the main dining floor of the restaurant, darting frantically through the legs of the tables and legs of the patrons, madly scrambling from the open space and heading toward the walls.

At the same time, a tiny ball of fur leaped from Solstice's roomy purse. Despite her attempt to hold back the tiny white dog, it wriggled to the floor and took off. With high-pitched yips of delight, its short legs pumping like pistons, the creature tumbled pell-mell after the frenzied rodents.

"Toodle-Lou!" screamed Solstice, terrified that her little dog would be mistaken for a furry white mouse and be smashed by the chair that one man was wielding as his hysterical wife climbed up on the tabletop.

Alexander jumped to his feet and wove through the melee and finally managed to scoop up Toodle-Lou.

Watching, Pilar calmly thought, "Psychic or not, I may have had a feeling something would happen but I didn't expect anything like *this*?"

The photographers and the news guys were filming and flashing.

JJ was snapping shots with her cell phone.

Slim had given his holler and Ed and Donny had burst into the room.

Leslie cowered against Birtchy, pretending to be horrified, while secretly smiling and giving a mental thumbs up to her cohorts who had already made their get-away.

Bob Smithers was staring around in disbelief and thinking that maybe he'd gone overboard with the alcohol.

Francine, for the first time in her life, was thinking, "I need a drink."

And Jessi, who knew Leslie was behind the whole disaster but also knew she could never prove it, instantly figured there was only one way to gain sympathy and capitalize on this catastrophe. Her eyes landed on Pearl Dupree, the chubby barmaid from Teddy's.

Without another thought, Jessi ran full tilt across the room and came to a screeching halt when reaching Pearl. With her shoulder mic still active, Jessi grabbed at Pearl's rounded arm and screeched at the top of her lungs: "Arrest this woman! She's from my arch-business rival, Teddy's Restaurant. Teddy has sabotaged my opening night!"

Just as the reporters with their visual and audio recording devices rushed toward the two women, a new figure appeared and his loud male voice broke through the air.

"Don't listen to Jessi Spellman! She's full of nothing but lies!"

The speaker was a man in a grey suit, who had made his way through the crowd when the rodent melee began and now stood next to Pearl.

He grabbed Jessi's mic and shouted to everyone: "Here's the truth! This restaurant is filled with rats and mice because Jessi Spellman got rid of the cats that kept them under control!"

Media people crowded avidly forward, storming the air with their questions. The man in grey bellowed, "I'm Geno and I know the truth because I'm an employee of the Carousel Restaurant."

"Fired employee," Jessi shouted over him, furious that he had grabbed the spotlight with his version of the story.

In time, cooler heads would acknowledge that the abrupt appearance of several hundred rodents, at a high point of the evening, could not have been accidental, although nothing was ever found to prove who'd been at fault.

As for Slim's look behind the building, what had he really seen? Unknown men, two of whom had driven off in a panel truck he couldn't identify, plus men rolling a crate inside the building. Leslie and her group had now disappeared. And, since she was the stepdaughter of a state senator and the fiancée of a man in Congress, who was going to tie her up with this mess anyway?

Slim would keep his mouth shut except maybe he'd share it with JJ. Amused, he thought they'd play one of their word games. He'd call the evening a *mess* and she'd say *disaster,* and he'd say *chaos* and she'd say *calamity,* and he'd say *catastrophe*, with the emphasis on *cat*. His pun would win the game and they'd laugh. Only not that night, dammit. He was back on the job.

Fortunately, the emergency workers who'd also been called had little to do. Despite the hullabaloo, there were only minor physical injuries, including a sprained arm. One woman did need to be treated for hysterics and another one, close to hysterics, had to be assisted down from the table on which she was standing. Most of the damage was spilled food, smashed crockery, and several broken chairs. The media people were still going strong in their interviews of those eager for their ten seconds of fame as the gathering was breaking up. Nobody knew where the little dog had come from, and only those at Pilar's table knew that it had now been safely returned to Solstice's purse and was finishing the leftovers that Solstice had been sneaking to it from the moment she'd brought it in from the car.

Laughing and chattering among themselves, the diners spilled out to the parking areas and scurried to their cars, eager to see what might be reported on social media.

* * *

When Darlene reached home, she called Acer, not thinking about the time difference until he answered and then she said in a mortified tone. "What time is it there? Did I wake you?"

He laughed. "Around two in the morning, but a call from you is always welcome. How did Jessi's grand opening go? Please tell me. I've wondered about it all evening."

At that, she laughed and told him of Jessi's latest disaster.

They spoke more about the opening and some of the details. Then she said something she had been thinking about for a long time. She took a breath and said, "I'm setting up a time for us to visit my daughter's house. You can meet Marie and her husband, Joe, and finally, meet my granddaughter, MacKenzie."

There was a moment of silence. Darlene's nerves tensed. Had she done the wrong thing? When he spoke again, his voice was husky with emotion. "You've invited me to go with you and you'll share your family with me. I cannot begin to tell you how honored I am."

At that moment, Darlene thought that despite the little she knew of Acer's past, he was a lonely man. A man, she suddenly realized, she was dangerously close to falling in love with.

Chapter 44

Over in another section of JumpRope, Pilar and Max were preparing for bed. Alexander and Solstice were to have stayed the night, but Solstice, embarrassed by Toodle-Lou's appearance at the dinner, insisted it was urgent to return to the familiar surroundings of her Brooklyn apartment because the puppy had been "traumatized."

Toodle-Lou, bouncing and eager to lick everyone's face, was about as traumatized as a feather in an April breeze, but Pilar was content to see them go. She had something to say to Max.

Turning from her dressing table mirror where she had been twisting her dark hair into a loose plait, she faced him. "Some time ago, you said there were two things."

Max lifted his brows expectantly. "Yes?" Where was this going? Pilar was always coming up with comments and viewpoints that delighted him, but there were times, as it was now, when it would take him a moment to gain the drift.

She said, "You told me that you liked it that I was youthful—" She paused, received his nod, and added, "You also said you wanted to marry me."

"I did and I do." This time, his nod was heartfelt. He had proposed a number of times and then decided to let the question rest for a while. This was the first that she had introduced it herself. He didn't want to get his hopes up, still—

She said, "You might want to revise one of those statements."

He angled his head, intrigued. "And which one would that be?"

"Well, I apparently am youthful, so that statement stands. I'm apparently even more youthful at age forty-two than I believed."

He frowned, feeling lost. She did have a winding way about her.

She said, "We were rather secure in starting a relationship out in midlife." She paused and added with meaning, "Able to enjoy many aspects of life, some more intimate than others."

A twinkle came into his eyes. "This is true."

"That just may be the problem. That and my evident youth."

"I'm afraid I don't follow you."

"So I see." Pilar thought of all she knew about him, his intelligence, his gentleness, his steadiness, and his desire to once again enjoy settled domesticity without in any way comparing her to his late wife. His only regret from that relationship had been the thwarting of their desire to have children.

Pilar knew that she loved Max and that he loved her. Now that she had confessed what had been holding her back, she had this new problem. She said, "I'm saying that you might want to make some revisions to your statement regarding your desire for marriage. I doubt that you ever considered it leading you into a delivery room."

He thought. He blinked. The light dawned. "*Pilar*?" He looked as if heaven had opened and a personal message had been delivered. "A child? Pilar, we're going to have a child?"

"Yes, but—" It had been confirmed. She was over two months along, having wrongly attributed her tiredness and other symptoms to her troubled indecision about marriage.

Stepping into his embrace, she allowed herself a small smile as she whispered into his ear, "You should know that twins can run in my family."

After

ℳAR-SEE-AH SPEAKS

𝒜ll secrets have been revealed.

Almost idly, Mar-see-ah moves the smooth river stones across the board. She sees the woman for whom she experienced fear was in a tranquil state; at long last, she has released herself from a deeply imagined guilt in exchange for newfound joy. Mar-see-ah sent good wishes. She sensed that the woman has received her message but in no specific way. She only feels it as an inexplicable sense of bliss.

As to the murders, they have been solved, the confessed killer put where that evil hand can strike no more. The pain and sorrow caused can never be undone, but there is satisfaction in finding justice.

Ah, look here at the newlyweds. A sense of warmth comes through Mar-see-ah as she sees the hearts that have been satisfied. Love has been found, love that will endure.

And then there are joys that have not yet been revealed. Time alone will tell.

Mar-see-ah lifts her hands.

All is at peace for the moment.

Enough for now.

Dear Readers

I hope you enjoyed *Death Wears Red Roses*, which reveals more about the character of Pilar, who has appeared in the three previous novels.

Some readers have asked what happened to Pilar's town newsletter, "The JumpRope Jive."

The most popular feature of the "Jive" was local happenings Pilar wrote about—without printing the subjects' names.

The subjects might have been embarrassed, but other residents were delighted when they figured out the subjects' identities.

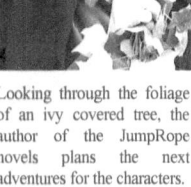

Looking through the foliage of an ivy covered tree, the author of the JumpRope novels plans the next adventures for the characters.

Pilar is no longer interested in writing the "Jive," but since town residents enjoyed it, maybe someone in the future will have the "Jive" flying high on social media.

We shall see.

Best always and happy reading,

Ivy C. Leigh

Don't Miss the Other JumpRope Novels

Mystery, Romancce and Murder in a Small Town Named JumpRope

And Take a Look at These . . . .

A mystic legend and a mismatched couple's search for a long lost diamond brings passion, danger and death in the wilds of the Yucatan jungle.

The sounds of children chanting are heard in the yellow house. Is the house haunted? Will mystery draw two people who love one another together or tear them apart? The future of the little girl they have come to love, depends on it.

Jersey Pines Ink publishes novels of mystery, suspense, romance and murder. We also publish short story collections and short story anthologies. More information follows..

JPI

We Are Short Mysteries

An anthology of WhoDunits and HowDunits.

JERSEY PINES INK
https://www.erseypinesink.com

JPI

We Are Horror
You've Been Itching to Read

Twenty-nine stories of internment, cremation and creatures that lurk in graveyards. These tales take place in cemeteries, graveyards, mausoleums, and those special places where creative people have cleverly gotten rid of the body.

JERSEY PINES INK
https://www.jerseypinesink.com